The Americans are Coming

The Americans are Coming

a novel by
Herb Curtis

Goose Lane Editions

Published with the assistance of the Canada Council, the New Brunswick Department of Tourism, Recreation & Heritage and the University of New Brunswick, 1989.

On the cover: "Wiener Roast on my Father's Farm" by William Kurelek, copyright The Estate of William Kurelek, permission granted by the Isaacs / Innuit Gallery, Toronto.
Book design by Julie Scriver.
Printed in Canada by Ronalds Printing Atlantic.

10 9 8 7 6 5

Canadian Cataloguing in Publication Data

Curtis, Herb, 1949-
   The Americans are coming

ISBN 0-86492-108-X
I. Title.

PS8555.U77A73 1989   C813'.54   C89-098656-8
PR9199.3.C87A73 1989

Goose Lane Editions
469 King Street
Fredericton, New Brunswick
Canada E3B 1E5

for Iris

Silas Gordon sold everything he had, boarded a heavily masted sailing ship and went to Saint John. In the inside pocket of his jacket he carried a royal blessing — a deed to a hundred acres of land in a place called Dungarvon.

In the year 1821, Silas Gordon built a house, store and a mill, fourteen miles west of a place called Blackville, and promptly named the three buildings "Gordon." The wagon trail that led from Blackville to Gordon was named "The Gordon Road." Gordon was three miles upstream from what was later called Brennen Siding.

Silas Gordon did not have it easy. There was an unlimited amount of massive pine needed for the building of ships, but his location was bad. He not only had to pay men to cut and yard the lumber to what was called "Silas Landing," but also had to pay men for the drive.

The prop was pulled, the large logs tumbled into the spring waters of the "Gordon Brook," floated two to five miles to the Dungarvon, another fifteen miles downstream to the Renous, ten miles down the Renous to the Miramichi, and then on to Newcastle fifteen more miles away. He was barely breaking even.

The sawmill was losing money. It was too small. He needed a pond and more settlers to buy his plank and shingles. Silas Gordon didn't have it easy, but he was optimistic. His optimism crumbled, however, in October 1825, when a fire lit in Juniper swept a hundred miles of Miramichi forest out of existence. It burned down everything from shipmasts to fenceposts, houses to sawmills. It burned down everything from Juniper to Silas Landing. It burned the store, the mill and every house, barn and outhouse in Gordon.

In 1827, Silas Gordon froze to death trying to find his way cross-country from Gordon to Renous. Because of the frozen ground and the lack of digging implements, they buried him in the soft clay of the spring.

Silas Gordon did not whoop.

one

Buck Ramsey got his name from the fact that he only showed up once a year, like a buck deer in mating season, made love to his wife Shirley, then headed back to Fredericton to his full-time woman. Buck Ramsey sired ten children that way.

"He's just like an old buck . . . ," said Lindon Tucker, remembering that someone had said it many years before. " . . . an old buck, yeah. An old buck, yeah, yep. Buck the buck. Yes, sir."

"Every time he comes home, he adds a point to his antlers," said Bert Todder. "Tee, hee, hee; ha, ha, ha; sob, snort, sniff."

When Bert Todder laughed, he sounded, at times, like he was crying. Bert's mother, Maud, had had the philosophy that it was not good to laugh too much. She believed that for every time you laughed, you cried; so she always laughed and cried simultaneously. The only time that Bert was ever seen to cry in his adult life was when Maud died. At the gravesite he went, "Tee, hee, hee; ha, ha, ha; sob, snort, sniff," and everyone thought he was laughing.

"Boys, I went into Shirley's to get the mail and she stunk some bad," said Dan Brennen.

"Poor bugger Shad sets beside some o' them young lads in school and, and, and, and I guess they're pretty coarse. He said that at times he kin hardly stand the smell o' that Dryfly and that, that, that Palidin." said Bob Nash.

"Well, they never took a bath in their life!" said Dan.

"They jist smell like a jesiless rag barrel," said Bert Todder and laughed . . . or cried.

"That Shirley don't look after them, ya know," said Dan.

"They claim that Buck's makin' all kinds o' money in Fredericton," lied Stan Tuney.

"Boys, if he is, he ain't spending it on her!" said John Kaston.

"No, no, no. He ain't spendin' it on her, is he, John old boy," commented Lindon Tucker, "no, sir. He ain't spendin' it on her, that's fer sure."

The Postmistress, Shirley Ramsey, and her family, was always a favourite topic of conversation at Bernie Hanley's store. The only time that the men didn't talk about Shirley, was when one of the Ramseys was there. The Ramsey boys seldom frequented Bernie Hanley's store; they couldn't afford to.

"That Shirley Ramsey'd be a good woman for you, Lindon," said Bert Todder. This was a way that Bert had of making fun of Lindon and Shirley at the same time.

"I,I,I,I,I,I, don't want want nothin' to do with the likes o' that old bag, so I don't. Kin git meself a better woman than that if I want, so I kin."

"Tee, hee, hee, ha, ha, ha . . . "

"Ya don't think she'd look too good in the mornin', do ya, Lindon?"

"Couldn't stand the smell o' her!"

And so went the conversation. When they exhausted Shirley Ramsey, the conversation drifted to the price of pulp, gold in the Yukon, cars, and whether or not they had enough potatoes in their bins to last them until digging time. Then, one by one, they reluctantly (the most reluctant of all was Bert Todder) sauntered off home.

*

Dryfly lay crying on the mattress amidst the coats and rags. They could not make him go to school. He would not go today, to-morrow or any other day. He would never go to school again.

For the tenth time Shirley yelled: "Git out here, Dryfly! Git out here n' eat yer breakfast afore it gits cold."

"Who ever heard of bread and molasses gittin' cold!" yelled Dryfly in a fit of temper, caught himself and moaned, "Besides, I'm too sick to eat. I'm pisoned, so I am!"

"Sick, me arse! A little bit o' rabbit shit never hurt nobody! If ya don't git out here and go to school, I'll give you to old Nutbeam and you kin live in the woods and be a hermit jist like him. Is that what you wanna be? Ya wanna be a hermit fer the rest of your life?"

"Bein' a hermit wouldn't be so bad," thought Dryfly, "it would be kind of nice to live alone in a snug camp in the woods and not be tormented with thoughts of school. And being alone would mean not having to face Shad Nash ever again. What's more, I'd never have to contend wit' the Protestants."

"Is that why Nutbeam lives in the woods," wondered Dryfly? "Could the giant Nutbeam be living in the woods alone because he'd been picked on by the Protestants?" Dryfly went through the events of the previous day.

*

Everything went well until noon hour when the sixteen children who made up the Brennen Siding school were set free by Hilda Porter to eat their lunch.

The March sun had weakened the crusty snow so that it gave way periodically beneath the feet of the four boys who wandered into the woods fringing the little school yard.

On the sunny side of a clump of jackpine the snow had receded several feet, and it was here, sheltered from the wind, on the dried pine needles (pine and spruce needles were locally referred to as sprills), the boys sat to eat.

Max Kaston and George Hanley were both in grade six. Shadrack Nash was in grade five and Dryfly Ramsey was in grade four. They were all the same age.

Max Kaston was fat with tiny shifty eyes that peeked over puffed and shiny cheeks. The style of his hair had obviously been simplified with a pisspot. He wore a blue checked hunting jacket, heavy green woollen pants and black rubber boots that came to just below his knees.

Max was the son of John Kaston, and perhaps because he was constantly being preached to, he was obsessed with and plagued by mistrust and fear. John knew that he, himself, would never become a preacher, but he was determined to make one out of Max.

Max had been told to respect and fear God; that Satan was forever present; that God was everything that was good and

Satan was everything that was evil. Fearing both God and Satan meant that Max feared everything.

George Hanley's ears, hands and feet all seemed too big for the rest of his body. The size of his ears, indeed, seemed exaggerated, because of the brush-cut style of his black hair. George played with the girls a lot, but because his father ran the store, he was never teased as being a sissy. He was too valuable a friend — he could steal things for you from the store.

Stealing was the only way George could get anything from the store, because Bernie gave him nothing.

Shad Nash had fiery red hair, cut by Dan Brennen for the price of a package of tobacco and a book of papers. He was slightly smaller than the rest and his tiny body was clothed neatly in a black windbreaker, blue jeans and leather-topped gumshoes. He had pale ivy eyes and a cluster of freckles that contrasted with his white skin. Shad was a fast talker and seemed forever in control. These were traits he'd developed coping with his father's frustrations and moodiness. Unlike the others, he'd been to the village, Renous and even Newcastle. He came from the first family in Brennen Siding to own an indoor toilet.

Dryfly was the mystery boy — not weird like his brother Palidin — but still, mysterious. Perhaps his mystery came from the fact he was a Catholic and God only knew what God they prayed to. Dryfly was thin, had broken teeth, a long snotty nose and a peaked chin. His clothing never fit him right (hand-me-downs from whoever took pity on him) and he smelled . . . like a rag barrel.

There, on the pine needles (the sprills), a rabbit had taken a meal the previous night, nibbling at the grass and blueberry bushes that yesterday's sun had uncovered. Shad eyed the tiny dung balls the rabbit had left. He bit into a large, round, hard molasses cookie. All the boys, except Shad, drank tea from pickle jars. Shadrack had a thermos with the picture of a cowboy twirling a rope on it. He ate from a square lunchbox that matched his thermos. Max and George ate from Ganong's hard tack candy buckets. The Ganong's candy bucket had a picture of a Ganong's candy bucket on it, which had the same picture on it, etc. . . into infinity. Dryfly ate from a chocolate box that had seen better days. The chocolate box with the barely distinguishable rainbow across the top had one soggy piece of bread and molasses in it.

A crow cawed, prophesying spring.

The four boys were saving hockey cards from the five-cent bags of Hatfield potato chips. Shad had found a second Bobby Hull card in last night's treat and knew that Max had two Andy Bathgates. With Andy Bathgate added to his collection, Shad would have the whole New York Rangers team. Shadrack endeavored to trade with Max.

"You wouldn't want to trade your Andy Bathgate for a Bobby Hull, would you Max, old buddy?"

"Can't. I already have Hull and I gave me other Bathgate to Dryfly."

"You gave your Andy Bathgate to Dry? What for?"

"I dunno. Thought he'd like it, I guess."

"I'll give you a Bobby Hull for it, Dry."

"I'm lookin' for a Boom Boom Geoffrion." said Dryfly, "Wanna play cowboy after school?"

"I'll throw in a Moose Vasgo," said Shadrack, "that's a Bobby Hull and a Moose Vasgo for one old Andy Bathgate."

"Nope. I might consider a Gordie Howe, though. Got a Gordie Howe?"

"Just the one," sighed Shad, wondering how he'd go about swinging a deal.

"Sounds like a pretty good deal to me, Dry. I'd trade with him, if I was you," said George.

"Ya wanna play cowboy after school, Shad?" asked Dryfly.

"I dunno. Maybe."

"I'll play," said Max.

"Me too," said George.

"Maybe," said Shad.

"I'll tell ya what," said Dryfly, "you gimme yer Bobby Hull and Moose Vasgo and let me play wit' yer cap gun after school and I'll give you me Andy Bathgate."

Dryfly wasn't very concerned about hockey cards anyway. His

family could rarely afford to buy potato chips, which made it practically impossible to collect any amount of cards. Nor did he know one hockey player from another. With no radio, he never got to hear a hockey game.

Shad gave the deal some thought. He needed that Andy Bathgate, but Dryfly was striking a hard deal. Moose Vasgo wasn't that easy to come by either, and giving up the cap gun would mean that Dryfly would get to be the "Good Lad." Dryfly would be Roy Rogers on Trigger, or The Lone Ranger. The best Shadrack could hope for, under the circumstances, was being Pat Brady, or Tonto. Shad hated using a stick for a gun.

"What if you broke my cap gun?" he asked.

"I won't break it," promised Dry.

"But you might."

"I won't."

"What would you do if you did?"

"I'd buy you another one."

"What with? What would you use for money, beer caps?"

"I won't break yer gun, pum me soul I won't."

"Well, I might let you use it for one short game, if you're careful."

"Nope. All evening. I never get to be the good lad."

"Me nuther," put in George Hanley, slurping his tea.

"I'm always the bad lad," said Max Kaston, "and it's always our barn that we play in."

"We kin play in our barn, if you want," said George with a glitter of hope in his eyes. It was true, perhaps because of his ears, or God only knows for what reason, he was never selected to be the good lad.

"You lads don't have a cap gun," snapped Shadrack, "like I told you a thousand times, you can't expect Roy Rogers or The Lone Ranger to go ridin' around with a stick for a gun!"

"Well, it ain't fair," grumbled George.

"Well, that's me deal. Take it or leave it," said Dryfly.

Shad couldn't handle the trading any longer. He wanted the Andy Bathgate too much. And he'd be ahead of the others anyway, with his full set of New York Rangers. It would be weeks before any of the others collected that many, and by the time they did, he'd probably have a set of the Toronto Maple Leafs or even the Montreal Canadiens.

"OK," said Shad, "ya gotta deal, but if ya break me cap gun, you're dead!"

"I ain't gonna break it. I wanna be The Lone Ranger the first game and Roy Rogers the second. If there's a third, I wanna be Matt Dillon. And you must cross yer heart and hope to die that you'll show up with the cap gun."

"Cross me heart," said Shad, "now give me the card."

The boys traded cards, all knowing that Dryfly, for the present, was the winner.

Shad was not about to be bettered by an Irish Catholic, however. Shadrack Nash had a new scheme. Shadrack Nash had thought up his new scheme while he was eating his first molasses cookie.

When he felt the time was right, Shad said, "Let's play a game, boys."

"Sure, what game?" asked Max.

"Let's see who can open his mouth the farthest," said Shadrack. "I bet I can."

"How much ya wanna bet?" asked Dryfly, feeling confident.

"I bet ya this marble," said Shad.

"Let me see the marble," said Dry.

"Nope. You have to take me word fer it. I'll give this marble to the one with the biggest mouth."

A marble was a rare thing in Brennen Siding, but the boys all knew that Shadrack Nash was the most likely one to have one, and he definitely seemed to be hiding something in his hand.

"OK," said Max, "I'll give it a go."

"Me too," said George.

"Count me in," said Dryfly, "I could do with a marble."

"OK," said Shad, "we'll judge each other. I'll count to three, then everyone gape as wide as they can. Ready? One, two, three."

Max, George and Dryfly all opened wide, revealing their

HERB CURTIS

cookie-coated tongues and teeth. Shad started to do likewise, but instead, he took careful aim and tossed the marble into Dryfly's mouth.

The marble was not a marble, however, but one of the dungballs the rabbit had left behind.

When he saw that his aim had been perfect, Shad snorted with laughter, spraying tea and cookie crumbs all over the blue-checked hunting jacket of Max Kaston.

The first thing Dryfly did was swallow.

Secondly, he gagged.

Thirdly, he ran home crying.

Dryfly could still hear the boys laughing when he crossed the railroad tracks. He felt he would never be able to face his friends again.

*

In his bed of old coats and rags, Dryfly could still hear them laughing. "I'll hear them laughing," he thought, "for the rest of my life." Dryfly sighed. "I'm a hermit already."

"If you don't git out here and go to school, I'm gonna go out and cut a switch!" yelled Shirley from the kitchen.

Dry relaxed a bit. Shirley's threat was idle, had lost its spark. "Her tail's probably waggin'," thought Dryfly and began to plan his day of freedom.

*

Dryfly was right about the spark. Shirley had lost it, but her tail was not wagging. Shirley had lost her spark the last time that Buck came home. In a manner of speaking, Buck's last visit was the last time she had wagged her tail to any degree.

"It's been . . ." Shirley counted, " . . . five, six . . . Dryfly's eleven . . . must be twelve years since Buck was here. No letters, no money . . . what's become of him, I wonder?"

Although Shirley was not aware of the anniversary, Buck had landed twelve years ago to the very day. Palidin was the baby, Junior was twelve . . . Bonzie was still alive.

Buck had taken her to the Legion in his old Ford. She drank three beers and Buck had a half dozen or more. They danced. She remembered he smelled of aftershave and his hair had been slicked back with that fancy grease stuff. When the Legion closed, they went to Bob Nash's and drank rye until four in the morning. Bob played the banjo and Buck played the guitar and sang Hank Snow and Doc Williams songs. Buck had been the hit of the night and Shirley had never been happier in her life.

Later they drove around to the pit and parked. Buck put his hand on her knee and told her how pretty she was; then he said he loved her and then he got serious.

"I suppose you're wonderin' why I never send you any money?" he asked.

"No, Buck, I know you ain't got any."

"Had me a job as a janitor for awhile. Good job, too. Only had to clean the ground floor."

"What happened, Buck?"

"Got caught stealin'. Took some old geeser's pipe and it fell right out of me pocket in front of the boss. Fired me on the spot. Livin' in Fredericton now. Workin' at the bottle exchange and junk yard. Breakin' batteries mostly. No money in it though. How you gittin' long?"

"Gladys sent me a bag o' clothes and Dad sent me a bag o' potatoes. Know what I'm thinkin' bout doin'?"

"Gettin' in the back seat?" Buck slid his hand up her thigh.

"Don't be foolish! No, I'm thinkin' 'bout takin' over old Maud's Post Office."

"Kin you do that?"

"Sure kin. All you have to do is collect the mailbag at the Siding, bring it home and give it out, stamp a few letters — anyone kin do it and Bert said he'd like me to do it. Thirty dollars a month."

"Why don't Burt do it?"

"Can't read. Maud did it all. I'm gonna set it up in the livin' room."

"I'd ask you to come to Fredericton with me, but there'd be no room for the kids."

"I know, Buck. I know you mean well. What d'ya think o' me runnin' the Post Office?"

"You'll have to do it, I guess. It'll be good for ya."

"You could come home and help me, Buck. I'd run the Post Office and you could go to work."

"Who for?"

"You could talk to Frank Layton. He might give you a job at the club."

"I ain't workin' for Frank Layton!"

"Why? Frank's a fair man!"

"I'd rather break batteries."

"You got another woman in Fredikten, Buck?"

"You know I ain't got no other woman, Shirley. You know I ain't that kind of man!"

"Then, why won't you come home?"

"Let's not talk about that now. Let's get in the back seat."

"You're crazy, Buck."

"If I do come home, I'll have to go back and get me clothes and me radio."

"You got a radio?"

"Yep. Heard the last Joe Louis fight, settin' right back in Fredericton. Ever hear of Hank Williams?"

The conversation continued. Shirley fell in love again and Buck negotiated seduction with promises and lies. Shirley was never happier. Buck was leaving and hadn't asked for her family allowance check.

They climbed into the back seat and Shirley wagged her tail to Buck's delight. Nine months later Shirley added another point to Buck's antlers and called it Dryfly.

*

Dryfly figured the time was getting on to nine o'clock. The rest of the children had already left for school and Dryfly was left to himself to enjoy the little room.

Dryfly shared his bed with Palidin and Bean. Jug and Oogan slept in the bed across the room. Naggie slept in Shirley's room and Neeny and Bossy slept in the room next door. Junior was married to Mary Stuart and lived with Mary's father, Silas. Digger, as usual, was tramping the road somewhere. Skippy, the oldest girl, wasn't married, but was shacked up with Joe Moon in Quarryville. Joe Moon had a dog that occupied more of his time than Skippy. Skippy was the homeliest one of the family and considered herself lucky to be living with a bootlegger. Bonzie, of course, was dead.

*

It happened on a Sunday. The family was having a picnic back of the big hollow. Some of them were fishing in the nearby brook, others sat in the shade discussing members of the opposite sex and some picked flowers. Palidin, Bonzie and Dryfly were pretending they were moose.

"I need to have a dump," said Bonzie and hurried into the woods in search of a roost.

Bonzie Ramsey found his roost (a broken down birch tree), and dropped his pants, sat and found relief. He was just pulling up his suspenders when he heard the sound of rustling leaves and the crackle of a dead alder bush giving way to a passerby.

The sound was nearby, but it was only a sound; he could see nothing but the trees and underbrush of the forest.

"Who's there?" he called.

No answer. Bonzie waited and listened.

"Who's there?" he called again.

"It would be just like Palidin and Dryfly to be watchin' a lad havin' a dump," he thought. "They're prob'ly tryin' to scare me."

"Alright boys, come out! I know you're there!"

He heard the sound again, but this time it had moved — it was more to the left.

Without giving what he thought was Palidin and Dryfly any chance to flee, he dashed into the bush, thinking he would take them by surprise.

There was nobody there.

He listened once more.

"Palidin? Dryfly?"

The song of a bird came up from the brook. He could not identify it.

"When I get my hands on you lads, I'm gonna interduce you to the rough and tumble!" he shouted. He hoped he sounded like The Lone Ranger.

There was a bit of a clearing ahead of him, where the sun

had nourished the ferns to waist height. He thought he saw an unusual movement in their midst. He went to check it out.

Nothing.

"Must've been a bird," he thought.

"The hell with yas!" he yelled, turned and headed back to where he thought the family would be.

He walked for half an hour, realized they couldn't be that far away, turned and walked for an hour, came to a barren and realized he was very lost.

He zigzagged back and forth for several more hours, calling "Mom! Palidin! Dryfly! Naggie!" Occasionally he got an echo, but that was all.

He grew warm and panicky; his pace quickened; he scratched his arms and legs on dead limbs and brush. The flies found him.

At dusk, he found himself at the barren's edge once again. He didn't know if he was on the near or the homeward side of it.

When you step into a barren, your foot sinks ankle-deep into a wet, moss-like vegetation. When you wander into a barren, you'd better mark your point of entry, for once you get in a few hundred yards, everything starts to look the same . . . look down, look up and you're lost.

Bonzie thought he saw something on the barren. Bonzie was already lost and had nothing to lose — he headed towards the something.

It took him a half hour to get to what he was looking at, and it turned out to be a huge boulder. Exhausted, he sat on the boulder to watch the stars, as, one by one, they appeared. He cried for a long while, slept for a little while, then cried some more.

He heard something walking, "splush . . . splush . . . splush," off to his right. He held his breath, for better hearing. He prayed a silent "Hail, Mary."

"Splush . . . splush . . . splush" — whatever it was, was passing him by.

At first he thought it might be a bear, or a moose, but he

wasn't sure. "It could be a man. It could be a man looking for me. I got nothin' to lose," he thought.

"Whoop! Over here!"

A game warden found the fly-bitten, crow-pecked body of Bonzie a month later, back of the barren.

As a result of Bonzie getting lost, Dryfly feared getting lost more than anything else in the world. The thought of being alone in the woods to battle the flies horrified him. He even had nightmares about it. The flies (the more you battled, the more you attracted), would be the worst thing of all. And to die and have your body exposed to the woods . . . ?!!

Years later when Dryfly was asked the whereabouts of Bonzie by an elderly, absent-minded teacher, he replied, "He went for a shit and the crows got him."

*

Dryfly was giving way to slumber when Shirley passed through the curtain that served as the bedroom door, to stand before him at the foot of the bed.

"I've made up your lunch, Dry," said Shirley, "and wrote a s'cuse to the teacher fer ya. I'm gonna need you home tomorrow, Dry, so's I want ya to go to school today. I got yer lunch all packed."

The emotional cloud over Shirley was thick and black and it spread over Dryfly as if instructed by a magic wand. His heart quickened, his stomach fluttered and tears of defeat commenced to flow.

"But, I can't, Mom!" he sobbed.

"You might have to stay home tomorrow, Dry. We've run out of grub, so's I want you to go today."

"But, I'm sick, Mom!" Tears, tears, tears.

"I'm gonna write yer father askin' him to send me enough money for that cap gun you like in the catalogue. C'mon, Dry darlin', be a good boy and go to school. I'm not gettin' any younger, you know. One day I won't be around to look after you and you'll need lots o' schoolin' so's you kin git a job."

"Ah, Mom!" Still more tears.

HERB CURTIS

"You kin stay home tomorrow, Dry, cause I ain't got the heart to send you to school on an empty stomach, but you have to go today. C'mon Dryfly darlin', git dressed, ya still have time."

"But, I don't want to go!"

"Poor Ninnie didn't take nothin' to eat wit' her. Said you could have it, Dry. Poor little thing was thinking of you and how you'd like a good sand'ich. So, c'mon, Dry."

Dryfly knew he was defeated and to make sure that Shirley's victory would be a difficult one, he cried all the time he was getting dressed. He cried in the kitchen and refused to eat his biscuit and molasses. He was still crying when he crossed the tracks.

When Hilda Porter opened Shirley Ramsey's excuse note for Dryfly's absence on the previous afternoon, it read:

Deer Mrs. Porter.

Dryfly stayed home in the afternoon yesterday, for he was sick from rabbit dung poisoning.

Yours truly,

Shirley

Hilda Porter already knew.

Shadrack Nash was not laughing as he watched Dryfly Ramsey enter the school, deposit his excuse on the teacher's desk and make his way to his seat; the memory of Hilda's two-inch-wide, foot-long piece of woodcutter strap on his stinging hands took care of that little pleasure.

Nothing was ever kept secret in Brennen Siding.

two

Shirley watched Dryfly until she was sure he would not run off into the woods.

Poor little lad, he's different from Palidin. Pal's only a year older, but he's a lot wiser. Palidin's smart, wants to be a somebody. Kind o' fruity, I'll admit, but he wants to be somebody. Kin read and write and do 'rithmetic better 'n me. It's more 'portant to keep Pal in school than Dryfly.

Shirley figured that Palidin would eventually get a job as a timekeeper or a store clerk in Newcastle or Chatham. To Shirley, being a timekeeper or a store clerk was having the ultimate good job. Anything more intellectual than these two occupations was beyond comprehension.

That's the way it was all over Brennen Siding.

When Jack Allen went off to Hartford with Dr. MacDowell and eventually became a dentist himself, everybody in the settlement disowned him — disowned him not so much because they didn't like him, but because Jack had become a different creature — looked different, spoke different, walked different and even smelled different.

When he came to Brennen Siding and put the word out that he needed a guide to go fishing, none of the local men would guide him. When Stan Tuney took the job out of financial desperation, he found Jack as alien as any other American sportsman. Jack Allen could have been Nelson Rockefeller sitting in the front of the canoe as far as Stan Tuney was concerned.

The people of Brennen Siding couldn't understand foreign places, wealth and formal education, and thought it pretentious to even try.

When the Connecticut lawyer asked Dan Brennen if the boys fishing across the river were natives, he replied, "No, sir, jist some of us lads."

To Dan, a native was a black man from Africa.

When the locals got together with the American sportsmen they were guiding, the common denominator was humor. Bert Todder did not know that all the food a salmon eats originates in photosynthesis. Bert Todder did not have a hunch that the life and death of algae depended on chlorophyll and its reactions to various colours of the spectrum.

When the American sport asked Bert why the salmon would not bite while there were bubbles on the river, Bert did not think of oxygen and carbon dioxide. Had he known of the existence of such words, he might have had a better answer to the American's question . . . . But, probably not.

"Why don't the salmon bite while those bubbles are on the river?" asked the American.

"They're on the toilet," said Bert, "them bubbles are fish farts."

Stan Tuney had grown up with Jack Allen and had recognized the difference in him immediately. Stan couldn't understand how money could change a man so much.

"How's she goin', Jack?" asked Stan.

"Great. What's happening with you, Stan?"

"Not too much. What are you doin' these days?"

Stan knew that Jack was a dentist. He didn't know that Jack was earning a hundred thousand dollars a year, but he could tell that Jack seemed rich. Like all the people of Brennen Siding, Stan was pessimistic and egotistical. When asked, "How's she goin'?" it was a rare occasion that one answered "Great." "Not too good" was the expected answer. Stan Tuney, like all the Brennen Siding dwellers, lived in isolation from the rest of the world. In Brennen Siding, life was difficult; being a timekeeper or a scaler was the ultimate success. Jack Allen was a Brennen Siding boy, but he had become a dentist. Stan couldn't understand how anyone could "become" a dentist. To Stan, dentists were born in foreign places like Fredericton, Saint John, and the

United States. Dentists did not come from Brennen Siding. Being "Great" was not the way a man from Brennen Siding should be.

"I'm still pulling teeth," said Jack.

"Doin' pretty good, are ya?"

Jack Allen had worked hard and was on a badly-needed and well-deserved vacation. He did not see a difference in Stan Tuney. Stan would never change. Jack wanted to fish, drink scotch and relax. He had worked hard to become a dentist and was proud of his accomplishment. Confronted with Stan Tuney, Jack couldn't understand why he was reluctant to admit he was a dentist. For some reason, he felt he might offend Stan by such an admission.

"Oh, not too good," Jack Allen, the dentist from Hartford, lied. "Just makin' ends meet." The lie eased the tension between them, but Jack could never call Brennen Siding "home" again.

*

Shirley hoped that Palidin would not become a lumberjack. She also hoped he would not become a dentist or a lawyer. A timekeeper at the mill in Blackville would be just right.

Although Shirley was somewhat puzzled about the future of Palidin, she had no doubts about Dryfly.

Dryfly hated school, hated books and teachers. Thoughts of the future went no further than this afternoon or tomorrow.

"I hope," thought Shirley, "he will not be afraid of hard work."

When Dryfly disappeared from her view, Shirley sighed and went to the cupboard. She knew there was nothing in it to eat, but she wanted to take inventory anyway. She pulled back the curtains and scanned the shelves.

No bread and no flour to make any.

No molasses.

No potatoes.

No brown sugar.

No milk.

No beans.

No tobacco.

Shirley Ramsey sighed as she picked up the empty yellow and·
red Vogue tobacco package. She shook the package over the
palm of her hand and a few dried, almost sand-like grains of
tobacco fell from it. She tore the package apart and in the folds
of the foil liner, she came up with a few more grains. She spied
a butt lying on the rim of a dish. The butt was only a half-inch
long, but there was tobacco in it. Shirley tore the butt apart and
added the contents to the grains she'd collected from the package. She closed her fist around the tobacco and blew gently into
it to moisten it. She then rolled a cigarette the size of a wooden
match into a Vogue cigarette paper. She sighed again as she went
to the stove for a light. She lifted the cover and added a stick of
alder to the fire. "Alder burns too quick," she thought. "Should
have maple, or beech." She broke off a splinter from a second
piece of alder and set it afire. With this she lit her tiny cigarette.
She pulled up a rickety, backless chair and sat by the table to
smoke and to think.

"No money, no food, no credit left at Hanley's store . . . " She
could charge a few things to her father's bill, but that was doubt-
ful. The fact of the matter was, her father hadn't any money
either.

"If it was a month later, the ice in the river'd be out and the
boys could ketch a salmon, or maybe some trout . . . even chubs
would be better than nothin'."

She contemplated setting a snare for a rabbit, but quickly
brushed the thought aside. "That could take days."

"I'll go to the store and lie," she thought. "I'll tell Bernie
Hanley that me check's comin' tomorrow and that I'll be right
up to pay 'im as soon's it comes. Surely the Blessed Virgin
wouldn' mind such a little lie."

She arose and went to the bedroom and grabbed her coat
from Dry's bed. The coat was green and old and smelled; it had
a frayed collar and cuffs, the pockets were torn and it had but
one button. It wasn't much, but it was all she had for protection
against the cold March wind. She put it on and went back to
the kitchen to size herself up in the piece of mirror that hung

on the wall above the water bucket. She removed what was left of the tiny cigarette from her mouth and dropped it in the slop pail and smiled into the mirror. Most of her teeth were missing, the remaining few decayed and dirty. "They won't matter. I've got no reason to smile anyway." She washed her face in the same dirty, soapy water the children had used earlier, ran a piece of comb through her greasy, straight brown hair and sized up the finished product.

"I'm a hard lookin' ticket," she muttered.

*

Ten minutes later, Shirley Ramsey was at the store pleading her case.

"I git me check tomorrow, Bernie, and me 'lowance check should be here in a week or two, so's I kin pay ya more. I thought maybe you . . . "

"Shirley, I know as good as you do, your check don't come 'til the end of the month! This is only the eighteenth. You owe me over a hundred dollars already and you didn' pay me nothin' last month. Everybody in the settlement owes me! Who ya think I am, Santa Claus?!! I can't afford to pay me own bills anymore! I'm gonna have to close down, if somebody don't soon pay up!"

Bernie was a big, good-looking Baptist with good teeth and wire-rimmed glasses. He wore leather-topped gumshoes, heavy woollen pants, a plaid shirt and a hat. Bernie was never without his hat.

Shirley hadn't wanted to say it and she had no intention of saying it, but she found herself confused and lost for words.

"Then, how's about chargin' a package o' tobacco and a book of papers to Daddy?" she blurted.

"Tobacco and papers? Tobacco and papers?!!"

"And a box o' asberns! . . . Dryfly's sick!" she quickly added. She was frightened and humiliated. She recognized her mistake. She should never have given tobacco priority to a Baptist. Tobacco had been the last thing on her list.

Bernie, too, was lost for words. He was amazed at the request. "Her kids are prob'ly starvin' to death, she hasn't got a stitch o'

27

clothes worth puttin' on, and she asks for tobacco!" he thought. He grabbed a package of Players tobacco (not even her brand) and practically threw it at her. The papers and aspirins followed in much the same way.

"There!" he snapped. "That's the last thing yer gettin' 'till I git me pay! Don't come back 'till ya got some cash!"

Shirley was about to cry and she knew it. To save perhaps a shred of dignity, she grabbed the items and left. "Thanks Bernie," she said.

Through the window, Bernie could see her walking, too fast for a woman, too masculine, towards the road.

"She smells like a rag barrel," mumbled Bernie. "God only knows why I'm so generous."

Bernie Hanley popped a peppermint into his mouth, sighed and added tobacco, papers and aspirins to "Daddy's" bill.

*

Shirley cried, but not for long. It was not the time for crying. It was the time for action. She wiped the tears from her eyes with the back of her hand. She wiped her nose on the green, tattered cuff of her coat.

"'Cludin' me, there's one, two . . . nine mouths to feed and there's nothin' to eat," she thought. She would not get a check for as long as two weeks. She could not starve her children for two weeks.

The north wind sweeping up Gordon Road was so strong that at times Shirley had to turn away from it and walk backwards, in order to breath.

A pair of men's long underwear hanging on Bernie Hanley's clothesline danced and flapped as if the spirit of their owner remained in them. The trees, too, bent and sighed in the howling wind as if possessed by some forbidding and tormented spirit.

With some difficulty (she was walking backwards), Shirley quickened her pace. She was determined to win the struggle against this devilish wind so set on holding her back, its cold breath its greatest persuasion.

"The line gales," she thought, "they come every spring, just like Buck use to. The whole world is gettin' screwed. What's the sense in having young lads, if they all gotta suffer and die?"

She turned and faced the wind once again and suddenly, eerily, she had the strange feeling the underwear was following her. She quickened her pace again and found herself nearly running towards the safety of her home.

"The whole damned country's full o' ghosts," she thought. "It's like that strange bird that keeps singin', but ya kin never see; and what do the dogs bark at at night?"

It had taken her ten minutes to go to the store; it took her five minutes to return home — home; the grey, weathered shingles; the tarpaper patches; the stovepipe with its wafts of smoke so quickly consumed by the wind. On a warmer day, the March sun had melted and deformed the dirty snowbanks lining the path to the door; today the pools, some foot-sized, some larger, were frozen so that Shirley half ran, half skated to the door.

Before entering the house, she glanced over her shoulder.

"I must be going crazy," she thought, but was thankful the underwear hadn't followed her.

Back in her kitchen, she went to the stove and placed a couple of sticks on the fire. The wind was rising with the sun and it slapped the plastic, threatening to tear it from the kitchen window. She sat by the table and opened the new package of tobacco, wondering who she might turn to for help.

She thought of the priest twelve miles away. It was very cold, the wind too strong. "Perhaps tomorrow, though."

She thought of the neighbors. "Damn near as poor as me."

She thought of prostitution, but dropped the thought with the recollection of the morning's portrait in the mirror.

She thought of Nutbeam, the mystery man who lived in the woods, seen so seldom, always hidden behind his collar, or hood. Nobody in Brennen Siding could say for sure what he looked like.

Everyone had a different opinion of Nutbeam. Dan Brennen thought he might be the mad trapper from the Yukon . . . . "Albert Johnson, or whatever his name is." Dan Brennen did not know that Albert Johnson had laid his last Mountie low and had been resting in the Yukon permafrost for many years.

Lindon Tucker thought Nutbeam might be a ghost, "or even the devil, yeah, yeah, yeah. The devil, yeah. Oh, yeah."

Stan Tuney claimed to know Nutbeam. Said he was a fine gentleman with lots of money. "Money to burn, so he does!" Nobody ever believed a word Stan Tuney said.

Whoever Nutbeam was, Shirley Ramsey knew she could not turn to him. Besides, she didn't even know where he lived. Nutbeam, to Shirley, was all of the above.

Then, Shirley thought of the Post Office. There was maybe as much as ten dollars in the Post Office float. She could borrow the ten dollars and manage until her check came and then pay the money back. But the stamps were due to arrive and she needed the stamps to keep the Post Office operating. If she took the money, she would not be able to pay for the stamps. Her supply would run out and people would want to know why they couldn't mail a letter. They'd report her. The head Postmaster from Blackville would pay her a visit and there'd be nothing for Shirley to do but tell the truth.

"Something came over me. I don't know what it was. I stole the money."

She'd be taken off to jail and maybe fined, the children trotted off to orphanages.

But the money was there. Handy. Accessible. Twelve dollars maybe, if she took the change, too. And nobody would know unless she ran out of stamps. If nobody mailed any parcels or letters for a couple of weeks, until she got her check, nobody would ever know. She fought back the temptation. "What's happenin' to me?" she asked herself. "Why am I settin' here thinkin' of stealin', when I should be on my knees prayin'?"

Then, as if to answer her questions, she heard the lonesome, distant whistle of the train. It was not the train they called the "Whooper." The Whooper had been replaced by a diesel years before. This was only the Express, the train that brought the mail every morning; the train that picked up and dropped off a few passengers going to and from villages and towns; the train whose whistle now seemed like a mournful cry from the forest, causing a chill to course its way down Shirley's back. The whistle seemed too timely, as if it had heard her, as if it was showing its approval or disapproval of her thoughts of stealing, its voice enhanced and amplified by the wind.

Shirley stood. "It's no time to be settin' around," she thought. "An idle brain is the devil's workshop, Daddy use to say." She went to the Post Office, retrieved the mailbag with the two letters locked inside, donned her coat once again and headed for the siding, the weight of poverty heavy on her shoulders, the winds no less haunting, no less cold.

When she arrived at the kempt little red building with the veranda that stood no more than a couple of feet from the tracks, she found she was right on time. The Express (a diesel engine, one passenger car and a caboose) pulled to a squeaking, grinding ten-second halt.

There were several people aboard, some of whom gazed down at her as though with pity; sad, unsmiling eyes, staring at her as if she was an animal in a zoo.

Shirley drew back her shoulders a bit, feigning dignity. But the attempt was feeble; she was too aware of herself; her ragged old coat; her fear. She looked away.

"Ya'd think they never saw a poor woman before in their lives," she thought. "Am I the only one? Why am I the only poor woman in the world?"

A tall, thin man dismounted from the train.

Shirley experienced a twinge of fear at the sight of him. She couldn't believe that so many things could be haunting her on the same morning. "What's goin' on here?" she thought, and "speak of the devil . . . ." The man was wearing a parka with an oversized hood. The hood was furry and hung low enough to hide his face, but she knew it was Nutbeam. She had never seen him before, but she knew.

"Lovely day," she said.

Nutbeam did not speak to her, did not nod his hooded head, did not even look at her. He strode swiftly away, carrying a black case under his arm.

Shirley traded mailbags with the porter and the train moved on toward its destination, Boiestown.

When she got back to the house, Bert Todder, John Kaston, Lindon Tucker and Dan Brennen were waiting for her. They stood in the sun, on the south side of the house away from the wind.

Shirley led them inside and unlocked the mailbag. The men waited. Dan Brennen eyed the untidiness of Shirley's house with disgust.

John Kaston got a copy of *Decision Magazine*, Bert Todder a letter from Linda who lived in Fredericton; Lindon Tucker, as usual, got no mail at all (Yeah, yeah, yeah, oh yeah, no mail's good mail, yeah, yes sir, yeah, yeah, yeah). Dan Brennen got a bill from Lounsbury's in Newcastle. Dan Brennen owed for the battery radio he listened to every night.

The men left and when they were a step further than an ear-shot away, Dan Brennen said, "Boy, she's a hard lookin' ticket, ain't she?"

"Hard lookin' ticket, yeah. Oh yeah, that's right, Dan old boy, old chummy pard, yeah, hard lookin' ticket, yeah." Lindon Tucker agreed with everything anybody said.

Back in the Post Office, Shirley sorted the rest of the mail: a letter for Helen MacDonald, a bill for Bob Nash, the *Family Herald* for Bernie Hanley and a bill for Lester Burns. She placed the mail in their rightful compartments, then opened the cash box and commenced counting the money inside. $12.60.

Then, she counted her stamp supply. Eight ten-centers, six five-centers and 19 two-centers.

She went into the kitchen, knelt before the only wall adornment in the house (the Crucifix), and prayed: "Hail, Mary, full or grace, blessed art thou among women . . . "

That night the family ate bologna and potatoes for supper. No one questioned where the food had fallen from, and only Shirley knew for sure.

*

Thursday night, the twentieth of March, Bert Todder was watering his horse (Queen) by the light of a kerosene lantern, when he heard the strange cry from the forest. It was a lonesome call that resembled nothing he had ever heard. It sounded neither human nor animal and it couldn't have been a train whistle; the railroad was in the opposite direction.

He was about to shrug it off as a car horn, when it came again . . . again . . . and again.

"It's comin' from back on Todder Brook," he said to Queen. "No cars back on Todder Brook. It's not a car horn anyway."

Queen didn't answer, sighed contentedly and continued to drink.

Lindon Tucker was "seeing a man about a horse" (which was his term for having a piss behind the shed), when he also heard the eerie call.

Both Lindon and Bert, as well as John Kaston and Dan Brennen, heard it on Friday night. On Saturday night, because nothing is ever kept secret in Brennen Siding, everyone in the settlement was out beneath the stars listening to the still unidentified scream from the distant forest.

Saturday night was the first night in Brennen Siding's history that every door was locked.

It was heard again on Sunday night, but only for a few moments.

On Monday evening, fifteen men and boys stood around in Bernie Hanley's store, eating oranges and drinking Sussex ginger ale.

On Monday evening in Bernie Hanley's store, the conversation was not about Joe Louis, the Saturday night jamboree, or the price of pulp wood. On Monday evening in Bernie Hanley's store, the conversation was not about Shirley Ramsey and Ford cars; nor did the men dwell on gold in the Yukon, or horses. Monday evening, the conversation rambled around everything from rabbits crying to the eerie screams of the eastern cougar; from the strange and numerous variations in the fox's bark, to ghosts and the devil.

"I wouldn't take a million dollars for goin' into that woods over there tonight," said Bob Nash. "Not even with me 303."

"No, sir! A panther kin climb and he'd git ya from a tree. Ya'd not know he was there 'till 'e was on top o' ya," put in Bert Todder. The panther was the cat that everyone decided upon . . . it, somehow, sounded better than cougar.

"Me? I don't think we're dealin' wit' a pant'er at all," began Stan Tuney. Stan Tuney always ate his oranges with the peel still on them. That's how they ate them in the Yukon, he'd been told. "I was back Todder Brook last Tuesday and I must've seen a t'ousand moose tracks. The biggest moose tracks I ever seen!"

"Are you sayin' we got us a moose runnin' round t'rew the woods blattin' his head off, Stan?" asked Bert. "I'd say t'was a pant'er, meself. Me father always said that the Dungarvon whooper was a pant'er!"

"There ain't been a panther in this woods for a hundred years!" said Dan Brennen with authority. "They never were panthers anyway. They were what you call eastern cougars."

"I ain't sayin' we're hearin' moose, or panthers," said Stan. "What I'm sayin' is, I saw tracks that I thought was made by a moose. Cloven hooves is what I saw, so I did, if ya know what I mean, like, see?"

"What would the devil want back Todder Brook?" laughed Dan Brennen, as if the whole idea was stupid and nobody could possibly know anything about this except himself.

But John Kaston was the true authority here. John had read the Bible, and only the Bible would have the answers to such a mystery. He demanded attention by thumping his fist on the counter in the way that Reverend Mather might thump the pulpit.

"Don't you know that the wilderness is the playground of Satan?!" yelled John, as if frustrated with their stupidity. "Did he not tempt the Savior in the woods?! Wasn't it in the woods where he tried to get the good Lord to turn the rocks into bread, and Jesus said that man can't live on bread alone? I tell ya, that he walks the Dungarvon jist the same as he walked . . . the Jordan. It's right there in the Bible! All ya gotta do is read yer Bible!"

Later, walking home, Dryfly was thankful he had his gun-shaped stick in his pocket. Somehow, its presence made him feel more secure. He was also thankful Palidin was with him. Palidin did not seem to be afraid at all.

*

The next morning when Constable Bastarache pulled up in front of Shirley Ramsey's house in his RCMP cruiser, Shirley experienced a twinge of fear like none other she had ever experienced before. The constable was the handsomest and most fearsome man she'd ever seen. He was six feet tall and muscular, wore a gun and big brown boots, and perhaps the most fearsome thing of all, the Royal Canadian Mounted Police uniform. The yellow stripes down the outside of his breeches screamed, "We Mounties always get our man . . . or woman!"

Her first thought was that she'd have to kill him and run off with his car. The thought dissipated quickly, however, for Shirley Ramsey knew she couldn't kill a fly and not feel guilt. She also knew she didn't know how to drive a car.

"How did he find out so soon?" she asked herself. "Who could've know'd I took the money from the Post Office? The kids must've guessed and told it at school."

Shirley had visions of bars and chains, of the kids being taken to orphanages all over the country, never to see her, or each other again. She grew so terrified that her legs began to tremble and weaken. She sat by the table and began to cry. When the constable knocked authoritatively on the door, she had already finished her second "Hail, Mary."

"Come in!" she sobbed openly. There was no sense in trying to hide the tears.

The door opened and there he stood like God himself. Three clunks of his big boots and he was in the kitchen looming over her.

She could smell his aftershave and thought she could even feel the warmth of his breath.

"Are you Mrs. James Ramsey?" he asked.

In the emotional condition she was in, she did not hear the gentleness in his voice.

She nodded. "I'm so very poor," she whimpered, "I needed food for poor little Dry and Pal . . . and everyone."

"My name is Constable Bastarache of the RCMP and . . . and, well it seems you already know. Anyway, I was to inform you. . . I'm sorry."

"You're sorry . . . it was me that did it."

"You shouldn't blame yourself, Ma'am, I'm sure you must have loved him very much."

"Him . . . who?"

"Your husband, Ma'am. I'm sure you will miss him terribly. I lost a loved one myself recently. We just have to be strong."

"My husband? Buck? Has something happened to Buck?"

"Ah . . . then, you don't know, Ma'am?"

"Know? Know what?"

"Ah . . . Mr. Ramsey has been found . . . ah, dead, Ma'am."

Shirley uttered something incoherent. What she was trying to say was, "My God, my God, my God!"

"I'm terribly sorry," said the Mountie. "Can I get you . . . a glass of water, a cup of tea, perhaps?"

"No, no, I'll be alright . . . how did it happen? When? How did he die?"

"He was found on a wharf in Saint John on the ninth of February. Exposure . . . he may have frozen to death."

"The ninth of February? That's six weeks ago."

"Yes, . . . he wasn't carrying any identification. It took the Saint John police until yesterday to track things down."

"Is he buried yet?"

"I'm afraid so, Ma'am. You could have him exhumed and brought back here, if you wished."

"No, no. I wouldn't do that. I suppose he should've been buried in Gordon . . . Buck's Catholic . . . but he never liked it around here much . . . he's prob'ly happy where he is."

"He was buried in a public cemetery, Ma'am, but we could arrange for a priest to sanctify the grave, if you wished."

"Yes, yes. Could you? And I'll see the priest in Blackville about a Mass."

"Of course, Ma'am."

"Thank-you."

"There's one more thing, Ma'am."

"Yes?"

"His belongings."

"Yes?"

"Mr. Ramsey had a room at 371 Collier Street in Saint John . . . there's this envelope," the constable handed Shirley an envelope, "and I've several items in the car."

"Yes, thank you very much."

Buck's worldly possessions consisted of a guitar, a radio, a pocket watch that didn't work and $163.82 in cash. The cash was in the envelope.

After Constable Bastarache left, Shirley Ramsey cried a few solemn tears, but the twinge of fear she had felt was replaced with a flood of relief.

*

A week later Shirley Ramsey's bill at Bernie Hanley's store was paid in full. There were ten dollars worth of new stamps in the Post Office and Dryfly was being The Lone Ranger more often than not, with his shiny, new cap gun.

Shirley's family allowance and Post Office check had arrived and she found herself sitting, for the moment, on the proverbial pig's back.

three

Shirley Ramsey, in a peculiar sort of way, was becoming famous. She was becoming a symbol of poverty, ugliness and untidiness for Brennen Siding, for all the Gordon Road area, and even mothers as far away as Blackville and Renous were telling their children: "You'd better get to school and learn, or you'll grow up to be poorer than Shirley Ramsey!" Because of her few yellow teeth and straight unkempt hair, her neglected figure and ragged clothing, she was literally becoming a household word in the community.

When Helen MacDonald was washing out the barrels she used for salting gaspereaux, she remarked: "smells worse than Shirley Ramsey!"

Bert Todder got drunk on rum one night and told Helen MacDonald that she was the prettiest woman in Brennen Siding. Helen promptly replied: "Git out with ya, ya drunken fool! I'm homelier than Shirley Ramsey!"

Bert once described the antlers of a buck he'd shot — "Pon me soul to God, they had sixteen points and were wider than ... than ... than Shirley Ramsey's arse! Tee, hee, hee, sob, sniff, snort!"

Dan Brennen drove all the way to Newcastle for a pair of boots for his son Charlie. When he entered the boot store, he realized he hadn't asked Charlie his boot size. Dan muttered: "Bejesus, I'm getting stupider than Shirley Ramsey!"

Shirley's name was used in other ways as well. For instance, if Shirley had a tool shed (which she didn't), it would have but two things in it, an axe and a dull rusty buck saw. Besides the chopping and sawing of whatever stove wood the Ramseys could collect, the saw and the axe were also used for the execution of whatever repair jobs were needed to be done. The outdoor toilet was built, for instance, with the saw and the axe. The porch over the door was also built with the saw and the axe, and so was the lean-to shed erected every November for a wood shelter.

These constructions did not go unnoticed. Most of the cuts were crooked, and many of the nails, driven with the back of the axe, were bent over.

John Kaston started the "Shirley Ramsey-the-bad-carpenter" ball rolling when he made a bad cut while making his kitchen cupboards. "Darn!" he swore, "I Shirley Ramsied it!"

While Buck was living, nobody in Brennen Siding would lift a finger to assist Shirley in any way. Buck was supposed to be responsible. If the Ramsey family starved to death, the inhabitants of Brennen Siding would not have felt the slightest twinge of remorse or guilt. After all, if a man can't look out for his family, he can't expect someone else to. "Buck went away and let that whole family starve to death," Dan Brennan might say, while cutting into a roast of beef.

When the people of Brennen Siding learned of Buck's death, however, Shirley Ramsey took on a different status: "the widow." Shirley Ramsey, the estranged wife, deserved nothing. Shirley Ramsey, the widow, needed help. Stan Tuney gave Shirley a bucket of potatoes and a bucket of carrots. "You kin keep the buckets," Stan told her. Dan Brennen gave Shirley a bucket of corned beef — "The bucket kin be used for carrying water from the brook," said Dan. "Water is good for bathin' in." Dan Brennen said this as though it was a great new revelation. He said a lot of things that way. Brennen Siding was named after his grandfather. He felt that made him special, that he was perhaps smarter and better than everyone else.

John and Max Kaston were cleaning out the summer kitchen. Max was gazing into a keg of brine.

"What'll I do with these old gaspereaux?" he asked. "They ain't no good for anything."

"Might as well throw them out. The gaspereaux will soon be runnin' anyway."

"Maybe we should give them to Shirley Ramsey."

"Good idea, Max. I'll take them down to her later."

John Kaston was religious; he wanted to be a preacher. When he got up to Shirley Ramsey's with a bucket full of gaspereaux, he said: "When the fish are gone, you can use the bucket for carryin' water. Cleanliness is Godliness, you know."

Shirley Ramsey was a Catholic and John Kaston was a Baptist forever trying to convert her. He had one reservation though; he wasn't sure if he wanted the likes of her associated with the church. Who'd want to sit beside her?

Lindon Tucker, who was never previously known to give anything away, gave Shirley an old galvanized tub he'd found in the barn.

"No, no, no, I want you to have it, Shirley old girl. Want ya to have it, yeah, yeah, yeah. Good tub, that. Yep. O yeah, yep, good tub, yep."

"Thanks, Lindon. It's awful good o' ya."

"Don't, don't, don't mention it, Shirley old girl. Glad, glad, glad to do it, don't, don't, don't mention it."

Bert Todder showed up, too, with a black salmon. Bert Todder was short and fat; he had a single tooth in the front of his mouth that you saw whenever he laughed. He'd show his tooth, squint his eyes and commence to jiggle and shake; the sound coming from within, more like sobs than laughter. Everyone liked him and he visited everyone in Brennen Siding once a week. He was the reporter. When he visited, he'd mean only to stay for five or ten minutes. When ten minutes was up, he'd stand and say, "Well, I gotta go." Then, he'd talk for five or ten more minutes and say, "Boys, I should be off." Before he got through the door, though, he'd remember that he hadn't told you about Lester Burns falling in the river and narrowly escaping drowning, the story taking ten minutes to tell. He might sit down again to tell it, at the end of which he'd say, "It's time to leave, I gotta go home."

Bert Todder usually stayed all evening.

Bert Todder even paid weekly visits to Shirley Ramsey. She made good news.

Because of Bert Todder, there were no secrets in Brennen Siding.

Todder Brook was named after Bert's grandfather and ran through Bert's property. Bert lived the nearest of all to the Todder Brook Whooper.

*

Shadrack Nash wanted to investigate the Todder Brook Whooper, but didn't want to do it alone.

He went to Max Kaston and was laughed at. Max snorted, said, "You're crazier than Shirley Ramsey.

"There ain't nothin' to be scared of," said Shad.

"Then go alone," Max eyed Shad over his chubby cheeks.

"You're just too lazy to go," said Shad and left.

Shad found George Hanley and Palidin Ramsey, smoking cigarettes, out behind Bernie Hanley's barn.

George Hanley's ears were too big, as were his hands and feet; but his teeth were white and even, he had long eyelashes and was almost pretty in the face.

"I wouldn't take a million dollars to step one foot into that woods!" said George.

The fair-skinned, brown-eyed, mysterious Palidin Ramsey (all the Ramseys were mysterious), said nothing. Palidin knew he was not being invited on the adventure. Shadrack Nash did not know that Palidin Ramsey had no fear.

Out of desperation, Shad went to Shirley Ramsey's. He found Dryfly sitting on the doorstep, strumming a G chord over and over again on Buck's guitar. Shad had learned a few chords from his father and had passed his knowledge along to Dryfly. He had traded the G chord for a Glenn Hall. By mid-June, he was on the verge of completing his hockey card collection. He was only missing Johnny Bower of the Toronto Maple Leafs. A Lou Fontenato and a Johnny Bucyk and he'd have the whole NHL. He was holding on to a C chord, just in case Dryfly might get lucky enough to get one of the cards he needed.

"What're ya doin'?" asked Shad, as if he didn't already know.

"Playin' me guiddar."

"Soundin' pretty good."

Dryfly shrugged. He was thin and needed a haircut.

"Don't know anymore chords, yet, eh?"

"No," said Dryfly.

"Gonna listen to the jamboree tonight?"

"Might."

Shad was referring to the Saturday Night Jamboree that was broadcast from CFNB Fredericton every week — Earl Mitton on the fiddle, Bud Brown the emcee, Kid and Ada Baker the guests more often than not.

"I am," said Shadrack. "Wanna come over and listen to it with me?"

"What for? I can hear it on me own radio."

"I got something I want us to do afterwards."

"Gonna be awful close to dark by the time the jamboree's over."

"I know," shrugged Shadrack. "I want it to be dark."

"What're ya gonna be doin' in the dark?"

"I'm goin' back to see what's makin' that noise."

"The Todder Brook Whooper?"

"Yep."

"What if it's a ghost?"

"I don't care."

"What if it's a panther?"

"Takin' Dad's 303."

"Yeah? How'd ya git that?"

"I know where it is. I'll just sneak it out. Know where the bullits are, too. Wanna come with me?"

"Nope. Ya'll never ketch me in that woods!"

"Why not?"

"Cause."

"Cause why?"

"Cause, ya wouldn'."

"Scared?"

"No, but I ain't goin'."

"Why?"

"I just told ya!"

"Yer scared!"

"I'm not!"

"I'm taken the 303."

"You'd be a pretty lad, shootin' a ghost with a big rifle like that! Knock ya arse over kettles!"

"Don't kick hardly at all. I'll let ya try it, if ya want."

"You fire it first."

"I'll fire it. It don't kick. Fire it all the time, so I do!"

"What if ya get lost?"

"All we'll do is follow the trail back and then follow it home again."

"The flies will eat us up, back there in the woods at night."

"No flies hardly at all. Work up a sweat and they never touch ya."

It was approaching the middle of June and Dryfly doubted very much that he could work up enough sweat to combat the forty-two thousand and one flies that would be attacking him back in the Dungarvon woods.

"Come with me and I'll tell ya how to put a C chord on."

"C chord?"

"Yep. Dad says if ya know C and G chords ya kin play any song at all."

"How far back ya goin'?"

"Not far."

"What if it's a ghost?"

"It's a panther."

"How do ya know?"

"Dad says."

"How ya gonna shoot a panther in the dark?"

"Takin' Dad's flashlight, too."

"Yeah?"

"Yep. You kin carry the flashlight and I'll carry the rifle. We'll jack 'im. You hold the light on his eyes and I'll down the bugger."

Dryfly thought of the rifle, the flashlight and the two of them gunning down a panther. Dryfly wasn't sure what a panther was, but he reckoned it was a throaty creature, by the sounds that came from it every night. He thought of the C chord and himself being able to play every song ever sung. He thought of the adventure and the stories that they'd tell everyone. He thought of being Shadrack Nash's friend; of being closer to Shad than George Hanley or Max Kaston were.

"I'll come over after supper," said Dryfly, "wanna come in and have some supper with us?"

"What're ya havin'?"

"Salmon."

"No thanks. Never cared much for salmon."

Shad left thinking that he wouldn't take a million dollars for eating Shirley Ramsey's cooking.

*

Sneaking the rifle and the flashlight out was almost too easy for any kind of interesting adventure. Bob Nash had gone fishing and Shadrack's mother was sewing in the kitchen. The rifle stood behind a chair in the livingroom. Shad hid the flashlight under his belt. To get the rifle, all Shad had to do was pick it up and go with it.

Outside, Shad gave Dryfly the flashlight. They reckoned they had an hour before it would be dark enough to use it.

The trail that led to Todder Brook country was an old, neglected trucking road, originally used for hauling out pulp, logs and boxwood, but it was evident that the road hadn't been used for years. The tire ruts were still there, but blueberry bushes and even the odd alder bush flourished in the center. Shadrack walked in one rut and Dryfly in the other. Neither boy felt like talking. Both boys were scared. Neither would admit it. Shad cocked the rifle the moment they entered the forest.

There was the odd bird singing and insect buzzing, the setting sun sat like a golden bonnet on the tops of the taller trees.

"How much further we goin'?" asked Dryfly after a while.

"I don't know. Maybe a mile. I don't know."

"Seems to me we've come a long way already. Do you think it's that far away?"

"I don't know."

They continued to walk until they heard the rushing sounds of Todder Brook. Here, they noticed that the ground was speckled with numerous hoof prints — some deer and some bigger prints they hoped were those of moose.

"I don't smell anythin'," commented Dryfly, staring at the hoof prints.

"What odds if ya smell anything?" asked Shad. "I doubt if a human could smell a panther, anyway, unless he had his nose right up against 'im."

"Mom told me that the devil's spose' to smell like shit."

"How's she know that?"

"Don't know. That's what she told me."

"That's foolish," said Shadrack, but he sniffed the air anyway.

Dryfly noticed that the sun had left the treetops and the twilight had replaced it. The anticipation of the approaching night and the inevitable darkness of the forest was not what Dryfly considered to be a good time.

"I think we should go home, Shad. I have to cross the footbridge tonight. It's tricky in the dark."

"You kin have the flashlight."

Dryfly sighed.

Shadrack and Dryfly found a big pine tree and after eyeing it to make sure there were no cougars in its midst, they sat close together with their backs against its trunk. They could not be attacked from behind.

Time ticked on and darkness fell.

There in the night, every sound (the snapping of a twig, the hooting of an owl, a breeze whispering in the boughs above them) quickened their imaginative young hearts. Every shadow, every form, seemed a potential threat, and sometimes what they knew was only a tree or shrub seemed to actually move. Dryfly checked out his surroundings with the flashlight about every ten seconds. Shadrack didn't complain.

"What's that?"

"Where?"

"There!"

"I don't see anything."

"There. I heard a thump."

"Where?"

"Listen!"

Dryfly couldn't hear anything, except his heart beating, but he wasn't sure. There might have been something. He might have missed something . . . he wasn't sure. "I think we should go home," he whispered.

"Why?"

"It's gettin' awful late."

"Shhhh!"

"Mom'll kill me."

"Wait a few more minutes."

Another deep sigh escaped from Dryfly.

A bird sang, its song piercing the silence, crisp and clear. Dryfly could not identify it — he hadn't heard it before. "Indians," he thought.

Palidin had read a book about cowboys and Indians, in which the Indians had used the songs of birds as a form of communication. Dryfly remembered Palidin's reference to the tale.

"I hope they're dead Indians," he thought.

The bird sang again and somehow sounded mournful and forsaken. "No," thought Dryfly, "I hope they are alive."

A Gander-bound plane rumbled far up amidst the stars, its flicker somehow reassuring as it crossed the Dipper.

A mosquito hummed by his ear. The bird sang once more.

"What bird is that?" whispered Dryfly.

"What bird?"

" . . . That one."

"Don't hear it."

A few minutes passed and Shad decided he'd had enough.

"Let's go," he whispered. The words "let's go" came like poetry to Dryfly's ears.

They followed the flashlight beam out on the trail, their feet thumping the ground and swishing the bushes as they hurried along.

Dryfly counted to himself, "One less step, two less, three, four, five, six . . . "

*

When a rabbit has lost the chase and finds himself cornered by a hungry fox, a strange phenomenon occurs. The rabbit gives up, goes into a trance-like state, a fear-induced state of paralysis, and sometimes even dies, robbing the fox of the thrill of the kill.

When Shadrack and Dryfly heard the honk from no more than a hundred yards off to their right, they stopped in a trance just short of death. The flashlight dropped from Dryfly's hand to smash the ground and go out at his feet. Darkness reigned supreme.

"Thump, thump, thump," went a heartbeat.

Dryfly wasn't sure if it was his own heart or Shadrack's.

Shadrack wasn't sure either.

"BEEP-BARMP-BARMP!" went the noise in the forest. The brief silence that followed was disrupted by a fart. Both boys knew that it had been Dryfly's release. For a moment it was impossible to say if, or if not, they were smelling the devil.

Shadrack gripped the 303 so tight that he might have been attempting to leave finger dents in the wood.

"What do we do now?" asked Dryfly in a tiny voice that seemed not to be his own.

Shadrack didn't know. He couldn't think. To run seemed to be the logical move, but in his confusion he prayed instead, silently. "Now I lay me down to sleep, I pray to God my soul to keep . . . "

"Thump, thump, thump," went a heartbeat Dryfly identified as his own. "Hail Mary, full of grace, blessed art thou amongst women . . . "

"BARMP! BARMP-BARMP, BEEP-BEEP!" went the noise that sounded like a sick car horn, an elephant, perhaps the scream of an eastern cougar, or all three.

"Got the gun, Shad?" asked Dryfly, his voice still very tiny in the great dark forest.

"Right here!" said Shadrack. "Want it?"

"You know how to use it?"

"Just pull the trigger, I think."

"BARMP, TWEEP, BLEEP!"

"You scared?"

"What'd you say?"

"You scared?"

"No. I don't think so."

"BARMP-BARMP HONK! BEEP-BEEP, BARMP-BARMP!"

As their eyes adjusted to the darkness, they were able to make out the trail before them — a navy line in a black-forested field, a mere reflection of the azure. Dew drops imprisoned the azure.

"The noise is coming from down by the brook," whispered Shadrack.

"Fire the gun! You might scare it off, if it's a cougar." Dryfly whispered back, spying for the first time since he dropped it, the flashlight. He knelt and picked it up. He pushed the button. The bulb was blown.

"Won't it work?" asked Shad, musing over Dryfly's suggestion to shoot the gun.

"The bulb's blowed," said Dryfly.

"Do you think a shot would do it?"

BARMP-BARMP! BEEP-BEEP! BARMP! continued the noise in the forest.

"It can't hurt!" said Dryfly.

Shad pointed the rifle at the sky. "I hope it's a cougar! I hope it's a cougar, I hope it's a cougar . . . " he chanted to himself. "I hope it runs away when I shoot, runs when I shoot, runs when I shoot . . ." He could have been memorizing a poem. "Oh God, make it run. I'll be good and go to church and everything," he prayed.

BARMP-BARMP-BARMP! BAR-AR-AR-ARMP!

"POW!!!" went the rifle.

Silence and the smell of gunsmoke.

*

Lindon Tucker never installed electricity in his house, but he had a battery radio. Lindon Tucker lived with his mother and an old tomcat called "Cat." When Lindon called Cat in at night, he called "kitty, kitty, kitty."

"Kitty, kitty, kitty," called Lindon.

"Meow," went Cat and zipped through the kitchen door into the dimly lit room, meowed as it scanned the dark corners for mice, then jumped onto the cot behind the kitchen range.

Lindon closed the door and went back to his rocking chair.

Everyone in Brennen Siding figured that Lindon kept his lamps turned low to save on kerosene. He may have kept the volume of his battery radio equally as low to save on batteries. Lindon Tucker wasted nothing. When he shopped at Bernie Hanley's store, Lindon saved every inch of twine from the parcels; he also saved the brown paper. He saved the aluminum foil from the inside of tobacco packages and the remains of used wooden matches.

Lindon Tucker picked his teeth with the remains of used wooden matches.

Lindon Tucker's mother sat with her ear not more than six inches from the radio speaker. From the CKMR station in Newcastle, Brother Duffy was busily condemning sinners. CKMR, the community voice of the Miramichi.

Hayshaker's Hoedown at 7:00 p.m. News, sports and weather followed by the marine weather forecast with its Brown's Le-Havres and Fundy Coasts, came on at 7:30. The exotic names mentioned in the marine forecast, the sound effects (ships bells and fog horns) were soothing, like poetry to Lindon. At 8:30 some heathen Catholic thing came on, which Lindon always turned off. He'd turn the radio back on at 9:00, set the dial at 550 and listen to the Saturday night jamboree on CFNB.

"The jamboree was better than usual tonight," thought Lindon. "Freddy McKenna, Freddy McKenna, that blind lad, Freddy McKenna was on it tonight. They claim he plays his giddar turned up on his lap."

At 10:00 p.m., Lindon had to oblige his mother and shift the dial back to CKMR for a Bible-thumping half hour of Oral Roberts.

Lindon didn't mind the preaching. At least it kept his mother from complaining for a half hour.

Claa, Lindon's mother, was eighty years old and hadn't been sick for forty years. The gift of health didn't keep her from complaining, however. Lindon was subjected to her complaining day in and day out, her voice whining and whimpering even when she was talking about it being a nice day.

"Bless us and save us," she whined. "Yes, yes, Lord. Dear Jesus!"

When Oral Roberts said "Hallelujah!" for the last time and went off the air, Clara leaned back in her chair and squinted her eyes to see Lindon. Her eyesight was good, but the lamp was turned down to a mere glow.

"My toe's botherin' me, Lindon. You think a person could git cancer in a toe? Some claim ya kin, some claim ya can't. You kin git gangrene in yer toe. Old Billy Todder died of gangrene in the toe. I've heard of people dying of cancer of the bowels and the stomach, but I don't know about the toe. I don't know about gangrene of the stomach either. Do you think a corn could turn to cancer, Lindon?"

"Oh yeah, yeah, yeah. Yeah. Cancer, yeah," said Lindon, reaching for the dial.

Lindon stopped turning the dial when he heard the rich and mellow voice of Doc Williams talking about a picture Bible. "Just write 'Picture Bible,' WWVA, Wheeling, West Virginia," Doc was saying. "And now I'd like to do y'all a song I very much enjoy and I hope y'all at home will enjoy too."

The guitar was strummed. It sounded deep and rich. Doc Williams was the best guitar player in the world—
Hannah! Hannah!
Hannah won't you open the door.
Hannah, Hannah, Hannah,
Won't you change you manna'
This is old Doc Williams,
Don't you love me no more?
— and Lindon thought that Doc Williams was the best singer in the world, too . . . with the exception of, maybe, Lee Moore.

When Doc Williams ended his show by picking "Wildwood Flower" and had gone the way of Brother Duffy and Oral Roberts, Lindon stood, yawned and headed for the door. He needed to have a leak before going to bed.

"Where ya goin'?" asked Clara.

"To see a man about a horse," said Lindon.

The night was moonless, the deep blue sky spangled with a million stars, the milky way straight up. The air was warm and scented with lilacs and grass. The songs of a million night creatures (peepers, Lindon called them) betrayed the presence of a swamp. The air buzzed and hummed with midges, blackflies and mosquitoes. A bird sang . . . like a robin . . . but not a robin; a swamp robin, perhaps.

Off in the east, back on Todder Brook, came the now familiar screams of what Lindon figured was the devil.

Then suddenly a rifle shot sounded from the same direction and the devil fell silent.

"Hmm, a shot in the dark," muttered Lindon.

Somebody standing behind him might have thought that Lindon was directing his comment at his penis.

four

Nutbeam lived in a tiny camp in the forest back on Todder Brook. He'd built the camp five years ago on somebody's land (he didn't know that it was the lumber section of the old abandoned Graig Allen farm) and none of the locals, as of yet, had located him. A couple of hunters came close a couple of times, but that was all.

Although Nutbeam could not read or write, he was not uneducated. He knew all there was to know about living in the woods. He was an expert trapper, hunter, fisherman and axeman. He knew every shrub, weed, wildflower, fern, berry, cherry, mushroom and nut; which ones were edible and which ones were not. He was an expert in a canoe and on a pair of snowshoes. He had gathered his knowledge from experience, mostly in the last five years.

Nutbeam was six feet, six inches tall and had a thirty-two inch waist. With a nose four inches long, big negroid lips and ears the size of dessert plates, Nutbeam was, indeed, homelier than Shirley Ramsey.

Although Nutbeam was independent, he was completely without confidence.

His appearance was the reason for it — his appearance and the fact that nobody normal could face him without laughing. His appearance was also the reason he had never gone to school, never liked people and had left his home in Smyrna Mills, Maine, to journey into Canada's Dungarvon country.

Although Nutbeam didn't like people, he wasn't necessarily uninterested in them. He liked to look at people, but he didn't want people to look at him. Nutbeam kept his distance from people, ran into the woods when he saw someone coming, hid behind his hood, or collar, when it was absolutely necessary to pass near someone.

Nutbeam sat in front of his camp, eyeing the tree tops adorned by the setting sun. He watched a mosquito feasting off the back of his hand.

"Gorge yourself and then you die," said he to the mosquito.

"That's about all there is to life," he thought. "A man ain't no different than a mosquiter. Yer born, ya eat and drink, ya dump it out again and then you die. If you're born ugly, or not too smart, ya might as well have your dump right away, die and get it over with."

"You, little mosquiter, are prob'ly pretty for a mosquiter," said Nutbeam and commenced to hold his breath. In a few seconds the capillary the mosquito was tapping tightened around its tiny proboscus, trapping it so that Nutbeam could reach out at his leisure, slap, pick off, or set it free. The mosquito's fate depended on Nutbeam's decision. Nutbeam's decision came with a sigh. He took a breath (the sigh), the mosquito filled his tank and flew off. It'll die soon enough Nutbeam thought and scratched the itch.

Nutbeam's first year on Todder Brook had been a difficult one. He nearly froze to death. Without the few rabbits he managed to snare, he would have starved. On several occasions he came very close to seeking help from the Brennen Siding dwellers.

"I'm sure glad I didn't have to do that," he thought. "I'm alright now. I don't need nobody now."

He remembered that he had frozen his massive ears so many times and to such an extent that they flopped over and stayed that way. The experience turned out to be a beneficial one, however.

"Ya kin hear better with big floppy ears," mumbled Nutbeam.

Nutbeam could hear a bird singing for a country mile. Nutbeam could hear a deer walking a hundred yards away. He could hear the mosquitoes humming outside his camp at night.

Nutbeam had no difficulty hearing Lindon Tucker's radio and frequently stood outside Lindon Tucker's house on Saturday nights, listening to Kid Baker singing.

Nutbeam recalled the night Lindon had taken an early break to see a man about a horse. Nutbeam had been standing in the shadows of a shed listening to Lee Moore sing "The Cat Came Back."

"Lindon didn't see me there in the dark, but he pissed all over me boot," thought Nutbeam.

As he learned and practised the art of survival, life grew continually easier. He began taking the train into Newcastle once a month (at the risk of being seen) to trade his furs. At first, he traded for traps and snares; later, he traded for food and ammunition, fishing tackle, aspirins and candy. Later still, he traded for boots and the wonderful parka with the big hood that protected his ears and hid his face whenever he looked down. Last winter, Nutbeam lived very comfortably trading mostly for vegetables, Forest and Stream tobacco and money.

"I spent a bunch of money on that trumpet," he thought, "and I doubt if I ever learn to play it."

Nutbeam had been trying to play the trumpet for nearly three months and still couldn't blow a recognizable melody. At first, he couldn't even get a noise out of it, but now, after three months practice, he was making more noise than he realized. He was making enough noise to send chills down the backs of everyone in Brennen Siding.

Nutbeam always waited until nightfall to practice his trumpet playing. Somehow, playing in the dark seemed easier. He didn't know why. Perhaps it was his fear of being caught. He didn't know why, but he knew he would die of embarrassment if anyone ever saw him playing an instrument. Nutbeam was very shy.

"I'm nearly a mile into the woods. Surely nobody kin hear me playing this far away. I might hear it, but I've got these big floppy ears. Nobody in Brennen Siding got big floppy ears." After three months, Nutbeam was convinced that nobody could hear the trumpet. Nutbeam underestimated the ears of Brennen Siding.

When he felt it dark enough, Nutbeam went into his camp and fetched his trumpet.

"Tonight, I'll practice that Earl Mitton tune," he thought. "What's it called? 'Mouth of the Tobique'?"

When fishermen waded down Todder Brook, they could not see Nutbeam's tiny camp embedded in the forested hillside twenty yards away, nor could the camp be seen from the bushy old truck road, a hundred yards to the south. If you were to stand thirty feet from the camp, looking directly up at it, you might not see it, unless you knew it was there. Nutbeam had built three quarters of the structure under ground, with the slant of the roof parallel with the hill. He built it down and into the hill like a mine shaft, so that he had to actually tunnel out a path to the door. All that could be seen from the front was a small door and two grey logs. Once a deer had actually walked on the roof. The tiny seven-by-ten-foot square camp contained a table, two chairs, a cot to sleep on, a barrel stove and three tiny kegs. In one keg he kept salty salmon; in another, he kept salty gaspereaux and in the third, flour. There was a shelf on the eastern wall, on which sat a can of tea, a can of Forest and Stream tobacco, a can of baking powder, two pipes and a can of molasses. On another wall hung two rifles and a wrinkled, frameless picture of the Virgin Mary. On a nail beside the picture hung Nutbeam's rosary beads. On a wall beside the stove were some more shelves occupied by pots, tin plates, cups, a frying pan, a box of matches, knives, forks, spoons and a tin can full of odds and ends — a pencil, a small magnifying glass, a ball of string, some fish hooks, one of a set of dice which Nutbeam called a "douce," a spool of thread, buttons and a red squirrel's tail. Clothing hung haphazardly on all four walls.

In a box in the corner he kept his traps, a revolver, ammunition and his trumpet.

There was no window in the camp, so that when he entered he either had to leave the door open so he could see, or light the lamp that sat on the table. Lit, the lamp was usually turned as low as Lindon Tucker's.

By the light of one tiny star, which shone through the open door, Nutbeam found his trumpet.

He took the trumpet outside, put it to his lips, pointed the horn at the star-spangled sky and blew.

"HONK, HONK, BEEP, BEEP, BARMP-BARMP!"

The sound of the trumpet echoed from hill to hill, crossed brooks and rivers and shot through windows and doors all over Brennen Siding. Nutbeam played what he hoped sounded like "There's A Mansion in the Blue" for several minutes.

Then the rifle shot went off, the retort slamming against his big floppy ear, startling him into a sudden, silent trance just a hair short of death.

Darkness reigned supreme.

*

Shadrack and Dryfly stood on the steps that scaled the east end abutment of the bridge, panting heavily from running all the way from the forest to the river. Shadrack was particularly tired from carrying the heavy 303 rifle. Both boys were very happy to see the lit windows of the little settlement. The sight of the river, calm, reflecting the starlit sky, restored their courage. The river, a symbol of home, strength and identity, would give them courage for the rest of their lives. At the age of eleven, they already loved it.

During their lives, Shadrack and Dryfly would travel to Vancouver and New York, Toronto and Nashville, England and Italy, but their hearts would always remain on the Dungarvon, the Renous and the Miramichi. At the age of seventy, they would still at times speak a little too fast and at other times a little too slow and would repeat the word "and" too much. At the age of seventy, they would still speak with a Miramichi accent, softly, as the river people do, and refer to themselves as "Dungarvon boys."

"You gonna be able to go home by yourself, Dry?" asked Shadrack.

"Yeah, I'll be alright."

"I have to sneak the rifle and flashlight back in. If I git caught doin' it, I'll be killed."

"What d'ya s'pose happened to the whooper thing?"

"Must've scared 'im, that's all."

"Me and you scared the whooper, Shad!"

"Yeah, I know. Can't be nothin' too dang'rous if me and you scared it."

"We gonna tell what we did?"

"What d'ya think?"

"I don't know. Maybe."

"What d'ya think it was, Dry?"

"I don't know. Panther, I guess."

"Well, we kin talk about it tomorrow. I gotta git home and try and git this rifle in the house without getting caught."

"OK. See ya later, Shad."

"Yeah. Night."

The boys separated.

Dryfly's fear might have climaxed back in the woods, but its memory still shook him from within. What was more, he was still out in the dark night and now he was alone. The boardwalk of the footbridge ribboned before him; the river swept below, another ribbon with its reflections of forest and sky.

Reasoning told him not to be afraid of the bridge. "It'll hold the devil," everyone always said, and he was accustomed to its bounce and squeaks; he'd walked it many times. But, in the day-light . . . always in the daylight.

When he reached the middle abutment, it loomed dark and menacing beneath. He quickened his pace and hurried by.

"I wished I was more like Palidin," thought Dryfly. "Pal's al-ways out in the night. Ain't scared a bit."

"How can Palidin do it? How kin he not be scared?"

"Scared?"

"Of what?"

"The dark?"

"A ghost?"

Dryfly didn't know why he, himself, was afraid. "Other people crossed the bridge and nothin' happened to them," he reasoned. "Why should anything happen to me?"

When he reached the west end abutment, he realized he was

confronted with a decision. "Cross the fields to the road, or go down along the shore to Stan Tuney's brook and go up through the woods." He knew the path along the brook better, but the thought of walking through the woods did not appeal to him. He dismounted the abutment and headed across Dan Brennen's field, passed the house, barn and sheds. He came to the road. "I made it to the road," he whispered, and headed north toward home. He passed Billy Campbell's farm and Bernie Hanley's store. He was nearing the railroad crossing when the bird sang — the same bird he'd heard in the woods.

Dryfly's heart leaped and began to drum in his chest. The hairs on his neck and back lifted, feeling like a chill. "I'm gettin' out o' here!" he gasped and ran as fast as he could all the way home.

It would be many years before he'd be man enough to admit that he'd been so afraid of a bird.

*

Shadrack climbed the hill toward home. His shoulder was sore from shooting the rifle, but he was not afraid of the devil himself. Shadrack had the rifle.

Outside the house, he peeked in through the window. His father sat in the kitchen, reading the *Family Herald*. That was a good place for him.

His mother was reading the Bible. Good enough, too.

"I'll sneak through the front door," thought Shadrack. "I'll have to be quiet, though."

Shadrack was just putting the rifle behind the chair, when his father yelled: "Where you been with that rifle?!"

Bob Nash was standing in the livingroom door, slapping the palm of his hand with a tightly-rolled *Family Herald*.

Shad turned to face his father, knowing there was no escape, that a severe application of the tightly-rolled *Family Herald* was about to occur.

"I shot the Todder Brook Whooper," said Shad, quickly. "You what?!!!"

"I shot the Todder Brook Whooper!"

"WHAT! What did I hear you say?!!"

Bob Nash had already decided upon his course of action and hit Shadrack, hard as he could, on the butt, with the tightly-rolled *Family Herald*.

"Don't Dad!" yelled Shadrack.

"Don't don't me!"

"Whack!" went the *Family Herald*.

"Take my rifle, will ya!" (WHACK) "Young lad like you!" (WHACK)

"OUCH! That hurts! Ouch! Stop!"

Bob Nash had a terrible temper. Bob Nash had fire in his eyes. Bob Nash's fiery eyes could almost see the *Family Herald*'s John Deere Tractor ad imprinted on Shadrack's behind.

"WHACK!" went the *Family Herald*. "WHACK, WHACK WHACK . . . "

Monday night in Bernie Hanley's store, Bob Nash took a drink of his Sussex Ginger Ale and said: "Yes sir, that boy of mine and that young Ramsey lad, Dryfly, took my rifle and went back in that woods alone, just the two of them, and scared that devil off. I haven't heard it since, have you?"

"No," said Bert Todder, "didn't make a peep last night, far's I know."

"Heard the shot, so I did, yeah. Not a peep last night, no. Heard the shot, so I did," said Lindon Tucker.

"I wouldn't even have the nerve to do that meself!" said Bob Nash, proudly.

"Them boys got good stuff in them, I can say that," said John Kaston.

"Did they see it, Bob?" asked Bernie Hanley, from behind the counter.

"Sure, they saw it! How would they fire at it if they didn't see it! Shad said it was as big as a moose and had horns like a cow. Said he saw his eyes shining and they were as big around as saucers!"

"I heard the shot, so I did. Yeah, yeah, yeah, I did, yeah," commented Lindon Tucker.

"Gimme a new flashlight bulb, would ya, Bernie? And a bag of them peppermints fer me young lad."

five

From the 15th of April to the 15th of October, Helen Mac-
Donald cooked for the Cabbage Island Salmon Club. The job
paid well. Helen was a good cook. She worked fourteen hours a
day, seven days a week for thirty dollars. Occasionally, one of the
club guests would tip her five or ten dollars. Helen MacDonald's
financial goal was to be able to afford an indoor toilet.

In order to have breakfast ready for the early-rising anglers,
Helen had to leave home at five o'clock in the morning. Rex,
her old brown dog, always followed her to work. Rex was fed very
well on the scraps left over from the Cabbage Island Salmon
Club dinners.

One hot July day in 1962, Helen MacDonald found herself
in a bad mood. She had baked a blueberry pie and had left it in
front of an open window to cool. An hour later she looked to
see how the pie was doing, and to her amazement and great dis-
pleasure, the pie had vanished. She had paid little Joey Brennen
fifty cents of her own hard-earned money for those berries,
hoping to impress a tip from the Americans with a pie.

It wasn't the first time she had lost food from that window
but it hadn't happened since the previous year. Helen thought
that maybe the thief had grown up and had developed some con-
science. "It's plain to see that Dryfly Ramsey ain't ever growing
up."

Dryfly Ramsey naturally got the blame. Dryfly Ramsey was a
Catholic and, therefore, bad enough to do it. Besides, earlier,
Helen had seen Dryfly snooping about the place. She should
have known enough then to remove the pie from the window
sill.

That night, Helen related her frustration to Bert Todder.

60

"I don't know what I'm ever going to do! That tramp! If a poor woman can't make a livin' without the likes o' that tramp botherin' her, what's the world comin' to!"

"Are you sure it was him?" asked Bert.

Bert Todder was making his rounds. Whenever Bert made his rounds, he always made sure to visit Helen MacDonald. Helen MacDonald was an old maid, Bert was a bachelor. Although Helen liked Bert, sexually she wouldn't touch him with a ten-foot pole. However, Bert thought there was always a chance. After all, he was male and she was female.

"Course, I'm sure! Who else would do it?"

"Did you ask anybody about it?"

"I saw 'im snoopin' around!"

"Ya can't leave stuff layin' around where he is."

"If ya can't leave a pie on a window sill without some no good tramp takin' it right out from underneath your eyes, it's gettin' pretty damn bad, I'd say! If I get my hands on that . . . that tramp, I'm gonna strangle 'im! I'll put him in his place, I tell ya!"

"You need a good man, Helen dear."

"There ain't no such thing as a good man, you old coot!"

Bert squinted up his eyes and laughed. Helen eyed Bert's lone tooth. "He sounds like he's cryin'," she thought.

"Ya know what I'd do, Helen darlin'?"

"What?"

"Well, I gotta go, but I'll tell ya. Must be gettin' late, ain't it? Anyway, what I'd do is, I'd make another pie and put Exlax in it. Put it on the window sill just like ya did before. Let 'im eat that and see how he likes it. That'll fix 'im!"

"Exlax," thought Helen. "It'll cost me fifty cents, but it would be worth it." Helen was glad she had thought of it. She liked the idea very much. It would teach Dryfly Ramsey a lesson.

*

William Wallace tied on a black bear hair with yellow hackle and green butt and picked up his eight-foot Orvis. The bamboo Orvis was the ultimate in fishing rods as far as William (Bill) Wallace was concerned. The Orvis had been a parting gift from the vice-president (Jimmy), the bastard who was after the presidency. Bill Wallace was the president of the company and had no intentions of stepping down.

"Here's a fishing rod for you," Jimmy had said. "Why don't you go fishing, get away for a while. I'll look after things."

Bill Wallace didn't know what Jimmy was up to, but Bill figured something was being schemed. Bill Wallace didn't trust the vice-president as far as he could throw him.

Bill accepted the rod and went fishing. He knew that something negative could happen, but he was not overly concerned. Bill Wallace had a fifty-million-dollar concept for Phase One of the new regional hospital that would leave Jimmy, the vice-president, gaping in awe. Bill Wallace was the president of a construction company, with a contract with the government of Massachusetts to build a hundred-and-fifty-million-dollar hospital in Pittsfield.

Bill Wallace waded ankle-deep into the Dungarvon River and stopped to look around.

"You have a beautiful river here, Lindon, ghosts or no ghosts. You say it was never heard after?"

Lindon Tucker (the guide) was lying amidst the shore hay, fighting flies.

"'Pon me soul, yeah," said Lindon. "No one around here's heard a peep since."

Bill looked at the river flowing peacefully by. He looked downstream to where the river bent and vanished behind a forested wall. He could see the hills, the fields, even the reflection of some houses on the mirror-like expanse before him. A swallow dipped and dashed, a salmon parr jumped, an unfamiliar bird could be heard scolding something, perhaps its mate, in a nearby spruce.

"Are we going to catch a salmon today, Linny? Is there anything in hea'?"

"Ya might, ya might, ya might. There ain't no amount o' fish, though."

"Well, I'll give it a try. Christ, there's got to be somethin' in hea'."

Bill Wallace waded in to his knees, released ten feet of his pink aircel line and made a cast. He pulled another four feet from his Saint John Hardy and cast again. He could feel the pressure of the current against his legs, dry in the canvas-topped Hodgemen waders. He lengthened out a few more feet and made another cast. The black bear hair with yellow hackle and green butt drifted past what Bill thought was a potential hotspot. Nothing. He moved downstream a few more steps and cast again.

"I hope Lillian likes it up here," he thought. "She's been wanting to come with me ever since she wrote that essay on the Dungarvon Whooper." Bill chuckled to himself, "The Dungarvon Whooper!"

Bill kept stepping and casting, stepping and casting until he had covered the whole rocky area the locals referred to as a pool, reeled in his line and waded back to where Lindon lay. Lindon was nearly asleep in the morning sun.

"Did the boys actually see the . . . the whooper?"

"Oh, yeah. Yep. Yeah, oh yeah, they seen it alright. Looked like a cow, yeah. Big as a moose, so it was, yeah. Took a shot at it, so they did. Heard the shot meself, so I did, yeah. Oh yeah, yeah, yeah, heard it meself. 303. Never even slowed 'im down."

"Stopped him from screaming, though."

"Yes sir, never saw 'im after. Never peeped since!"

"Where's this young . . . what did you say his name was?"

"Shad? Peelin' pulp, I think. Back with John. Workin' with John Kaston, yeah."

"And the other one?"

"You'd prob'ly find Dryfly home. Home, yeah. Playin' guiddar. All he does is play guiddar. Good at it, too, yeah. Another Hank Snow, that lad, yeah. Gonna give it another try?"

"I think I'll give it one more try, then head back to the club. What do you think, Linny?"

Lindon yawned. He wanted a break from sleeping on the shore. The sun was too hot and the flies were bothering him. Lindon knew that there were very few, if any, salmon in the river and that Bill Wallace's chances of catching one were close to nil.

"Can't ketch 'im wit a dry line," said Lindon.

Bill Wallace started the procedure again in much the same

fashion. Bill knew that his chances were very poor, too. The weather was too hot for good, productive fishing. But Bill Wallace was standing in the cool water away from the flies. Bill Wallace liked being on the river and liked the scenery and the fresh air. He changed flies, went to the squirrel tail with yellow hackle he'd purchased from Bert Todder.

"Bert Todder ties the best damn salmon fly in the world," thought Bill. "So delicate, yet so strong and durable."

Bill took his eyes off the colorful little flyhook and scanned the scenery again. "So scenic and peaceful," he thought.

Across the river stood a massive log cabin, with two stone fireplaces, a breezeway between the kitchen and the living quarters, a full length veranda, shaded in a grove of pines.

"Nice little place," thought Bill. "Belongs to Sam Little. Sam's a Yale man, I think. Out of Hartford. Made his money in the hotel business. He's got the best salmon pool on the Dungarvon and I'm casting directly into it from Lindon Tucker's shore. I wonder why he never bought Lindon Tucker out?"

"Does Sam Little spend much time at his lodge?" asked Bill.

"Too much, too much, too much. Like the, like the, like the feller says, too much."

"Did you ever guide for him?"

"Yeah. Oh yeah. I guided the old sonuvawhore, so I did. Yeah, I guided him, alright. Guided him too much."

Bill Wallace waded deeper in the river, smiling to himself.

"Lindon Tucker wouldn't sell Sam Little anything," thought Bill.

*

A freshly peeled stick of pulpwood is as slippery as a greased eel, or, in the words of Bert Todder, "slipperier than Shirley Ramsey's slop pail dump." Shirley Ramsey dumped her slop pail on the grass, ten feet east of the house, and on more than just a few occasions, while waiting for the mail, a man would go around the house to "see a man about a horse" and slip and fall on the accumulated grease. The only way to identify a slop pail dump is the longer grass that grows from its constantly enriched situation.

THE AMERICANS ARE COMING

The pulpwood stick slipped from Shadrack's hands, taking a fair amount of the skin with it. Shadrack didn't swear. He was too hot and sweaty and fly-bitten to swear. He was beyond swearing. He was speechless! He was fourteen and his mind was on more interesting things. If he'd been in a state to speak his mind, he'd have yelled: "That American girl at the Cabbage Island Salmon Club is the prettiest thing on earth! I hate this jesiless job," and "There's gotta be a better way to make a livin' than this."

"Hurt yer hand?" asked John Kaston. John Kaston was but a few feet away, trimming the limbs from a fir he'd just felled.

Shad analyzed the scratch amidst the dirt and pitch on his palm. "Just a scratch," he thought.

"I cut it damn near off!" he said. "I'd better go home! See ya later!"

That was how Shadrack Nash quit his first job.

John Kaston shook his head in dismay.

"The lazy bugger only lasted three days!" muttered John to his axe.

*

Dryfly Ramsey sat in the shade behind the house, playing his guitar and singing Hank Snow's "Sentimental." It was a pretty song. It had nice chords in it. Dryfly liked it.

Dryfly felt somewhat embarrassed when Shadrack rounded the corner. Although Dryfly had played and sang a thousand times to the accompaniment of Shad and his banjo, he still didn't want Shad to think he played alone. Dryfly was shy. He stopped immediately.

"How's she goin' today?" asked Dryfly.

"The very best," greeted Shad.

"Not workin' today?"

"Naw. Quit. Got ugly."

"Yeah?"

"Told old John Kaston to shove his spud up his arse!"

"Ya didn't, did ya? Wha'?"

"Got any makin's? I'm dyin' for a smoke. Never had a cigarette all day."

"Yeah. Awful dry though," said Dryfly, handing Shadrack the package of Vogue tobacco and papers they referred to as "makin's."

"See that little lady at the club?" asked Shad.

"Hasn't everybody?"

"Let's go down."

"Now?"

"Why not?"

"Liable to get shot."

"What for? We never did nothin'."

"You didn't, maybe, but I did."

"What ya do?"

"Stole a blueberry pie."

"Where from, the kitchen?"

"Off the window sill."

"Was it good?"

"The very best."

"Ya git caught?"

"No, but ya never know who might've seen a lad. They'll blame me anyway. They always do."

"That's because it's you that always does it."

"You do it, too."

Shad shrugged and grinned. "There might be another one today," he said. "Let's go down."

"You ain't scared of gittin' caught?"

"Naw. What're they gonna do, put us in jail for stealin' a blueberry pie?"

Dryfly sighed. "Guess it won't hurt to go down," he said, leaning his guitar against the house. He rose from the grass, leaving a bum print where he had been sitting.

The two boys crossed the tracks and Stan Tuney's field. They came to Tuney's brook and took the shaded path that followed the brook to the river. The large spruce and elms that grew beside the brook sighed in the dry summer wind.

Just before they got to the river, they crossed the brook on a footbridge Stan built and went up the hill to where the six log cabins that made up the Cabbage Island Salmon Club sat. Like Sam Little's lodge, the Cabbage Island Salmon Club camps sat in a grove of gigantic pines. From the front of each camp, one had a view of a mile of river in either direction.

In the shade, outside the dining camp, sat Bert Todder, Dan Brennen and Stan Tuney. They were waiting for the Club owners to finish lunch. The guides might have as much as three hours before they would be obliged to go back into the glaring sun of the river. The guides all were thankful that the Americans took a long time to eat their lunch. Lindon Tucker still hadn't returned with Bill Wallace. Bert Todder, Dan Brennen and Stan Tuney all were thankful that they weren't guiding the "fish hog," the name they called Bill Wallace.

Lillian Wallace sat in a snug bathing suit, on the lounge veranda, reading *Gone With The Wind*. High up in a pine tree, a red squirrel chattered. The good-time voices of the Americans came in bursts of shouts and laughter from the dining camp. A jeep, a Ford station wagon and a Cadillac sat in the driveway.

When they neared the kitchen, Dryfly was delighted to see another blueberry pie on the window sill.

The boys, hidden behind a nearby tree, eyed the pie.

"Looks kind o' s'picious to me," said Shad.

"Why's that?"

"Well, if you had a pie stolen from you yesterday, would you put another one out in the very same place today?"

"No, I wouldn't, but there's a pie there. Same kind o' pie, too, by the looks of it. Blueberry."

"It's blueberry, alright, and maybe a little poison mixed in with it."

"They wouldn't poison a man, would they?"

"Damn right they would."

"So we just leave it there?"

"Damn right. I ain't eatin' no poisoned pie. I'm gonna go up and striker up a say with that little darlin'. You wait here."

"Why can't I go, too?"

"She can't be with the both of us, kin she?!"

"Why not?"

"Damn, you're stupid! I wanna maybe pass the hand. Can't do that with you watchin' us, can I?"

"Well, don't be all day, then."

"I won't be no time. Jist gonna feel things out."

"OK, I'll wait."

Shad walked from behind the tree and rounded the camp to where Lillian Wallace sat reading. He was unsure of what his approach should be, but he feared he'd mess it up if he got too near her. He moved to within ten feet of where she sat, and with hands in his pocket and shoulders back, he pretended to be eyeing the river for something or other. From the corner of his eye, he could see her watching him. He knew he would have to acknowledge her sooner or later, but was hoping she would make the first move.

Luck was with him.

"Is something wrong?" asked Lillian.

"Naw, jist lookin'. Nice day, eh?"

"Yes, it is." Lillian had the strong, confident, arrogant voice of an American. Shad was thrilled with the sound of it.

"You from around here?" asked Shad.

"No," smiled Lillian, "I'm from Massachusetts."

"Heard of it. Big place?"

"Yes, it's quite big. Where do you live?"

"See that house down there on the bend, the one with the blue bottom and the pink top?"

"Yes."

"That's where I live. It's got an indoor toilet."

"Really?"

"Yep. Only one around here."

"Well! How wonderful."

"You stayin' here long?"

"We can only stay a week, I'm afraid."

"Doin' any fishin'?"

"No. I'm not a fisherwoman, I'm afraid. I'm leaving the fish for my father."

"Is yer father gettin' any?"

"Not yet."

"Must be usin' the wrong fly."

"Perhaps you could point him out something more productive."

"Is he around?"

"He's still out, but he should be back any minute."

"Like to meet 'im. Hear he's a nice lad. Gotta big salmon this
morning on a fly he might be wantin' to know about."

"Really?! You caught a salmon this morning?"

"Oh yeah, I kin ketch 'em any time at all."

"Well! You should, indeed, talk to my father. He's not very
productive when it comes to salmon, I'm afraid."

"Usin' the wrong fly. Gonna be here tonight?"

"I imagine so."

"I'll come up."

"Well . . . alright. He likes to fish in the evening, but he'll be
back about dusk."

"Good. That a Gene Autry book you reading?"

"No, it's called *Gone With The Wind*. Have you heard of it?"

"No, read a lot o' Gene Autry, though. Any good?"

"It's not bad. Not as good as Gene Autry, perhaps, but it's not
bad." Lillian smiled so beautifully that it quickened Shad's heart.

"Well, I gotta go. I'll come up later and talk to yer father."

"Good. I'm sure he'll be delighted."

"Yeah, well OK then, see ya' later."

"Bye."

Shad went around the camp to where Dryfly was waiting behind the tree. The first thing he noticed was Dryfly petting
Helen MacDonald's dog. The second thing he noticed was that
the blueberry pie was gone from the kitchen window.

"What happened to the pie?" asked Shad.

"Fed it to the dog. Hope it don't hurt 'im," said Dryfly.

*

That night when Shadrack went to the Cabbage Island
Salmon Club, he did not take Dryfly with him. He would meet

Dryfly later. Shad had no intentions of going to work in the morning and that meant that he and Dryfly could play on the river for as late as they wanted. Shadrack and Dryfly's favourite pastime was playing on the river at night. Dryfly would be somewhere on the river (he always was), and all Shad would have to do was whistle and wait for an answer. Dryfly would eventually answer and they would swim or just canoe about until the wee hours of the morning.

"Good evening, my boy! Come in! Have some lemonade. You're just the man I've been wanting to see. I hear you have a fly to show me."

Shad didn't have a fly to show Bill Wallace, but he had prepared himself.

"Yeah, but I kin only tell you of it," said Shad. "I lost it in a big salmon earlier this evening."

"Really! Christ, I've been whipping the river all day and never had as much as a rise."

Shad sat on the sofa beside Bill Wallace. Lillian sat at the table eyeing her father and the strange boy with the greased red hair. The boy had cleaned up since the afternoon and had changed his awful clothes for a plaid shirt with the collar turned up, blue jeans and sneakers. Lillian saw in Shadrack's icy blue eyes a certain zest for life . . . and naughtiness perhaps. She thought she kind of liked him.

"It's what you call a green-arsed hornet," said Shad. "Jist looks like a hornet, 'cept it's got a green arse 'stead o' yellow."

"Well, I'll have Bert tie me up a few. A green-assed hornet, huh?"

"Yep. Best fly on the river!"

"Lillian, I don't know if you've heard, but young Shadrack here is somewhat familiar with the Dungarvon Whooper."

"Really!"

Shadrack leaned back on the sofa, put his arm on the back, crossed his legs and made ready for whatever lies he might have to conjure up. He wished he had brought Dryfly, afterall. Dryfly was good at lying and stuff.

"Lindon Tucker told me about it this morning," continued

Bill Wallace. "Young Shadrack here is quite a hero in these parts."

"Tell me about you being a hero, Shadrack," said Lillian in the same way Shadrack reckoned she would talk to a child. Shadrack was losing confidence. These people were very different from the people he was used to. He couldn't read their faces. He couldn't decide whether they were making fun of him or not.

"What did Lindon tell them?" was the question on Shadrack's mind. He tried to remember all the stories. Shad decided he would go into the story in a roundabout way. That way, he'd have time to remember things.

"Well," breathed Shad, "this thing was screamin' in the woods, see, and . . . "

"What did the whooper sound like, Shad?' asked Lillian.

"Well, sort o' like a . . . a . . . a train whistle . . . a panther hollerin' . . . and the . . . the devil screamin', all in one . . . only louder. Everyone was scared to death of it."

"So one night when the moon was full and the thing was makin' more noise than usual, me and Dryfly thought we'd better be doin' somethin' about it. So, by God, I grabbed the old 303, and, and, and Dad's flashlight and strucker for the woods."

Both Lillian and Bill were smiling friendly smiles. Shad thought that they might be swallowing his yarn and it gave him a bit more confidence.

"So, anyway, we didn't get no more than a mile or two in the woods when we smelt this awful smell. 'Pon me soul, it just smelt like . . . like Shirley Ramsey's arse and, and I had to swing and throw up right then and there. And, and, and then this awfulest scream struck 'er up and Dryfly turned as white as a ghost."

"I said, by God, Dryfly, we're done for."

"So, what did you do?" asked Lillian.

"Well, I said the only way we'll be able to git rid of it is to go down to the brook where the thing seemed to be, so we went down. Well, sir, you never heard anything like it in all your life!"

Lillian and Bill exchanged glances.

"Anyway," continued Shad, "I saw this big black thing down through the woods and I said to Dryfly, I said, I said Dryfly, I think I see it. Dryfly never said aye, yes or no. I didn't know what it was, but I could tell that it had horns like a cow and was about the size of a, of a bull elephant."

"Dryfly said ya'd better shoot the sonuvawhore before it sees us, or we're as good as dead. So I pulled up the old 303 and let 'er drift. Well, anyway, the noise stopped right up and that thing swung and took a look at us, I could see its eyes shinin' in the flashlight beam and, and, and they were about as big around as that ashtray. I thought we were dead men but it didn't do a thing, just swung and trotted off down through the woods. I wanted to go after it, but Dryfly said, he said, he said, we'd better not. We might get lost, so we swung and come home. We never heard it after, but you could smell it for three days."

"Did anybody else ever see it?" asked Bill.

"Not that I know of," said Shad.

"Did anybody else ever go back to look for it?"

"I don't think so. Not that I know of, anyway."

"Do you think it was a ghost?" asked Lillian.

"I dunno, maybe."

"Or, maybe Satan?"

"I don't know. Could've been."

"Did you go back after to look for its tracks or anything?" said Bill.

"No, no, I never went back."

Shadrack was beginning to feel uncomfortable with all the smiling questions. "They're makin' fun o'me," he thought. "They think I'm lyin'. Course lyin's what I'm doin', so I might as well stick with it."

Bill Wallace got up from the sofa and went to the bar, poured himself a double scotch and tossed it back, grunted the hot liquid along to his stomach, then poured himself another. He was moving away from the kids. He was not interested in the Dungarvon Whopper, as he called it. The Dungarvon Whooper was Lillian's thing. Bill Wallace commenced to think about salmon pools and a place of his very own, private, away from this club of cabbage heads.

Between the chair where Lillian sat and the sofa where Shadrack sat, it commenced to rain electricity.

Shadrack was unprepared. He wanted to get outside with Lillian so that he might get a chance to pass the hand.

Lillian, on the other hand, experienced a feeling of bewilderment as she eyed the thin, red-haired boy. "He's lying about the whooper," she thought. "He's a liar, just like every other boy. Except . . . he's not the same. I'd hate to see this one in an Elvis Presley haircut."

"Ever hear of Elvis Presley?" she asked.

"Yeah," said Shad, thankful for the fact the topic had changed. "I heard 'im on the radio."

"Have you ever seen him?"

"No."

"I have a picture of him in the bedroom. I'll get it."

Lillian went off to get the centerfold from the *Teen* magazine she'd brought from home. Shad removed his wallet from his hip pocket and slid it between the cushions of the sofa. "An excuse to come back, in case I don't get invited," he thought.

Bill Wallace stood at the window, eyeing the river. "I should fish for an hour before dark," he thought, "but I can't leave Lillian alone with this hick . . . or would it matter? Lillian's not about to get involved with the likes of him . . . she's only fourteen . . . I could talk with Lindon . . . " Bill Wallace was still thinking about his very own salmon pool.

Lillian returned with the picture. She placed it on the coffee table in front of Shadrack.

"That's Elvis," she said.

Shad looked at the greased black hair, the black leather jacket with the turned up collar, the tight black pants and the jet boots. Shad looked at the smooth tanned skin with not a freckle on it, the sideburns and the slightly curled lip. "So, this is Elvis," he thought. "He's a good lookin' lad, alright." ·

Shad had heard that Elvis had his hair greased back, and had tried the grease himself, but Shad hadn't known that Elvis' hair was so much longer . . . and the sideburns . . .

"The girls are wild about him," said Lillian. "Don't you think he's wonderful?"

"For a girl to look at, maybe," said Shad, and to himself, thought, "I'll have to let my hair grow."

A knock came at the door. It was Lindon Tucker. Lillian let him in.

"You wanna fish this evenin'?" Lindon asked Bill.

"By God, Lindon old buddy, I'm glad you're still about. Do you have a good fishing rod, Lindon?"

"Well, yeah, I got an old one that's seen better days, as the feller says. Seen better days, an old one, yeah."

"Well, I have this Shakespeare I'd like for you to try."

"Sure, sure, the very best. Love to try it. Nice one, nice one, nice one, ain't it?"

"Let's go fishin'," said Bill, putting his arm on Lindon's shoulder.

As the two men were leaving the camp, Bill Wallace was saying, "I like you, Lindon! I'd like for you to come down to Stockbridge and visit us sometime! Would you like to have a rod like that, Lindon?"

"Sure, sure, sure, yeah, love to, yeah, nice one ain't it?"

Bill Wallace stopped at the door, looked at Lillian, gave a quick, dark glance at Shadrack and said, "I'll only be gone for an hour or so, Lillian."

Lillian Wallace knew that the quick, dark glance meant that Shadrack Nash had better not be there when Bill Wallace returned.

Although Shadrack was quite pleased with the situation, he was also somewhat confused. He'd never been alone with a pretty girl before.

Lillian Wallace was tall for her age and was physically well advanced in the transition from girl to woman. She had short blond hair, big blue eyes and an easy smile that revealed perfect white teeth. Earlier, while reading on the veranda, the mosquitoes had found her and she had sprayed her body with repellent. Shad was very fond of the repellent's perfumey smell. Shadrack found himself lost for words.

"You go to school?" asked Shad.

"Yes. I'll be starting high school this September."

"Me, too," lied Shad. Shad quit school when he was twelve.

"How many kids in your class?" asked Lillian.

To Shad, a school was the one room building called the Brennen Siding School — a blackboard, a woodstove, desks, a bucket in the corner for water and not much more. Shad had never stepped foot in the high school in Blackville. Shad didn't know what a class was.

Resorting to his knowledge of the exterior of Blackville School, he said, "Ninety-two."

"Wow! That's a big class!" said Lillian.

"Blackville's a big place," said Shadrack.

*

And so the conversation between Shadrack Nash and Lillian Wallace continued. Shadrack grew more relaxed as he became more familiar with his luxurious surroundings, with Lillian's accent, tone of voice and smile, but part of him still wanted to get closer. A hug? A kiss? Pass the hand? Shadrack didn't know what to do first.

For ten minutes, Shad sat on the sofa and she in the chair. Then, Lillian moved to the sofa, but sat at the other end.

For another ten minutes, Shad debated whether or not he should move closer to her; then he moved an inch.

He waited ten more minutes for her to make the next move. Finally, she crossed her legs, and maybe (he wasn't sure) moved slightly toward him. He couldn't say whether it was an intentional aggression or not.

She offered him a beer.

"No thanks," he said, "I'm trying to quit."

"You got a girlfriend?" she asked.

"Yeah," he lied, "two or three."

Lillian moved back to her chair.

Ten minutes later, Lillian moved back to the sofa. They both knew they were running out of time. There was a couple of moments when you could hear a pin drop. Shadrack's heart quickened and he made the giant plunge; an unpremeditated, graceful, three-inch glide toward her.

"There's no turning back now," he thought.

Lillian had just had a ten-minute debate with herself, too. The move back to the sofa, for her, had taken a great deal of strenuous reasoning. She had forced herself to favour optimism. At least I can say I was "with" a boy in Canada, was the crux of her drive.

She turned slightly toward him.

"What occupation will you eventually pursue?" she asked.

"I don't know," answered Shadrack. "A half dozen maybe."

"I'm considering anthropology, myself. Are you familiar with the Leakeys?"

"No, but I had the measles and the mumps."

"What's your friend Dryfly like?" she asked.

"I like Dry. Didn't use to. Dry's cleaned up a lot."

"You mean he had an addiction?"

"Oh no. Dry's healthy enough. Poor, that's all. Dryfly's pretty near as smart as me and he ain't scared o' nothin'."

"Is he still in school?"

"No, quit a long time ago . . . two years, grade five."

"So, what's he planning on doing?"

"Nothin'. Play guiddar."

Lillian was going to make another move to get nearer to Shadrack, but she changed her mind. She heard Bill Wallace's footsteps on the veranda steps.

"There's Dad," she said. "You'd better go."

"Oh . . . OK."

"But . . . come back tomorrow night"

"Sure," said Shad, rising from the sofa.

"And . . . why don't you bring your friend Dryfly along?"

"Maybe," said Shad.

six

Shirley had become a byword, but Brennen Siding had many bywords, some of which were meaningless adages that would leave
an outsider totally confused as to what the insider was talking
about. Some of the bywords had been passed down from previous
generations, so that even the present day residents of Brennen
Siding didn't know why they were using them. For instance,
someone might say: "He grabbed the bag o' flour and never 'cried
crack' till he hit the top o' the hill." A beautiful women was described as a "Martha Lebbons." Martha Lebbons had been dead
for a hundred years, but obviously, she had been very beautiful.
Something expensive and new was referred to as a "cream o'
tarter."

"I hear ya got a new canoe?"

"Yep."

"Is it a good one?"

"She's a cream o' tarter!"

A conversation outside Bernie Hanley's store might go:

"Would ya like a drink o' rum, Dan?"

"Sure would, Stan. I'm dryer than a corn meal fart."

"How ya like it?"

"(Cough) Trip a ghost."

"How ya like that Ford ya bought?"

"She's a cream o' tarter!"

"Fast?"

"Blue Streak!" It didn't matter if the car was red or yellow, if
it was fast, it was a blue streak.

If anything moved slowly, one might say, "Slower than cold
molasses."

After Shadrack fired the 303, the two boys held their breaths and listened to a silent forest. Then they ran a blue streak all the way to the river.

Nutbeam, on the other hand, went into his camp, removed his 30-30 from the wall and went creeping about the forest. He crept as silent as an undertaker's belch, as slow as cold molasses.

Nutbeam had heard the two boys running and was very afraid. "That trumpet must've been louder than I thought. The whole country's been listening to me play." Nutbeam was not only afraid, he was also embarrassed. He vowed he'd never play the trumpet again. Like Dryfly, Nutbeam was shy about playing in front of anyone.

Living in the forest was changing Nutbeam. It was making him very timid. He may have been taking on the way of the animal, for, like an animal, the sound of the rifle shot had spooked him into an even deeper hiding, made him even more cunning, and, in a word, wild. He stopped practising his trumpet playing. He stopped boarding the train at Brennen Siding. Instead, he went to Gordon, two miles upstream. He continued to stand in the shadows listening to the radio, but he stopped listening to Lindon Tucker's. Instead, he crossed the footbridge, always on the darkest nights, to stand outside of Shirley Ramsey's house. The Ramseys always played the radio at a much greater volume than Lindon Tucker, and with Nutbeam's acute hearing, he could hear Freddy McKenna sing from thirty yards away.

On some nights, Nutbeam got a very much appreciated bonus. Those were the nights when Dryfly stepped onto the porch with his guitar. Dryfly still had a lot to learn on the guitar, but to Nutbeam, Dryfly was, "The very best! Great! A-1! Couldn't be better! Pretty near as good as Doc Williams! He'll be famous someday!"

*

Doc Williams did not come from Brennen Siding. Kid Baker did not live twelve miles up the Gordon Road. Hank Snow did not include Brennen Siding in his song "I've Been Everywhere." Elvis Presley did not stand on the Brennen Siding footbridge on moonlit nights, singing "Love Me Tender" to Neenie or Naggy Ramsey.

Nobody from Brennen Siding could claim fame or fortune. A store clerk, scaler or a timekeeper was the ultimate goal. Old men and women never talked about what they'd achieved, but instead talked about what they "could have" achieved.

"I could've been a doctor," Stan Tuney said at the store one night, then added, "If I had've gone to school."

John Kaston was "this far" from becoming a Preacher. "But Dad needed me to work in the woods with him." "This far" was a very, very long way.

"I could've been a great musician," said Bob Nash. "All I needed was the proper training, practice and something to work with."

It was that way all over the Miramichi area, tributaries included.

David Thornton from Millerton would have been rich if the "nine" (the last number on his sweepstake ticket), had've been a "four."

"That lad from Doaktown . . . what's his name?"

"John Betts?"

"No, not John. That other lad there. You know the lad . . . he would have been the Premier had he won the election?"

"Oh yeah, that lad."

And, of course, Yvon Durelle. Yvon Durelle was never thought of in Brennen Siding as the boxer who was the light heavyweight champion of the British Empire, covering Britain, Canada, Australia, a smidgeon of real estate in South America, and a third, or more, of Africa. Yvon Durelle was that lad from Baie Ste. Anne who would've been the champion of the world, had he beaten Archie Moore.

At the post office one morning, Bert Todder said, "Dryfly, me boy, you could be a singin' star some day, if ya had half a chance."

Dryfly wondered which half of which chance Bert referred to, and if Bert knew.

"The Miramichi would've been a great center, only for the Miramichi Fire of 1825."

*

When Shad left the Wallaces' cabin, he met with the warmth of a July evening. He took the path that led from the Cabbage Island Salmon Club to Judge Martin's camp. Judge Martin rarely came to his cabin, and because it was a private and peaceful place, endowed with a terrific view of the river, Shad often went there to think and relax.

Shadrack Nash sat on Judge Martin's veranda to watch the night settle in on what he thought was the prettiest place in the whole world.

Shad couldn't decide whether he felt happy or sad. That he felt different was all he knew.

"God, she's a pretty thing!" he thought. "Got lot's o' money, too. Marry that one and a man would never have to cut pulp for a livin', that's for sure."

Shad had a vision of a big white house in the city, a new car in the yard and maybe a pickup truck for him to drive whenever Lillian needed the car to go to work. Shad never thought of himself as ever going to work. "But, Lillian'll work," he thought. "She'll be a clerk or a teacher and I'll just look after things. Lillian'll come home from work, all pretty and dressed to kill, and I'll be settin' right back in me big chair, with me feet up, smokin' me pipe, waitin' to tell 'er that I made a hundred dollars sellin' somethin'. I'll be a salesman and not have to work. I'll live in a big city like New York or Bangor . . . or even Wheelin' West Virginia and play the banjo with Bill Monroe."

"All I have to do is git Lillian to fall in love with me. To do that, I'll have to git her to . . ." (he didn't know) " . . . kiss me? One kiss . . . sure would be a good start. A woman would have to love ya, if ya kissed her . . . wouldn' she?"

It wasn't long before Venus showed itself in the sky, said, "OK gang, the sky's clear! You can come out now." Pop-pop-pop, pop, pop, pop-pop, the stars commenced to shine.

"Thump," came a noise from downstream. Shad recognized it as a pole making contact with the side of a canoe.

"Moooooo!" went Shad.

"Moooooo!" answered Dryfly, from down in front of Sam Little's lodge.

Shad knew that Dryfly was in the process of borrowing Sam Little's canoe for the night. "Borrowin' without askin'," thought Shad, "What's the difference between that and stealin'?" He could hear the plunk, plunk, plunk of the pole, as Dryfly pushed his way through the Dungarvon current until he hauled up in front with a scraping sound against the rocks.

"Shad?"

"Yeah, up here."

Dryfly could not see Shad in the shadow of the veranda. He tossed the anchor onto the shore and headed toward the camp.

"How'd ya make out with Lillian?"

"The very best. Kissed her twice. Once in front of the fire-place and once on the veranda."

"On the lips?"

"Course!"

Dryfly sat beside Shad, his breath laboring from his climb up the embankment to the camp.

"Lillian showed me a picture of Elvis Presley," said Shad. "We'll have to let our hair grow more and he's got a little curl to his lip . . . like this."

"Like what?"

"Light a match."

A match was struck.

"Like this."

"Huh! How's this?"

"A little more . . . well . . . " Shad realized that Dryfly could never look like Elvis. Dry had a long head, a big nose, a peaked chin and a very thin upper lip. Dryfly's hair was brown and fine and combed over from a part on the left side. "He's homelier than Shirley Ramsey," thought Shad and chuckled to himself. "The lip looks great," lied Shad, "but you'll have to start combin' your hair back and let your sideburns grow."

"You really kiss Lillian?"

"I was alone with her for four hours! What do you think?"

"You in love with her?"

"I think so."

Dryfly was very disappointed. He, too, was in love with Lillian, although he hadn't spoken to her.

"What do you want to do?" asked Shad.

"I dunno. Go home and go to bed, maybe."

"What d'ya want to go to bed for? It's summer."

"I dunno. Tired, maybe."

"I thought we might pole up to Gordon."

"What for?"

"Somethin' to do. Ya don't git many warm nights like this around here," said Shad.

"You gonna see her tomorrow night?"

"Pretty likely. Me and Lilly would kind o' like to git married."

"Kind o' young, ain't ya?"

"Not right away. Couldn't now, if we wanted to."

"Why?"

"Lillian's a Cath'lic and I'm a Baptist."

"You could turn with her."

"Lillian said she'd turn with me if I went to church on Sunday," Shad sighed. "But old Bill's gonna be hard to deal with. Would've been easy, if it hadda been you, Dry. I'm the man she loves and we're gonna have to do the best we kin."

Shad hadn't spoken a single word of truth, but what he was saying added a nice wing to his fantasy. Marrying Lillian and moving off to live the life of the rich was the "best" thing that could happen, but simply knowing and being in love with this rich girl, was an important attention-getter in itself. Even if they never married, or saw each other again, the intimate contact with her would be good for his reputation.

"Poor Shadrack," people would say, "His poor heart's been broken. He loved that American girl! Never seen him with another woman after . . . his heart will always be in the States."

"Yes, I know, and him so brave too. Shadrack Nash, the one that shot the Todder Brook Whooper! He would've been a rich man today, if her mean old father, the fish hog, had've thought of the poor girl's happiness!"

"Got any more of the dry tobacco left, Dry?"

"Got a new pack. Made fifty cents today pickin' blueberries."

Dryfly handed Shad the tobacco.

"The blueberries ripe yet, Dry?"

"Not quite. They're still red because they're green."

Dryfly really didn't want to spend this warm summer's night at home in bed. He wasn't really tired. Dryfly was envious, jealous and hurt. "I didn't even get a crack at her," he thought.

"Lillian wants you and me to go visit her tomorrow night. Wants you to take yer guiddar. I told 'er you was a good singer."

"I'll take the guiddar, but I ain't singin'."

"Let's go to Gordon. I'll pole."

"OK. Why not?"

It took Shad forty-five minutes to pole the canoe to Gordon. He didn't mind the work. "Being on the most beautiful river in the world" was all the reward he needed.

Shadrack pushed the canoe ashore; they both jumped out and pulled it up on the rocky beach.

"So, what're we gonna do now?" asked Dryfly.

"Let's have a smoke," said Shadrack.

Dry started walking back and forth and in circles.

"What're ya lookin' for?" asked Shad.

"A soft rock to set on," said Dry.

"Ya fool!" laughed Shad.

The boys sat on a rock and rolled cigarettes, lit up and eyed their surroundings. There was the starlit sky overhead, the barns and houses of Gordon on the hills on both sides of the river and, here and there, a sport camp. Randall Brook murmured as it entered the river across from where they sat. They watched the lights in the houses going out and knew it was bedtime in Gordon. Everything, other than the murmuring brook, was very quiet.

The boys sat and smoked until the last light was out and all fourteen houses and eight sport camps were in darkness.

"The time's about right," said Shad.

"Yep."

"OK, let's give 'er hell."

"Bark, bark, bark! Yip, yip, yip! Yelp, yelp, yelp!" went the two boys as loud as they could, so that their voices echoed off the hills.

Somebody's dog started barking; then, somebody else's; then another and another until every dog in Gordon (and there were a good many of them) started barking.

A light came on, then another and another. Windows were lifted, doors were opened, dogs were cussed and called.

When the inhabitants of Gordon had calmed their dogs into silence, they switched their lights off and went back to bed.

"We'll giver a while," said Shad.

"Here, have another smoke."

"Thanks."

"Know any jokes?"

"Who killed the Dead Sea?"

"I dunno. Who?"

"Same lad painted Red China."

"Lillian tell ya that?"

"No, Dad."

"I like it. Funny."

"Know what I'm gonna be when I grow up?"

"What?"

"Salesman for potato bugs."

Dryfly chuckled. He liked that joke too. "I'll have to remember that one," he thought.

"Ready?" asked Shad.

"Ready."

"Bark, bark, bark! Yip, yip, yip! Yelp, yelp, yelp!"

Again their voices echoed off the hillsides and started the dogs barking. It took a little longer this time, but again lights came on, windows were lifted, doors were opened and dogs were cussed and called.

"Is that a star up there?" asked Shad, pointing to the big dipper.

"I don't know, I'm a stranger around here."

"Ha, ha, ha, ha, ha, ha, ha, ha! You just think o' that?"

"Yep. Just sort o' popped into me head. Good one, eh?"

"Yep. It's a good one. Have to remember it."

"They've all gone to bed again."

"Yeah. Give it a few more minutes."

"No hurry. Here, have another smoke."

"Know what I heard, Dry?"

"No, what?"

"Heard yer brother Palidin's a fruit."

"Where'd you hear that?"

"Everybody's sayin' it."

"He might be. He sure does act fruity. Reads all the time."

"Acts like a woman, too."

"He'll get his head kicked in one o' these days."

"I'll kick his head in, if he ever touches me!"

"He won't touch ya. He's my brother."

"Bark, bark, bark! Yip, yip, yip! Yelp, yelp, yelp!"

Lift, lift, lift. Slam, slam, slam. "Git in here you old sonuva-whore!"

"Here Skippy, Skippy, Skippy!"

"Here Pal, Pal, Pal!"

"Here Spot, Spot, Spot!"

Lights out. Back to bed.

Shad and Dry smoked and played this game for an hour or so, then headed back to Brennen Siding. They didn't paddle, but drifted on the current, watching the stars. When they drifted past Helen MacDonald's farm, they did not know that Helen's dog, Rex, was relieving himself for the third time on the kitchen floor. The blueberry pie with the Exlax was taking its effect. Rex was shitting a blue streak.

seven

Palidin Ramsey was different.

He was not just different from Dryfly, but was unlike anybody else in Brennen Siding. If you searched the whole Miramichi area, you would not find a single person like him.Being effeminate was not the only unusual trait that set him aside from the other boys. He was gentle, kind, imaginative and ambitious. Perhaps the greatest difference, though, was his curiosity. He was not superstitious, for he did not fear what he did not understand; he was too curious for that. For instance, he had checked out the Todder Brook Whooper long before Shadrack and Dryfly and had kept it as his very own secret. His trek had been alone at night. He had watched the lonely man trying to play his trumpet and had left him to live his life as he chose. He found the fear, the superstition of Brennen Siding, the stories of Shadrack and Dryfly amusing. The Todder Brook Whooper was a form of entertainment for them all and he chose not to take it away from them.

Palidin went as far in school as Hilda Porter could take him, which was grade eight. To go to high school, he would have had to move to Blackville, to live there and pay room and board, to dress better. Of course, such extravagances were beyond Shirley Ramsey's pecuniary means. So, Palidin borrowed what books he could (Hilda Porter was his greatest supplier), and read. John Kaston had felt certain that he had converted Palidin to the Baptist fold when he was approached for the Bible. Palidin read the Bible and returned it, but his face was never seen in the little church.

"Thank you, John. It was interesting," said Palidin and left before John had a chance to preach.

Palidin had taken great pains and much time in the reading of both the New and the Old Testaments. It had been difficult for him, but the crux of his drive had been simple — "At least it's reading matter." He'd found The Gospel According to St. Matthew the most interesting of all, and read it twice. This accounted for another difference in Palidin: he was, unlike the others, aware of the prince of devils and the lord of flies, Beelzebub.

"You don't have to be Beelzebub, or wicked either, to control flies," he told himself.

Palidin saw nothing wrong or unusual in running naked through the forest, sitting naked in swamps eyeing birds and insects. He had a calmness about him, so that when he sat in the fly-infested swamps of Dungarvon, the blackflies and mosquitoes, as well as the other animals, seemed to accept him with a casual indifference. He could walk through fields of goldenrod where thousands of busy bees cluttered the blossoms, theorizing: "Take your clothes off and stay calm and nothing animal will bother you." He liked the bees and the bees seemed to like him. He never once got stung. "If you fear them and feel hostile toward them," he thought, "they'll feel it and not like you. It's goodness, not evil that helps you through the field."

Palidin's favourite toy was a dime-sized magnet. "It's like holding a little planet," he reasoned. He played with it for hours, picking up needles and nails; spinning it, pondering it, toying with theories of energy, circles and echoes. He had a theory that if you shouted at a star, your voice would take thousands of years to return, but would, eventually, do so.

West of everybody's property line, deep in the forest, was a valley that everyone in Brennen Siding referred to as "The Big Hollow." Because the property was government-owned, Shirley Ramsey often took her family there on picnics. "Nobody'll bother us back there," she always said. Of course, when Bonzie got lost just back of the barren beyond The Big Hollow, the picnics stopped. Nobody in the Ramsey family had the heart to go back there again. Nobody, except for Palidin.

Palidin liked the barren and went there frequently. The barren was like a lake you could walk on. It was swampy so that the moss and water would take you to the ankles with every step, but visually it was like a prairie that stretched for several miles, its wild rice and reeds blowing in the wind. There was a huge boulder in the center of the barren where he often sat to think. On that rock, alone, naked, he would tan his body and wait for echoes to return. He fantasized that perhaps a wise old prophet had shouted something from the rock when the barren was still a lake, and that one day the prophet's echo would return. Palidin did not want to miss the prophecy.

It took him a great deal of time and effort, but with a stone and chisel, he hammered out the inscription:

Probe the atom;
Ponder the echoes of the wise.
There lie the secrets of the universe.

Palidin Ramsey had but one friend to play with — George Hanley. George was also growing up to be different. When he was a little boy, his hands, feet and ears had seemed too big for his body, but as he grew, everything seemed to take on the proper dimensions. He was developing into a very tall and handsome man and that, in itself, was one difference. Brennen Siding men were rarely good looking. George's teeth were even and white, and that, too, made him different. He was also a good friend of Palidin Ramsey and was more than just a little infatuated with him. They travelled together constantly; their friendship was faithful and true. None of the other boys in Brennen Siding wanted to be seen with Palidin Ramsey.

When he was younger, George spent much of his time playing with girls. He felt girls were more honest and interesting. Girls didn't ask him to be a thief for the sake of buying friendship. He palled around with Max Kaston for a few years, but Max was becoming more and more introverted. Max was scared of everything, would not leave the house at night — had been that way ever since he quit school, and John, fearing Max would never become a preacher, tried to break his spirit by working him long and hard in the woods.

But then, George became drawn by the magnetism, by the

eyes of Palidin Ramsey. Palidin triggered his curiosity, was easy to talk to, told him things about earth, man and the universe — interesting things that whirled his mind to greater heights.

He told himself: "I'll be a friend to Palidin, no matter what anyone thinks!"

*

Lindon Tucker sat by the kitchen table. The kerosene lamp was turned up a little higher than usual. Lindon Tucker was figuring on a used envelope, with an inch long pencil. "No sense wastin' good paper," thought Lindon. "No, no," thought Lindon, "and I kin light the fire, as the feller says, yes sir, yes sir yes sir, I kin light the fire with it in the mornin' and nobody'll ever know what the figures are about. No, no, no, nobody, not a soul, no one will ever know." Lindon was working on the extremely confidential state of his economy.

"Seven dollars a day for guidin'," he figured. "I'll be on the job for seven days . . . seven days, yeah. Seven days on the job, yeah, oh yeah, yeah, yeah. Me pay check should be . . . 7+7=14, 14+7=21, 21+7=28, 28+7=35, 35+7=42, 42+7=49 . . . forty-nine dollars, yeah, yeah, forty-nine dollars, yeah. If I git a five dollar tip . . . 49+5=54 . . . I'll have fifty-four big ones, oh yeah, yeah, yeah."

Lindon opened his checkbook and thought of his mother. She had passed away the previous spring and Lindon had been very upset. "It cost me nearly . . . " he looked at the checkbook . . . "Damn! $1200.00 to bury her! $1200.00 for puttin' somebody in the ground!"

The checkbook read $3962.17. "Add the $49.00 for guidin' and I'll have . . . " (he figured) " . . . $4011.17."

"Damn!" he swore. "When Mom was alive, we had over $5000.00!" Clara's senior citizen's check once a month and Lindon's penny pinching over a period of fifteen years were the reasons for the $5000.00, but Clara's death . . . "Damn! $1200.00 for puttin' somebody in the ground is robbery, robbery, yeah, robbery!"

To Lindon, five thousand dollars was the magical figure.

Lindon Tucker thought about his riverfront property. "I could sell him all the way to the bottom of the hill. That's about five hundred feet. Me lot's about ninety rods long . . . ninety rods by five hundred feet. Wonder what it's worth?"

"If it had good hay on it, it'd be worth a lot more," he thought. "If it had lumber on it, it'd be worth more agin, but thar ain't nothin' on it. No ain't nothin' on it, no, no, no, nothin' on it, no."

"Damn!" he swore at the table, the envelope and his pencil. "I should've had it ploughed and seeded! Land ain't worth nothin' if there's no hay on it!"

"Bill Wallace is Amurican . . . he might have a figure in mind," thought Lindon. Lindon eyed his checkbook and wondered if Bill Wallace would give him enough for that old shore to bring the figure "$4011.17" back up to "$5000.00."

"I'll ask him for $1200.00 and let him think he's beatin' me down to a thousand," decided Lindon.

*

Across the river and upstream, another gentleman (Bill Wallace) sat pondering figures.

"That much river frontage on the Connecticut, or the Housatonic would go for half a million. Up here in the sticks, it's not worth a penny more than fifty thousand. I'll have somebody build me a nice cabin on it . . . another fifty thousand."

Bill Wallace wondered if Lindon Tucker was capable of negotiating.

Bill Wallace sipped his scotch and envisioned the Lindon Tucker Salmon Pool . . . "The Bill Wallace Salmon Pool" he said to himself. "Ninety rods of private river frontage. The pool's got hundreds of boulders in it, a strong current, deep water, a gravel beach for landing salmon on . . . it's perfect! One of the best pools on this damn river, . . . maybe the world. $50,000.00 would be a steal . . . a tax writeoff."

*

Dryfly Ramsey had fine brown hair and a natural part in the middle of his scalp. In Brennen Siding, it was not cool to part your hair in the middle. If Dryfly Ramsey combed his hair over from a part on the left side, it would hide the natural part in the middle. When Dryfly greased and combed his hair back like Elvis, his hair went "flip-flop" and there was the part, like a zipper, streaking back the middle of his head. More grease would hold everything in place, but only until he moved. Although Dryfly didn't know it, he was confronting a problem that would always keep him "homely" and "without confidence" for a great deal of his adolescence. Dryfly knew by the shape of his head, the big nose and the peaked chin, that he could never look like Elvis Presley, but he felt the hair, at least, would help. As Dryfly labored in front of the piece of mirror that hung on the wall above the water bucket, he was very discouraged. If Dryfly had had a closet, he would have hidden in it.

"Maybe I can train it to lay back," he thought, "and I'll hold my head very still."

He turned very slowly away from the mirror.

"How's it look, Mom?"

"Looks good, dear. Don't use up all me lard."

"Well, what am I gonna use, Mom? Ya won't buy me any Brill Cream!"

"How's about the tobacco? Who buys you the tobacco?"

"No argament there," thought Dryfly. "See ya later," he said and left. As he stepped off the porch, his hair went "flip-flop."

Palidin sat quietly in his bedroom with a book in front of him. He was reading. Palidin was looking in the men's underwear section of the T. Eaton catalogue. He heard Dryfly leave.

"I wish Dryfly would have some sense!" he thought.

Shirley was sitting by the kitchen table, thinking and smoking a cigarette.

"Maybe I should do something with meself," she thought. "The girls are all off and Palidin's the only one home. It's gettin' lonesomer all the time. I should have a man. Maybe I'll wash me hair. Maybe I'll wash all over."

"Palidin!"

No answer.

"Palidin, you go out somewhere. I wanna take a bath."

No answer.

"Palidin?"

"I'll be out in a minute, Mom!"

"NOW, Palidin! I want to take a bath!"

"Why . . . why don't you go to the river, Mom?"

"'Cause I want to take it here!"

"OK, Mom . . . I'm comin'."

*

When Dryfly met Shadrack at the meeting place (the foot-bridge), he saw that Shad hadn't forgotten the empty pickle jar. Shadrack and Dryfly had plans for the pickle jar.

"Here, you carry it. You're the one's gonna be usin' it," said Shadrack, passing Dryfly the pickle jar. "Remember the plan?"

"I know, I know, I know!" said Dryfly.

They landed at the Cabbage Island Salmon Club at eight o'clock, Dryfly dressed in his best shirt (a black cowboy shirt with snap buttons), blue jeans and sneakers. Shad had on a blue plaid shirt with the collar turned up and the sleeves rolled in wide, well-ironed cuffs to just below the elbow. Shad's bright red hair was greased back and staying nicely in place. Shad's lip was already feeling tired from holding it in the unaccustomed "curled" fashion.

Lillian was sitting on the veranda in sandals, blue jeans and a red haltertop blouse. She was writing a letter, and when she saw Shad and Dry approaching, she put her pen down and closed the writing pad.

"Hi guys," she said.

"Go'day. How's she goin'?"

"Godday."

"How are you boys?"

"Good."

"Good."

"It's a warm day, isn't it?"

"Hot."

"Hot."

"Would you like a soda?"

Both boys, being accustomed to calling it "pop," thought of the "cow brand" baking soda, used also for a seltzer for indigestion.

"No, that's alright."

"Not right now," said Dry.

"I have some nice cold soda in the fridge, if you want some," said Lillian.

"I might have a glass o' water, maybe," said Shad.

"You sure you don't want a Pepsi, Dryfly?"

"Yeah, I might have a Pepsi," said Dryfly.

Shad wondered why Lillian hadn't offered him a Pepsi.

Lillian stood and offered Dryfly her hand, "I'm Lillian Wallace," she said.

"Dryfly Ramsey."

Lillian smiled. "I'll get the Pepsi and water," she said and went inside.

"What'd ya do with the pickle bottle?" asked Shad.

"Behind me."

"Remember the plan?"

"Yep. I got 'er."

"Here you go, boys."

"Thanks."

"Thanks."

"So, what's your real name, Dryfly?"

"Driffley," said Dryfly.

Shad chuckled and Lillian smiled.

"There's something about Dryfly," thought Lillian. "Honesty perhaps."

"And you play guitar?" she asked.

"Naw, a few chords, that's all."

"And modesty," thought Lillian.

"You should hear him! He's some good," put in Shad.

"Well, I'd like to," said Lillian.

The three sat in the shade of the veranda, consuming the view and feeling the caress of the warm summer breeze. From here, they could see a man beaching a salmon over on Cabbage Island. They could hear the faint whine of the reel and see the sunlight dancing on the pressured bamboo rod.

"Doctor Saunders," said Lillian.

"Looks like a big one," said Dryfly.

"Do you fish?" asked Lillian.

"Some," said Dryfly.

"Do you catch many big ones?"

"Now and agin."

"Do you guide?"

"Some."

"Never caught a salmon in his life," said Shadrack, "ain't old enough to guide, either!"

"Am too!"

"You're not!"

"Am too! Might go guidin' this fall!"

"Play guiddar's all you do!"

Shad didn't like the way things were going. Lillian was directing too much of her conversation at Dryfly. "Lillian's my girl," he thought. "Surely she can't be interested in Dryfly!"

"There's something mysterious about Dryfly," thought Lillian.

Shad didn't like the way the conversation was going, but he had brought it back to where he wanted it as far as the plan was concerned.

"You should have yer guiddar here. Play us a song," said Shadrack, winking at Dryfly.

"Later, maybe," said Dryfly.

In all actuality, Lillian Wallace was not the prettiest girl in the world. It was just that Shadrack and Dryfly thought she was the prettiest girl in the world. They were like two dogs mooning and sniffing a bitch in heat. They saw magic in her smile, mystery in her accent, wisdom, honesty and sophistication in her eyes.

A dark cloud was creeping up the western sky.

"Looks like we might get a shower," said Dryfly.

"Not for a couple o' hours," said Shad. "The birds are still out."

"Do birds know when it's going to rain?" asked Lillian.

"Birds are like hens," said Shad. "A hen will go under a shed or somethin' when yer about to get a shower. If yer about to get a day's rain, the hen will stay outside, pay the rain no mind at all. Them birds will go and hide in an hour or so, just you watch."

Shad was feeling very wise and grown up. His father had told him about hens, but Shad wasn't sure about birds in general. It didn't matter though. If the birds stayed out, he'd say they were in for a big rain. If the birds took shelter, it was late enough in the evening so that they'd be in for the night anyway.

Shadrack stood up and walked to the veranda railing, sat on it and stared at the river. Shadrack loved the river as much as he loved Lillian Wallace. The angler had landed his salmon and was casting for another. Shad saw a salmon jump, down on the bend.

"That lad landed his fish and I just saw another one jump down on the bend, Dry. Is there a run on?"

"Someone was tellin' Mom that the Renous was full o' fish," said Dryfly.

"That's good," said Shad. "Too bad we didn't have a net."

Shad was commencing to formulate another plan. If it didn't rain all night, he and Dry might borrow a net somewhere and go drifting for salmon — a perfect excuse for being out on the river.

"Netting salmon is against the law," thought Shad, "and that makes it more fun. We'll have lots of cigarettes and whiskey. . . . Dry and me will have some fun tonight!"

"Is Helen MacDonald still here?" asked Shad.

"I think she's finished for the day. She'd be down in the kitchen, if she's still here," said Lillian. "Did you want to see her?"

"Oh no, just wonderin'."

"You suppose I could use your bathroom?" asked Shad.

"Of course. Go through the living room and down the hall. It's at the end."

Shad winked at Dryfly. "I'll be right back," he said.

As Shad was going through the door, he stopped. "You didn't find a wallet here today, did ya, Lillian?"

"No."

"I think I left it here last night. It's prob'ly on the sofa."

"Well, take a look around. I haven't seen it, though. Dad might have found it."

"It don't matter. There wasn't any money in it. I'll just take a quick look."

Inside, Shad went directly to the sofa, reached between the cushions and came up with the wallet. He took the opportunity to scan the room. A carton of Lucky Strike cigarettes lay on the table. In the corner, on another table (the bar), sat bottles of rum, rye, gin, bourbon, vodka, scotch, Dubonnet, sherry and Canada Dry Ginger Ale. "All's well," thought Shad, went to the bathroom, peed, then returned to the veranda.

While Shad was inside, Lillian asked, "Shadrack tells me you're not in school. Do you have a job?"

"No place to work around here," said Dryfly. "I might go guidin' in the fall."

"What does your father do?"

"Me father's dead," said Dryfly. "Never saw 'm in me life."

"I'm sorry. Does your mother work?"

"No. Runs the Post Office."

"Really? There's a Post Office in the area?"

"At our house, yeah."

"Good, I'll have to mail a letter and some postcards, tomorrow."

"I'll come over and git them for ya," said Dryfly.

"Oh, you don't have to do that."

"I don't mind. Ain't doin' nothin' anyway."

"OK, tomorrow then."

Lillian was thinking of herself and Dryfly being alone without Shadrack. "I could say that I was with two boys, then," she thought.

Dryfly was nervous. He could not look Lillian directly in the eye. He was feeling not so much shy as guilty. He was feeling that maybe Shad's idea was not such a good one. "What if they miss it? What if we get caught?"

"Did you find your wallet?" asked Lillian as Shadrack came through the door.

"Yep," said Shad, holding up his wallet.

Shad sat on the veranda railing once again. "Why don't we go and get your guiddar?" he asked.

"Naw. Not feeling too good."

"Oh, is there something wrong?" asked Lillian.

"No, just tired, I guess. Had a late night last night."

"Maybe me and Lillian could git the guiddar for ya," recommended Shadrack.

"Maybe you don't feel like playing," said Lillian.

"Oh, I don't mind playin', I just don't feel up to goin' after it."

"Me and Lillian will go for it," said Shad.

"I would love to hear you play," said Lillian. "Would you, if we went and got it for you?"

"Yeah, but you lads will have to do the singin', I jist play, I don't sing."

"Ya do so sing!"

"I don't!"

"Ya do!"

"Don't!"

"Wanna go get it Lillian?"

"How far is it?"

"Just a little ways. Take about ten minutes."

"Well, OK. Will you be alright here, Dryfly?"

"Yeah, I'll just rest here while yer gone."

"OK. We'll be right back," Shad reassured Dryfly with a wink. The wink said, "It's all there, Dry, just like I said."

When Shadrack and Lillian had gone over the hill and had disappeared into the foliage of Tuney Brook, Dry rose and went into the cabin. Inside he found himself wanting to luxuriate for a while in the richness — the beautiful sofa and chairs, the mahogany tables, the fireplace. Dryfly found himself having to control his fantasies. The plan came first and he didn't want to screw it up.

Dryfly went to the table where Bill Wallace kept his liquor supply. "He must be havin' a party," thought Dryfly, "there's so much of it."

As planned, to make sure that Bill would not miss anything gone, Dry poured a little from each bottle until the pickle jar was full of rum, gin, bourbon, vodka, scotch, Dubonnet, sherry and Canada Dry Ginger Ale. He then went to the other table and took two packs of Lucky Strike cigarettes. "He won't miss two packs," he thought.

Carefully, so as not to be seen, Dryfly sneaked out the back door of the cabin. He scanned the surroundings. "All's clear. Everyone's fishin'."

He stashed his booty in the tall grass at the edge of the woods and went back into the camp.

The camp was cool and smelled of pine. He sat in a big upholstered chair for no other reason than to test its quality, wanting to experience for the first time in his life what it was like to sit in a comfortable chair. He sighed, "This is the life!" and tried out the sofa. Then he tried a chair at the table. He ran his hand across the smooth surface of the table, gently, feeling its coolness. He then reluctantly went back outside.

Back on the veranda, Dryfly noticed that the thunder clouds had progressed considerably in their approach. They were deep and fluffy, the horizon blue as steel and periodically swept with lightning. The silence seemed deeper too, between the grumbles of distant thunder.

"It's gonna be a heavy storm," thought Dryfly and checked to see if he was positioned in a safe place.

"In a storm, you should never set near a window," he thought. "People draw lightning, so it's good to git indoors. Stay away from bulb sockets and plug-ins. Stay away from stoves. Lightnin' is apt to come down a stove pipe."

"There's danger all around," he thought. "No escape."

When a lightning storm hovered over Brennen Siding, half the population ran to a neighbor's house. If the storm was particularly heavy, they got on their knees and prayed.

John Kaston always led the prayers, saying things like: "Dear loving Heavenly Father, smite the tempest!" "The voice, mighty in the wilderness," and "Thank thee for removing the cancer from me bowels!" John Kaston loved to preach. John Kaston was "this far" from being a preacher.

"If she's gonna hit, she'll hit," thought Dry. "No sense worrying about it."

Often when a storm approaches Brennen Siding from the northeast, depending on the preceding barometric decline, ahead of it comes the smell of sulfur, the smell of the smoke from the pulpmill in Newcastle. The storm pushes it and spreads it like a monstrous fart over the area. It spread over Brennen Siding this night and reached Dryfly's nostrils.

Dryfly knew what it was; he'd smelled it many times. "The pulpmill," he thought. "You kin always smell it before a storm. Smells like a fart."

Whenever Dryfly smelled the pulpmill on the air, it always reminded him of Shirley's description of the devil: "He's got big horns and a long tail with an arrowhead at the end of it. His eyes are yellow . . . like a cat's and they shine at night. He smells like . . . like . . . like shit."

"Smells like the devil," thought Dryfly. "Maybe he's comin' to get me for what I just did. The lightning could be the light from the fires of Hell, the thunder could be the sound of the big doors slammin', or the devil's growl. Maybe that's why everyone prays when there's a storm comin'."

Dryfly did not like thoughts of the devil and shrugged them off. He didn't even know if the devil existed — or God, for that matter. Thunderstorms only came at the end of hot summer days and Dryfly loved hot summer days. There was too few of them in this north land, and when they came, he felt obliged to enjoy every minute of them, thunderstorms included. Down deep inside, he liked the thunder. Liking the thunder was one of the few things he had in common with his brother Palidin.

*

When Shadrack and Lillian were crossing the bridge over Tuney Brook, on their way from Shirley Ramsey's, Shadrack stopped and looked into the water.

"Sometimes ya kin see trout in here," he said.

"Really!" Lillian moved closer to Shad and peered into the water. "There's one," she pointed, "There!"

"And there's another one," said Shad, inching toward Lillian.

Shadrack eyed Lillian: "God! She's a pretty little thing," he thought.

If there was the smell of sulfur in the air, Shad was not aware of it; all he was smelling was Lillian's perfume.

"If I don't make a move tonight, I might never git the chance," thought Shad. "So, what do I do? Pass the hand? Say something mushy?"

"That's awful good smellin' perfume ya got on there," tried Shad.

"It's fly repellent."

"Still smells good."

The sound of thunder tumbled in from the northeast. The smell of sulfur settled. Lillian sniffed the air and looked at Shadrack with disgust.

"I wish I could say the same thing about you right now," she thought. She turned and walked toward the Cabbage Island Salmon Club.

Shad, carrying Dryfly's guitar, followed.

Lillian was thinking of Shirley Ramsey.

Their visit had been a brief one; just long enough for Shirley to get them the guitar. Shirley had been proud of the fact she had something to give and had shown Lillian great respect and courtesy. Lillian, however, only saw the slop pail, the broken mirror hanging over the sink, the backless chairs.

"How can people live in such a place?" she thought. "I've never seen such a place! And that's where Dryfly lives? Poor Dryfly."

*

"I've had enough fishing for one day, Lindon. Let's go back to the camp and have a drink. I'd like to discuss that property."

"Good, good, good. Gonna rain, gonna rain anyway. Might as well, might as well."

When Lindon and Bill got back to the camp, they found Lillian being entertained by Shadrack and Dryfly. Dryfly was play-ing guitar and Shadrack was singing: "George Hare shot a bear, shot 'im here, shot 'im there; George Hare shot a bear, shot 'im in the arse and never touched a hair."

"Godday Bill, Lindon! How's she goin' old boys?" yelled Shadrack.

"Good, good, good."

"Hi boys, Lillian."

"Shad and Dry have been singing for me, Dad," explained Lillian.

"Well, don't let me stop you. Lindon and I have some busi-ness to discuss. We'll join you lata'."

The two men went inside. Bill poured them a couple of stiff scotches and sat across the table from Lindon.

"I should've had that salmon, Lindon. What d'ya think I did wrong?"

"Nuthin', nuthin', nuthin'. Held 'im too tight, maybe. Knot in yer leader. Never did a thing wrong."

"Damn!"

"We'll git 'im tomorrow. Yep! Get 'im tomorrow, we will."

"Let's drink to that," said Bill. "Bottoms up!"

Bill emptied his glass. Lindon put his glass to his lips, opened up and tossed the two ounces back, sloshed it around as if mouth washing and swallowed.

"HEM! AHEM! Trip a ghost!" he said.

"Have anotha'," said Bill and replenished the glasses.

"Well, Lindon, I've decided I'd like to buy that property. Do you, or don't you want to sell?"

"Well I've been thinkin', as the fellei says, as the feller says, if ya know what I mean, I've been thinkin'. Sell if the price is right."

"Well Lindon, old buddy, let's hear your price."

"Well, I know, I know, I know, I know there ain't no lumber on that old shore; I know that, I know that; and I know there ain't no hay on it, I know that. And, and, and I, I, I, know it might sound dear, but, but, but, I was thinking, I was thinking,

I was thinking, I'd sell, if the price was right. Was thinkin' maybe, I know it might sound dear, and all that, but was thinkin' maybe I'd sell it for twelve hundred dollars."

"Twelve hundred dolla's !" Bill Wallace had been expecting fifty thousand.

"Well, I, I, I, couldn't let it go for a cent less than a thousand, No, No, not a cent, not a cent, not a cent less than a thousand, if ya know what I mean, as the feller says, not a cent less than a thousand." Taking Bill's response negatively, Lindon thought: "He thinks I'm askin' too much."

Bill Wallace wanted to laugh and whoop and holler. Instead, he tossed back the second double of scotch. "Twelve hundred is giving it away. I'm getting this property for almost nothing," he thought.

"Are you talking the whole front?" asked Bill.

"Oh yeah, yeah, yeah. Oh yeah, yep. The whole front. No good to me. No lumber on it. No hay, no lumber. Good place to fish though. Good place to fish. Go over the hill anytime at all and ketch a salmon, so ya kin. I wouldn' lie to ya! Ketch a salmon there anytime at all, so ya kin, ya kin yeah."

"How far back you talking?"

"Back about, about, about, about, about, about five hundred feet, five hundred feet back to the top of the hill."

Bill sipped his drink. He had been thinking two hundred feet. "This man doesn't have a clue what he's doing," he thought. "At this rate, I could buy up the whole river."

"A thousand dollars, you're asking?"

"Well, I wanted twelve hundred, but like I say, there ain't no lumber on it, no lumber to speak of, like the feller says, like I say, no hay on it either. Guess I could let it go for a thousand."

"Tell me, Lindon, you wouldn't be interested in selling the whole place, would you?"

"No, no, couldn' sell the house and the lumber land. No, oh no. Couldn' sell the house and the lumber land."

"Has the property been in the Tucker family for long?"

"Ever since the, as the feller says, ever since the great fire of

1825, yeah 1825, yeah 1825, I think it was. Me grandfather, or me great grandfather, now I ain't sure, I don't know which."

"It was your grandfather that cleared the land?"

"Either him, or me great grandfather, I, I, I, as the feller says, I ain't sure which. All I know is, the old feller, one of them, come here from Ireland after the fire o' 1825 and couldn' find a tree big enough still standin', if ya know what I mean, a tree big enough after the fire, for a fence post."

"Who owns the property next to yours?" asked Bill.

"Well, Sam Little, Sam Little, Sam Little owns across the river from me and Lester Burns owns to me left and Frank Layton owns to me right."

"How about the Lester Burns property? Is that a good pool?"

"Good fishin' yeah, good all along there, yeah, oh yeah."

"And who owns upstream from Lester?"

"Bert Todder. Bert Todder, yeah. Bert ain't got much of a fishin' hole though. Ain't much of a pool in front o' Bert's. Back side o' Cabbage Island. 'Muricans own the island and all this side. Bert just got a little trickle 'tween him and the island."

Bill Wallace poured some more scotch into Lindon's glass.

"Would you consider shaking hands on a deal tonight, Lindon, old buddy?"

"Sure, sure, sure, if you got the money, sure, sure I'd shake hands, if you got the money. Thousand dollars. Wanted twelve hundred, but I'll sell to you for a thousand. A thousand, yeah."

"Well, Lindon, you drive a hard bargain, but I'd really like to have a place up here."

"OK, OK, OK, we got a deal, got a deal, shake hands on 'er, shake, put 'er there!"

Bill and Lindon shook hands aggressively. Both men were grinning happily. Both men were getting what they wanted and both men were beginning to feel the effects of the liquor.

"We have a deal," said Bill Wallace.

"A deal, yeah."

They drank to the deal.

"You'll be buildin' a camp?" asked Lindon.

"Yes."

"You might be needin' someone to look after yer place when yer not here, if ye know what I mean, someone to look after the place?"

"Yes, by God, Lindon old buddy, maybe I will!"

"Well, sir, I'd do it for ya, so I would. I'm just yer man! I'd do it for ya. Wouldin' mind. I'm right there. Right handy, so I am."

"That sounds like a good idea," said Bill Wallace, then thought, "And so is this Lester Burns fellow whom I'd like to convince to sell."

*

"Gotta have a leak," said Shadrack. "Comin' Dry?"

"Yep. Could do with one meself."

Dryfly put his guitar down and followed Shadrack around to the back of the cabin. This was the fourth time they excused themselves and went to the place where Dryfly had hidden the pickle bottle and cigarettes.

"Startin' to rain," said Dryfly, "We'd better put these cigarettes in our pockets."

"Yeah, but don't make a mistake and smoke one while we're inside. Here, have a drink."

Both boys took substantial slugs of the concoction in the pickle bottle. Both boys were feeling a little woozy and starting to lose their inhibitions. The pickle bottle was only half full.

"Good stuff, eh?"

"Let's get back. I'm gettin' wet."

"Who gives a jesus! I don't care if I git wet! You care if you get wet, Dryfly? A little water wouldin' hurt you, Dryfly! Here, have one more little slug."

"Hem! Ahem! Don't know if I can handle much more of that!"

"I can handl'er. I'll drink'er if you can't, by God!"

"C'mon, let's get back."

"You gonna play us another song?"

"Shhhure, why not!"

Back on the veranda, Dryfly picked up his guitar.

"We should go inside," said Lillian. "The rain's starting to come in here."

"Very best with me, darlin'!" said Shadrack.

"Sure! Let's go in," said Dryfly.

Inside the teenagers found Lindon Tucker and Bill Wallace feeling very happy. Shad and Dry were also feeling very happy. Lillian Wallace, although she wasn't drinking, was picking up on the good time vibrations and was also having fun. A celebration was commencing to brew.

"Ah! Boys! Come in, come in! I see you have a guitar! Let's have another drink, Lindon!"

Lindon Tucker was grinning from ear to ear. "Don't mind if I do," he said. "A little drink wouldn' do us any harm!"

"Sing for us, boy. Sing us a song!" said Bill.

Dry sat on the sofa and strummed a G chord. "What would you like to hear?" he asked.

"Anything you know is fine with me."

Dryfly strummed the G chord once again.

> *Roses are blooming*
> *Come back to me darlin'*
> *Come back to me darlin'*
> *And never more roam . . .*

Dryfly sang loud and clear and strummed smoothly. Dryfly was giving his first performance in front of an audience. He sang: "Roses are Blooming," "Beautiful, Beautiful Brown Eyes," "The Cat Came Back," and "Hannah Won't You Open The Door." Everyone listened and everyone enjoyed.

Much later, Bill Wallace said: "You know (hic), back home in Stockbridge, there's this hotel. (hic) The Red Lion, it's called. (hic) I know the manager. You'd go over (hic) well there. Dryfly. I could arrange to get you (hic) a booking."

"A booking."

"Sure! (hic) You could entertain there. You could come down and stay (hic) with us for a week and entertain at the Red Lion."

"No, I ain't good enough to do that."

"Yes you are, my boy! There's a bunch o' (hic) young people

playing there all the time, that aren't any better than you are. (hic) In fact, you're better than most of them."

Bill Wallace, though intoxicated, was serious. He liked Dryfly's singing, he liked Dryfly's guitar playing, and he liked Dryfly. "He parts his hair in the middle . . . not like all these Elvis Presley freaks. And I could get him a booking."

Dryfly thought of the Red Lion many times, but that was all. He was too shy, too backward, and loved the Dungarvon River too much to leave it for a week.

In Stockbridge, Massachusetts, people like Arlo Guthrie and Joan Baez were starting to get bookings at the Red Lion.

*

The lightning flashed and the thunder boomed and rumbled. There was so much static on the radio that Shirley Ramsey not only turned it off, but unplugged it as well. Shirley Ramsey was very afraid of thunderstorms. She sat in the kitchen, smoking and fingering her rosary beads. Palidin was back in his room. Shirley hoped Dryfly was not on the river. "Water draws lightning," she thought.

Nutbeam, on the other hand, was not at all afraid of the storm. He liked it. It added excitement to his life. Nutbeam found the warm summer rain refreshing and often showered himself in it. Nutbeam was standing outside of Shirley Ramsey's window. He had gone to Shirley Ramsey's house to listen to the radio, but had lost all interest in listening when he saw Shirley Ramsey remove her clothes to take a bath.

He moved closer, so that he was actually spying through the window a few inches from the glass. Nutbeam found Shirley Ramsey very exciting.

"The most beautiful woman I ever saw in my life," he whispered to himself.

eight

Palidin Ramsey sat on his bed reading an *Outdoor Life* magazine he'd borrowed from George Hanley. He was reading an article on the Atlantic salmon and was very much interested. "The Atlantic salmon," the article stated, "lay their eggs in the upper reaches of the fresh water rivers such as the Cains, the Renous and the Dungarvon. When the young have grown to about a pound in weight and are called 'smolt,' they take a little journey. They swim a couple of thousand miles to dine in the ocean waters off the coast of Greenland. When they've stuffed themselves to satisfaction, they head back to their place of birth to start another generation. They lay their eggs behind the same rock, or in the same bed where they themselves were conceived."

The questions asked in the article were: "How do salmon find their way to Greenland and back? How do they recognize the same old rock, or the same old bed where they themselves were born?

"Four thousand miles through the dark ocean waters to return to the same nest, on the same river! Why? Why not some other river, or at least some other rock?" One of the article's contributing scientists theorized that salmon may have the ability to sense magnetic forces, that they follow magnetic fields from magnetic rock to magnetic rock, from magnetic coast to magnetic coast. "Salmon do tend to follow coast lines and even river banks," stated the scientist.

Magnetic was the magic word that started Palidin's quick mind to work. Lately Palidin had been thinking that voices (the echoes) were drawn back magnetically. Perhaps one's voice is thrown from a hillside by antimagnetic forces. Perhaps the ear is the magnetic force that attracts it home again. Perhaps magnetic forces account for the homing instinct in all creatures, for instance, the Monarch butterfly, the swallow . . . and the salmon.

Palidin had learned at a very early age how to stroke metal with metal for the purpose of creating magnets. "If salmon are attracted to magnets," thought Palidin, "why wouldn't a magnetic hook work better than just your everyday, ordinary hook?"

Palidin decided to pay a visit to George Hanley.

Palidin found George sitting in the shade of the barn, smoking a cigarette. George always went behind the barn to smoke.

"How's she goin' Pal?" greeted George. "What's up?"

"Was thinkin' I might go fishin'. Was wonderin' if ya had any hooks."

"Not me, no. There's some in the store, I think."

"Thought maybe you could steal me a couple."

"Shouldn' be any trouble. Where ya goin' fishin'?"

"I dunno. Someplace where it's good."

"Trout or salmon?"

"Salmon."

"Ya need flyhooks and a rod n' reel to fish salmon."

"Thought I might borrow Shad Nash's outfit. You sure ya need flyhooks for fishing salmon?"

"Yep. That's what everybody's usin'."

"Ya think you could steal me a flyhook?"

"It's hard to say. Flyhooks are a lot more costly than baithooks. Why don't you just go trout fishin' back the brook?"

"Because I have an idea about catching salmon."

"What idea?"

"Get me a flyhook and I'll tell ya."

"What makes you think the idea is worth it?"

"I don't. I have to experiment."

"Well, I might be able to get you one flyhook. What kind do you want?"

"It don't matter. I don't know one from the other."

"OK. I'll see what I can do. Wait here."

In less than five minutes, George returned with a fly called "Blue Charm" and handed it to Palidin. George was always giving Palidin things. George Hanley and Palidin Ramsey were good friends.

"Want to play in the hay?" asked George, gesturing to the inside of the barn.

"I was thinking about you last night," said Palidin.

*

Dryfly found himself pacing restlessly. He couldn't quite figure out what was happening to him, but he knew that something strange was in the making. For the tenth time he found himself pondering the facts. "She spent a lot o' the night talkin' to me and hardly spoke at all to Shad. True, they walked all the way here for me guiddar, but they didn' take long in doin' it. They couldn' do nothin' in that short o' time. Shad didn' seem to know what he was doin'. He got drunk, too, and puked off the veranda . . . almost didn't make it. Shad drank a lot more than I did. No wonder he got drunk. Lillian was prob'ly makin' fun o' us, but . . . she seemed to like me."

On the way to the Cabbage Island Salmon Club, Dryfly picked a daisy. "Mom says all women like flowers," he thought. "Mom says she carried daisies when she married Buck."

As Dryfly neared the cabin where Lillian Wallace was staying, he found himself thinking that maybe he had arrived too early. "It's still mornin', she might not even be out of bed." He didn't knock on the door, but sat on the veranda to wait and watch the river. He heard robins and chickadees and crows. He could see the river and the forest. He could smell the morning, fresh, radiant in the sun, cleansed to sweetness by the recent rain.

"Good morning, Dryfly," greeted Lillian from behind the screen door. "Am I a sleepy head, or are you early?"

"The train goes at eleven o'clock . . . you said you had a letter to mail and I thought . . . "

"Oh, yes. I haven't finished it yet. Would you like some orange juice?"

"Sure."

"I'll bring it out to you." In a moment Lillian reappeared with two glasses of orange juice, handed one to Dryfly and sat at the table. She was wearing a blue and white checked blouse, blue shorts and sandals.

"I picked you a daisy," said Dryfly, handing her the flower.

"Oh, how nice! Thank you! How thoughtful of you!"

Dryfly was feeling a little bit embarrassed about giving her the flower, but he was glad that he had given it to her. Lillian put the daisy in her hair. She had just taken her morning shower; fresh, clean and radiant, she complemented the morning itself. Dryfly could not take his eyes off her.

"Did you have a good time last night?" she asked, waving at the mosquitoes and blackflies that were already commencing to seek out her sweetness.

"Yeah," said Dryfly.

"My father really enjoyed your singing. It would be nice if you could come down and play at the Red Lion."

"You never know, I might."

"Have you seen Shadrack this morning?"

"Not yet."

"Ouch!" Lillian slapped a mosquito that was feasting on her thigh. "The bugs are terrible! Don't they bother you?"

"Sometimes."

"Only sometimes? I think they're out to devour me. How do you put up with the things?"

Dryfly wanted to tell her what Palidin had told him; that insects were very tiny; that insects had tiny eyes that restricted their vision to but a couple of feet; that insects were attracted to smell and body heat and that by waving and slapping and getting excited, one was only attracting more of them.

"They don't bother me that much," he said.

There was a can of repellent sitting on the table. Picking it up, Lillian said, "They sure bother me!"

Lillian sprayed her legs and arms. She sprayed some into the palm of her hand, then rubbed the back of her neck and face; she closed her eyes and sprayed her hair, and then she sprayed the air about her.

"Your father gone fishin'?" asked Dryfly.

"He and Mr. Tucker went to Newcastle to see a lawyer. My father's buying some property."

"From Lindon?"

"It's right on the river. Dad tells me it's beautiful."

"Good salmon pool there," commented Dryfly. "Only one left around here."

"What happened to the others?" asked Lillian.

"Oh, they're still there, but us lads can't fish in them."

"But, why?"

"Lads from Fredericton and the States and stuff own them. They don't want us lads fishin' in their pools . . . ketch all the fish."

"But, there's got to be plenty for everyone, isn't there?"

"Yeah . . . I don't know. I don't fish much anyway. Most of the people around here fish with a net."

"But that's against the law, isn't it?"

Dryfly shrugged. "If you want salmon, that's how ya gotte get 'em if ya don't have a pool to fish in."

"Don't people get caught by the wardens?"

"Sometimes. Hardly ever."

"Well, my father will let you fish in his pool, Dryfly. Don't you worry about that."

"Not worried. I hardly ever fish anyway."

"Dad wants to build a cottage next year."

"That's good. You'll be able to come up more often."

"I guess so. I'd really like to see the property sometime."

"I know where it is."

"Is it far from here?"

"The other side o' the river. Just cross the bridge and down the other side a little bit. See that house down there on the hill?"

Dryfly pointed at the paintless house, barn, woodshed, outdoor toilet, pigpen, toolshed, binder shed, henhouse and well-house that sat on the hill, across and downstream a half a mile or so.

"Could we get over there to see it?"

"No trouble. Cross the bridge and down the path. Wanna go?"

"Sure. I'd love to."

Dryfly and Lillian left the Cabbage Island Salmon Club and went over the hill to the river. They followed a riverside path upstream for several hundred yards until they came to the foot-bridge.

The footbridge consisted of four steel cables that spanned the river, two on top and two on the bottom. The sides and the bottom were held together by fencing wire. The two bottom cables were crossed with four-foot lengths of two-by-four lumber. Three strips of six-inch board were nailed to the two-by-fours, giving the bridge an eighteen-inch walking space. The cables were connected to pillars of stone and concrete on either side of the river and were stabilized in the middle of the river by a similar abutment. The bridge had to be high to escape the spring torrents and ice flows, so there were stairs of about thirty steps leading to the top of each riverside abutment. The bridge was sturdy enough to hold the weight of, perhaps, a thousand men, but it "looked" shaky and tended to bounce and sway when walked upon. For Lillian, walking the bridge was a new experience and scary business. She doubted its durability. When she got to the middle abutment she stopped to gather herself.

The morning breeze, cooled by the rains of the previous night, played in her hair and brought gooseflesh out on her arms and legs. Lillian eyed the river, the forested hills in the distance, the little farms, a swooping osprey in the cloudless sky. Dryfly eyed Lillian, her golden hair, her smooth tanned skin, her big blue eyes.

"You scared walkin' the bridge?" he asked.

"Well, it's a new experience," she said. "It's kind of shaky."

"Hold the devil himself."

"Yes, but will it hold two devils?" laughed Lillian.

"In a thunderstorm one night, a lad got beat to death on one of these things," said Dryfly. "Up the river. Above Gordon. The wind came up, started the cables flappin' and beat him to death. You can bang these top cables together hard enough to cut you in two with a little help. It'll bounce, too, and damn near throw you off of it."

"Must be scary."

"Scary enough. See right down there on the bend? There's a hole down there. You can drop an anchor from a twenty-foot rope and it'll hang straight down. 'Corpse's Hole' it's called, 'cause that's where they always find the bodies of anyone that's drowned. There's a whirlpool there and the bodies just go round and round. Mom says it's prob'ly haunted. Old Bill Tuney said he heard a ghost there one time."

"A ghost? What did the ghost sound like? What did he say?"

"Don't know. He never said, I don't think. He's dead now. Whoopin' prob'ly."

Dryfly looked at Lillian and felt a little bit ashamed; felt he was perhaps sounding like a superstitious old woman, that his choice of topic was perhaps too morbid a thing to have been dis-cussing with a young lady.

Lillian was eyeing 'Corpse's Hole' thoughtfully. "This whole river seems haunted," she said. "Did you and Shadrack really see the whooper?"

"I . . . I . . . No."

"I didn't think so. Shadrack lies a lot, doesn't he?"

"He doesn't mean to lie. He just always does it . . . and we did hear the thing . . . right in the woods beside us. We were just little kids and ran home."

Lillian turned to face Dryfly. Dryfly turned away to watch the river.

"He's funny looking," thought Lillian, eyeing the worn shirt and jeans, the dirty sneakers, the hair parted in the middle and the long nose.

"Would you hold my hand the rest of the way?" she asked.

"Ah . . . sure." Dryfly looked self-consciously back and forth along the bridge, a little embarrassed that someone might see him holding her hand.

When their hands touched, their hearts quickened. Dryfly's hand was warm and perspiring — so was Lillian's. They walked on, slowly, Lillian being careful to walk the center boards, to minimize the sway. Dryfly, close behind her, reached awkwardly ahead to hold her hand.

When they got to the far side, Dryfly wondered if she would let go of his hand. He left it up to her to make the decision. As they went down the steps and crossed Billy MacDonald's field, Bob Nash's field and Todder Brook, they were still holding hands.

"Do you plan to go back to school?" asked Lillian.

"I dunno," said Dryfly. "Maybe."

"What's your plan for the future?"

"I dunno. Not much to do around here."

"Will you move away?"

"Prob'ly. Everyone else does. Around here, you're either too young or too old to leave, or you're gone. Me brother Digger's livin' in Ontario. I might go and live with 'im in a year or so. Lots to do in Ontario."

"What does . . . ah . . . Digger work at?"

"Don't work hard at all. Packin' tomatoes in a place called Leamington . . . makin' two dollars an hour."

"You could play music for a living."

"Naw."

On the south side of Lindon Tucker's house grew an apple tree loaded with juicy green crabapples.

"Would you like an apple?" asked Dryfly.

Lillian and Dryfly, still holding hands, walked up the hill to the apple tree. Dryfly picked a few and offered one to Lillian.

"They're awfully green, aren't they?"

"Won't hurt ya. Hardly ever give ya the shits."

Lillian giggled a giggle that Dryfly found very pleasing.

"Why ya laughin'?"

" 'The shits,' " she said.

Dryfly laughed too.

They stopped laughing when they bit into the apples. They squinted their eyes, the muscles in their cheeks contracted, they wrinkled their noses — the apples were very sour.

They walked around Lindon Tucker's house and sat on the swing.

"It's very pleasant here," said Lillian, "and very quiet."

"Pretty place, yeah," said Dryfly.

"Look! There's a butterfly!" A big yellow butterfly played on an air current that eventually led to the arm of Dryfly's swing.

"Hmmm," said Dryfly, "what's this?"

"It likes you," said Lillian.

Dryfly said nothing, thought: "Everything's very pretty."

"How old are you?" asked Lillian.

"Fifteen."

"Do you have a girlfriend?"

"Naw. Ain't many girls around here."

"Shadrack said he had several girlfriends."

"Naw. He didn't mean it."

"Shad lied about girlfriends," thought Dryfly. "Shad lied about everything."

"Do you have a boyfriend?" asked Dryfly.

"No. I'm only fifteen, too."

They were eyeing each other and feeling very warm inside.

"Thank you for the daisy," said Lillian. "You're the first boy to ever give me a flower."

Lillian reached out and gently placed her hand on Dryfly's knee. Dryfly stared into her eyes and saw Heaven.

Something very emotional was sweeping over Lillian — a combination of happiness, sadness and bewilderment. It excited her to the point of tears.

"The butterfly and I both like you," she said.

Dryfly, swept by similar emotions, swallowed, said: "I . . . like you, too."

"The appropriate thing to do," thought Lillian, "would be to kiss him. The appropriate thing to do is for him to kiss me."

A hundred wild horses hooked onto Dryfly's nerve endings. They tugged at his nerve endings, his inhibitions, his shyness and his heart. Every one of the hundred wild horses seemed to be saying: "You haven't got the nerve, Dryfly! She's rich and pretty and you're poor and ugly. She'll laugh at you and you'll feel like a fool! You'll be lucky if she doesn't slap your face." The hundred wild horses pulled so hard that the chains connected to

Dryfly snapped and broke.

Dryfly leaned toward Lillian and placed a gentle crabapple-scented kiss on the smooth, cool cheek of Lillian Wallace.

*

Shadrack Nash awakened to his very first hangover. Shadrack Nash didn't feel very well at all. His head was aching, his mouth was dry and he had a guilt complex to no end.

"I made a fool of myself," he thought. "I talked too much, I sung too many dirty songs and to top it all off, I got sick. Lillian Wallace will never want to see me again!"

In the kitchen, Shad sat to a breakfast of tea and toast. He spread some of his mother's fresh strawberry jam on the toast.

Shadrack was very unhappy about something else. Lillian Wallace seemed more interested in Dryfly than she was in him.

"Why?! . . . Dryfly was showin' off on the guiddar, for one thing! And he didn' talk too much, or git sick!"

"You home, Shadrack?" The voice of Palidin Ramsey came through the screen of the kitchen door.

"No, I'm in Tracadie fishin' smelts!" said Shadrack.

Palidin entered.

"What're ya up to, Pal?" asked Shadrack.

"Wanna go fishing?" asked Palidin.

"Naw. Don't feel too good," said Shad.

"Would you mind if I borrowed your rod?"

"Fishin' trout or salmon?"

"Salmon."

"How long ya gonna be?"

"An hour . . . two, maybe."

"I don't care. Take it. It's on the porch."

"Thanks, Shad. I'll look after it. Bring ya back a salmon," said Palidin and left, taking Shadrack's rod and reel with him.

Shadrack's mother (Elva Nash) was washing dishes and humming "Rock of Ages." She hadn't spoken to Palidin. Elva Nash did not like the Ramseys. The Ramseys were trash and Elva Nash did not like her son to associate with trash.

"You shouldn't have given him that fishin' rod, Shad," said Elva. "Ya give 'em an inch and they'll take a mile. He'll be back agin, you mark my words! He'll be naggin' ya every day for some-thin'!"

"Ah, Pal won't hurt it."

"No odds! I don't want him around the place! They're Catholics! They don't know the word o' God! I pray for you Sha-drack, darlin'! I pray every night that you will stop hangin' around with the likes o' them Ramseys. They'll jist git you in trouble, mark my words!"

"They're not so bad, Mom."

"NOT SO BAD! NOT SO BAD! THEY'RE TRASH, THAT'S WHAT THEY ARE!! Never go to church on Sundays, runnin' the roads like . . . like cattle. 'Pon me soul, Shad, I don't know what's becomin' o' you? Yer gettin' jist like them! That old Shirley Ramsey never took a bath in her life and I could smell that Palidin as soon's he walked through the door. They'll never see the kingdom o' God, Shad, you kin mark my words!"

Elva Nash was warming up for one of her sermons and Shad knew it. She was washing dishes and Shad was sitting at the table. Through the window over the sink, Elva could see the river. Through the window, Elva could see Lillian Wallace walk-ing down the path with Dryfly Ramsey.

"Now look o' there, would ya! There's that sport's daughter walkin' down the flat with that . . . that . . . that tramp! Boy's, she must think a lot o' herself! What do you suppose the world's comin' to!!"

"Who?" Shad dashed to the window. "Dryfly and Lillian," he muttered through the thick black curtain that seemed to have fallen.

Shad ran outside and around the house. Spying from the corner of the house, he could see Lillian and Dryfly walking through the field, holding hands.

Shad was hungover and a little dizzy. The sight of Dryfly and Lillian almost made him sick. "Damn!" he thought. "Damn! Damn! Damn!"

Shadrack Nash was very hurt and wanted to cry. Shadrack was not hurting so much just because of the girl. There is more to heartbreak than losing a girl. Shadrack Nash was hurting for the same reason all losing lovers hurt. Egomania. How could he face Dryfly?

Shadrack Nash went for a walk through the woods. He needed to think. Shadrack took a walk back to Todder Brook.

*

When Dryfly removed his lips from Lillian's cheek, he could taste her fly repellent.

"She tastes and smells better than the DDT they spray over us in budworm season," he thought.

"We'd better be going back," said Lillian, getting off the swing and reaching her hand out for Dryfly's.

As they walked over the hill and back through the fields toward the bridge, nothing was spoken. Dryfly broke the silence in the shadow of the bridge abutment. There in the shadows, with a thousand blackflies swarming about his head, he stopped and swung in front of her. He looked into her big blue eyes and wanted to say, "I love you." Instead, he said, "Flies like the shade."

Dryfly was hot, inside and out and excited to a single point shy of panic. He forgot Palidin's teachings and waved at the on-slaught of flies, attracting a thousand more. But being there with Lillian was a precious moment and he wanted it to last. He wanted to say something, something intelligent, something romantic, anything. "Tell her that you love her," came a tiny voice from deep inside. "Tell her that she's beautiful! Tell her that you think she has the most beautiful eyes in the whole world! Tell her how wonderful she is!"

Lillian was protected by fly repellent and not being attacked, but she was as excited as Dryfly. "Just do what they do in the movies," she thought, parted her lips slightly and closed her eyes.

Dryfly didn't know it, but he was the son of a fabulous lover. Although Dryfly never met Buck, Buck's genes flowed in his veins; the same hereditary instinct was bubbling forth. It was the Buck in Dryfly that took control. Dryfly leaned forward and kissed Lillian, gently; as gentle as the butterfly that had rested on his hand. There was no pressure, no desire-driven fondling. Just a gentle, cool kiss — one heartbeat and it was over.

Dryfly withdrew a few inches and looked at the beautiful young girl. Lillian opened her eyes and looked at Dryfly.

"You have awful blue eyes," said Dryfly.

"You have awful brown eyes," said Lillian.

A mosquito drove its proboscis into the back of Dryfly's neck; another feasted on his forehead and another on his arm.

"C'mon! There's plenty for everyone!" yelled the mosquitoes.

One old mosquito zeroed in from the north and jabbed the thin, worn material of Dryfly's shirt, getting him in the back; another (a cowardly-bastard-of-a-mosquito) sucked on Dryfly's wonderfully exposed earlobe.

Without taking his eyes off Lillian, Dryfly battled and scratched. He moved in again and kissed Lillian for the second time, and once again tasted her repellent.

Withdrawing and looking at the wonderful girl with the big blue eyes, the same girl who was smart enough to protect herself from the cursed flies of the Dungarvon, Dryfly whispered: "No flies on you."

*

There was another precaution Dryfly could have dwelled upon: "If you keep walking, the mosquitoes and blackflies won't bother you as much."

Shadrack Nash kept walking through the fly-infested forest of Todder Brook until he came to the exact spot where he and Dryfly Ramsey had done away with the panther, or the devil, " . . . or whatever the Todder Brook Whooper was."

For the first time since he left his mother's kitchen, Shadrack was not thinking about his broken heart. Shadrack found himself preoccupied with the Todder Brook Whooper.

"What was it?" he asked himself. "Was it the Dungarvon Whooper? Was the Dungarvon Whooper a devil that wandered from place to place? Where is it now?" It hardly seemed conceivable that the devil, or anything else, could be so wily that a single shot fired into the air by a small boy would scare it off.

"We were standing right here," thought Shad, "and the thing was right down there by the brook. There was moose tracks all over the place . . . or devil tracks."

119

When Shadrack Nash scanned the rain-drenched clay about his feet, he did not see any moose tracks. What Shadrack did see, though, was the tracks of a human.

"Who else could be back here?" Shadrack asked himself. "Them tracks have been made since the shower last night. Someone must be back here this mornin'."

Shadrack, for no other reason than curiosity, started following the tracks. There weren't many and they didn't go far until they turned down a barely distinguishable path. Shad followed the path for about thirty seconds and came to a place where the path branched off. Now, confronting Shadrack was a path to the right, a path to the left and one down the middle. Each path that lay before him was less distinguishable than the one he was standing on.

The three paths reminded Shadrack of a John Kaston sermon.

"When you die," commenced John Kaston, sounding all the world like a southern American, "y'all will come to a branch in the rewd. Ya won't know which rewd to take unless yer one with the Savior! One path leads to Heaven, one leads to the pits of hell, and one leads to purgatory. Us Protestants don't have to worry about the one to purgatory. Know the Savior and you won't have to worry about the path to hell either!"

Shadrack took the path down the middle, hoping he would at least be accepted into Catholic Heaven. He followed the path for about a hundred yards and came to a dead end — the brook.

"At least it didn't lead to hell," thought Shad and retraced his steps back to where the paths branched.

He eyed the two paths that were left. He had a fifty-fifty chance of going to heaven. He took the path to the right. This path went a little further, three hundred yards or so, but again, Shad found himself eyeing the swift waters of Todder Brook.

"It ain't Heaven," thought Shad, "and it ain't hell either. I wish Dryfly Ramsey would go to hell and leave my woman alone!"

Shad went back to the branch of the path and took the third and last one. Again, he came to the brook.

"Oh well," he thought, "they must be just fishing trails. Whoever made them tracks, must be wading down the brook."

Shad was half way back to the junction of the paths when he heard someone sneeze. The sneeze was followed immediately by a bigger sneeze and the word "shit."

Nutbeam was standing behind a fir tree watching Shad. He had heard Shad coming. Nutbeam had stood in the rain for too long on the previous night and had caught a cold.

At first Shad could see nothing, but he knew that the sneeze had come from the vicinity of the fir tree. Examining the tree more carefully, he spotted a big old floppy ear.

"Who's there?" asked Shad.

No answer.

"I can see ya. Who are ya?"

No answer. The ear withdrew from sight. The other ear appeared.

"You got awful big ears," said Shad. "You an elf?"

"What d'ya want?" came a voice from behind the fir tree.

"Nuthin'."

"Then, go home!"

Shad contemplated the words "Go home!" He did not know if he was in danger or not. "Go home," he thought. "Maybe I should . . . but, who is it?"

"Who are you?" asked Shad.

Nutbeam was very depressed. He had been found. Out of curiosity, people would visit him. They'd laugh at him and bother him and he'd have to move.

"Why don't you go home?" Nutbeam groaned petulantly. Nutbeam hoped there was still a chance that Shadrack hadn't seen the camp.

Shad could not see Nutbeam's camp, but he heard the whimper in Nutbeam's voice, and he heard the fear. The whimper and the fear in the fir tree's voice restored Shadrack's courage.

"What're ya doin' standin' behind a tree?" asked Shad.

"None of yer bus'ness!" said Nutbeam.

Shadrack had often heard Americans running people out of

121

their salmon pools and in the way of an American, said: "Oh, I don't know about that! My father owns most of this brook and you ain't my father! What're ya doin' back here?!"

"I ain't doin' nothin'!"

"Come out so I can see ya!"

Nutbeam was indeed a timid creature, but he heard the command in the boy's voice. He stepped out.

"Nutbeam!" whispered Shad, amazed. "You're Nutbeam!"

"How do you know that?" asked Nutbeam.

"I don't know," said Shad. He could have added, "There are no secrets in Brennen Siding."

Nutbeam stared at the red-haired, freckled boy. Shadrack was fifteen, but Nutbeam guessed him to be twelve, not a day older. Shadrack was amazed to see Nutbeam and Nutbeam was amazed at the fact that Shadrack was not laughing. It was simple: Shad was too amazed to laugh.

"You back here fishin'?" asked Shad.

"I ain't fishin'."

"What happened to your ears?" asked Shadrack. "You look like an elf, or a monkey, or somethin'." Shad was not intentionally making fun of Nutbeam, he was simply in awe.

Nutbeam didn't answer. Nutbeam simply dropped his head in shame.

Shad gathered more courage and moved closer. "His nose is awful big, too," thought Shad, "and so is his mouth." Shadrack could not imagine why such a big, tall man would seem so afraid.

The next time Shad spoke, his voice was more gentle.

"No one's seen you in a long time, Nutbeam. Where've you been?"

"I ain't been nowhere," said Nutbeam. His voice was barely audible.

"You live around here?"

"Why don't you go home?" Nutbeam's voice had calmed too and sounded mellow and sad.

"Listen," said Shadrack, "if you don't live too far from here, I sure could use a drink o' water. I was drinkin' last night, and I'm sort o' hung over. Sure could use a drink o' water."

"Drink from the brook."

"Oh, brook water's bad fer ya. Beaver shit in it."

"Please, go home."

"What's the matter? You ain't scared o' me, are ya? You a crim'nal?"

"No, I ain't scared and I ain't a criminal! I just want to be left alone. You'll tell everyone where I am and they'll all come to visit the freak!"

"You a freak, Nutbeam?"

"Well, I ain't exactly normal!"

"Look normal to me. Now me, the lad yer lookin' at, I ain't normal. There's somethin' wrong with me."

"What's wrong with you?"

"Well, I had this girlfriend, the prettiest little lady I ever seen, and she left me for a lad as homely as you are. She don't seem that stupid, so there's got to be something wrong with me."

"How much would you take to keep yer mouth shut?"

"What's that?"

"I said, how much money will you take to keep quiet about me?"

Shad thought for a moment, then almost sang: "I wouldn't take yer money, Nutbeam."

*

Palidin Ramsey sat on a boulder at the edge of the water. In his right hand he held a lodestone the size of a dime, and in his left hand he held the flyhook he'd borrowed from George Hanley. He stroked the lodestone across the point of the hook for a few minutes, then touched the hook to the reel of Shad's rod. The hook was magnetized and clung to the reel. "Good," he thought, "now for the experiment."

He kicked off his sneakers and rolled up his pants, carefully crossed the gravel beach and stepped into the water. The water in the Dungarvon is amazingly warm in the summer (about 75°) and it felt good on Palidin's feet and ankles. He then waded until the water was encircling his waist.

"If nothing else, I'm getting washed," he thought. He was not very enthusiastic about his experiment. He had thought it up in a moment; it had probably been tried before. "It'll never work in a thousand years," he thought, "but it's worth a try."

Palidin was fishing in Dr. MacDowell's pool. Dr. MacDowell had purchased Graig Allen's shore ten years ago, built a cottage and put the run to every one (local) who tried to fish there. Dr. MacDowell owned one of the five productive fishing pools in Brennen Siding. Three of the other four pools were also owned by Americans. Bill Wallace from Stockbridge, Massachusettes, was in the process of buying the last one (The Lindon Tucker Pool) at that very minute. Graig Allen had sold his pool for five hundred dollars, spent it on moving to Fredericton, and never came back. Times were changing — Lindon Tucker was getting a thousand dollars for his "property."

In 1962, most of the local residents of the Dungarvon River, the Cains or the Renous did not fully appreciate the value of their property. "That old shore ain't worth much to me," was the general attitude. With a million dollars, one could have purchased the whole Dungarvon river valley. "A million dollars for the Dungarvon river!" The locals did not see the approaching change. Bill Wallace would sell the Lindon Tucker Pool in 1986 for three-quarters of a million dollars.

Dr. MacDowell did not allow anyone other than himself and a few friends from back home to fish his pool. Neither did the Americans that owned other pools in the area. Dr. MacDowell was in Florence, trying to get far enough away from the Duomo to photograph it. He wouldn't bother Palidin until September.

Palidin made a cast. A salmon swirled for the fly (a roll) and missed it.

Palidin made another cast.

SPLASH!

Palidin was busy for the next fifteen minutes. He landed a twelve pound Atlantic salmon. Palidin Ramsey would be hooked on salmon fishing for the rest of his life.

nine

Bill Wallace walked through the field he'd purchased from Lindon Tucker, looking for a suitable site to build a cottage on. On the north end of the field was a knoll that Bill thought had a lot of potential. There was a great view and it was high enough to be above any above-average spring torrents. Lindon Tucker's old house and buildings sat on the hill to the east — quaint, grey, serene and picturesque amongst the elms and apple trees. An old swing sat beside the lilac bushes in front of Lindon's house. It was plain to see the house was going in the ground, falling down.

When Bill Wallace stood on his knoll and looked southwest, he could see at least a mile of river, maybe more. The immediate river was lined on both sides by the green fields of Brennen Siding. In the distance, the river seemed to flow from beneath the forested hills.

"It could be a scene from Vermont," thought Bill Wallace, "but it doesn't have the mountains. Fine with me! I never cared much for mountains, anyway. A river's all I need. If the river happens to have Atlantic salmon in it, that's a bonus."

Bill Wallace had spent many happy childhood days playing, fishing and canoeing on the White River in Vermont. The White was a tributary of the Connecticut. The Connecticut hadn't had a salmon in it for a hundred years. The Connecticut River had gone the way of all New England rivers, with the exception, maybe, of the Penobscot in Maine. Over-fishing, electrical dams and industrial pollution had turned what used to be some of the greatest Atlantic salmon rivers in the world into sewers for human waste — into dumps for humans to throw their old tires, sometimes whole cars, mattresses, bean cans, dead animals and the occasional human.

"It'll happen here, in time," Bill predicted. "It's the American way. Industry will move in, people will follow and that will be it — bingo, the fifty-first state."

Bill Wallace left his knoll and headed south until he came to the cedar fence that separated the Lindon Tucker farm from the Lester Burns farm.

"The Lester Burns farm," thought Bill, "another gold mine."

Bill Wallace was amazed that nobody had jumped on the opportunity and purchased this land before now. "Unknown to most Americans, thank God," he thought. "And the rich Canadians? Are there any? Sure there are. Do they not know what they have here? Probably not. They probably go to Disneyland on vacations."

"It's an investment that you'd have to be a fool to ignore," thought Bill. "Christ! This is one American that won't ignore it! I'm buying the Lester Burns property, regardless of the cost. The cost — ha! I'll probably get that for nothing, too!"

Bill Wallace wanted to be alone for a few minutes and had convinced Lindon Tucker to "take it easy. Have a nap in the canoe, I'll be just a few minutes." Bill, once he was satisfied with his exploration of the newly-purchased property, went back to where Lindon was waiting, half-asleep in the hot July sun. Lindon climbed from the canoe and held it steady for Bill to climb in the front. Then Lindon stood in the back and poled (plop-swish . . . plop-swish) back toward the Cabbage Island salmon club.

"Newcastle's a nice little town, Lindon," said Bill.

"Oh, yeah, yeah, yeah. Stinks awful bad though."

"I guess they should've built that pulp mill further away from the town."

"Further away, yeah. Should o' built it further away."

"That pulp mill is American-owned, I'll bet on that," thought Bill.

*

Helen MacDonald was making a corned beef and cabbage stew in the kitchen of the Cabbage Island Salmon Club. Although Helen was occupied with peeling potatoes, carrots, turnips and parsnips, she was being more "the detective" than "the cook." She could have been Sam Spade, Sherlock Holmes, or Charlie Chan. Detective Helen MacDonald was fitting together the "Blueberry Pie" mystery.

"Somebody took me pie from that window sill," she thought. "And the next day, somebody took the second one — the one with the Exlax in it. Rex, me dog, had a bad case o' the runs, and the somebody that took the pie didn't seem to have a complaint in the world. Seems clear to me that that someone might have fed the pie to poor old Rex. Now that someone has the gall to be hanging around here all day with that young Lillian. Boys, she must think a lot o' herself to be hanging around with the likes of that . . . that . . . that tramp!"

"I can't let him get away with it," she thought. "I have to teach 'im a lesson."

Helen MacDonald would get her opportunity to get even with Dryfly Ramsey sooner than she thought. A knock sounded on the kitchen door.

"Come in!" called Helen.

In stepped Lillian Wallace followed closely by Dryfly Ramsey.

"Hello, Miss MacDonald," said Lillian.

"Goodday, Helen," said Dryfly.

"Hello. I was just puttin' together your supper, Miss."

"Oh, good! What are we having tonight?"

"We're havin' good old fashion corn beef and cabbage."

"Oh! Good!"

"Your father likes me corn beef and cabbage. I cook it for 'im every time he comes up. What kin I do for ya, young lady?"

"Well, would you mind putting on an extra plate tonight?"

"No trouble. Who's stayin' fer supper? Lindon?"

"I've asked Dryfly to dine with us, and he's accepted."

"Oh! . . . Well . . . sure!"

"You don't mind?"

"Oh! . . . Well . . . no!"

Helen MacDonald thought: "How can they stand havin' that no good weasel around? I'd put the run to 'im, if it was me!"

"Good," said Lillian. "You sure you don't mind?"

"No, no, not at all."

"Thank you, Miss MacDonald. I appreciate it."

"Does your father know that Dry's stayin'?"

"Not yet, but he won't mind."

"Hmmm."

"Will we be having dessert, Miss MacDonald?"

"Well, sure. What would you like?"

"Oh, I don't care. Whatever you decide, is fine with me."

"Well, I don't have any more of the blueberries I spent good money on," said Helen, looking directly at Dryfly, "but I could make some chocolate puddin'. You like chocolate puddin'?"

"Oh, yes, very much."

"Do you like chocolate puddin', Dryfly?"

"Yep. Anything's OK for me."

"Good. You kin have all you want."

*

"See? I told you she wouldn't care if you stayed for supper, Dry." said Lillian.

"I didn't like the way she looked at me when she mentioned the blueberry pie. I think she's out to get me."

"What makes you think that?"

"I dunno. She don't like me very much."

"Dryfly Ramsey, I do believe you have an inferiority complex!"

"Maybe," said Dryfly. Dryfly hadn't the slightest idea what an inferiority complex was, but he liked the sound of the words. "I'll have to remember inferiority comprex," he thought .

The two teenagers went to the veranda of the cabin Bill and Lillian occupied and sat on the railing to watch the river.

"When your father gets his camp built, you'll be able to come up here all the time," said Dryfly. "Would you like stayin' up here?"

"I like it up here very much."

"Are you from a big city?"

"Stockbridge? No, it's a little town . . . not much bigger than Blackville. You'd like Stockbridge."

"Have you ever been to a big city?"

"I've been to New York and Boston. I went to Los Angeles once and Miami a couple of times."

"Ever been to Wheeling?"

"No. Where's Wheeling?"

"Down around where you live somewhere. Wheeling, West Virginia."

"Oh, West Virginia. That's in the south. Who do you know in West Virginia?"

"Nobody. We just hear it on the radio all the time."

"Does anyone around here have a television?"

"No." Dryfly had only heard of television. He would not get a chance to watch a television for another year. Bob Nash would be the first person in Brennen Siding to get a television. "I never saw a television in me life," said Dryfly.

"Television is wonderful. You'd like it," said Lillian. "What do kids do around here?"

"Walk up and down the road mostly. Shad and me spend a lot o' time on the river, in the summer."

"You love the river, don't you?"

"Yeah, the river's all there is around here."

"Could you ever leave it?"

"Mostly everybody that ever leaves, comes back . . . I don't know, maybe."

Lillian eyed the thin, homely boy. "His hair is greasy," she thought. "A little shampoo would change his whole appearance."

"Where do you take a bath, Dryfly?" she asked.

"In the river during the summer. In the winter, we don't bathe much. Once a month, maybe."

"Can you swim in the river?"

"If ya kin swim, ya kin swim in the river. It's no different than any place else. There's a little bit of a current."

"But it isn't polluted?"

"No. Ain't polluted . . . I don't think."

"Would you like to go for a swim, Dry?"

"Yeah, sure. OK."

Lillian went inside, grabbed a comb, a towel, some soap and a bottle of shampoo. "I'll clean him up for dinner," she thought. "I'll wash that smelly shirt for him, too. It will dry quickly in the sun."

Lillian and Dryfly walked hand in hand to the river. They swam and bathed and Lillian washed Dryfly's shirt with shampoo, rinsed it and washed it again. They took one last swim, then sat on a boulder to dry off. Lillian combed Dryfly's hair, parting it in the middle.

"I like how you part your hair in the middle," she said.

*

Shadrack had been looking almost directly at it and still hadn't seen it. Then, when he did see it, he couldn't believe his eyes. "A lad could walk by it a million times and never see it," thought Shad, amazed. "It's like a part of the hill."

He asked, "Is that your camp?"

"Damn! Now I'll never have any piece and quiet!" thought Nutbeam. "The little bugger sees it!"

"It's great!" Shadrack was still feasting his eyes on the little half-cave, half-cabin Nutbeam called home. The camp, two-thirds buried into the hill, with the moss-covered roof running parallel to the hill, was the smartest hideout Shadrack had ever seen.

Nutbeam was very proud of the camp. He had put hundreds of hours into its construction. But Shadrack's open, boyish enthusiasm was something Nutbeam had never anticipated. The awe and admiration in Shadrack's eyes was soothing to Nutbeam, and he found himself turning to face what Shad was seeing.

"Made it myself," said Nutbeam.

"Wow! How long ya lived here?"

"'Bout . . . . Never mind!"

"Some lot o' work in a camp like that!" said Shadrack.

"Hard work," said Nutbeam.

Nutbeam sighed. "What's the use?" he thought. "The little bugger sees it. The game is up."

"Just wait 'till Dry sees this!" said Shadrack.

"I don't want you bringin' no one else here, ya understand!"

"You a crim'nal?" asked Shad.

"No! I just don't like people around me!"

"You wouldn' mind a few people, would ya, Nutbeam?"

"No! I don't want no people, I tell ya!"

"Just maybe me and Dry and Dad and a few more."

"How much to keep yer mouth shut?"

"Oh, I couldn' take yer money from ya, Nutbeam . . . ," said Shad once again in that singsong how-much-ya-willin'-to-pay voice.

"How much?"

"Well . . . kin I look inside it, Nutbeam?"

"No!"

"What's the matter, Nutbeam?"

"You'll bring everyone back here and they'll laugh and make fun o' me!"

"Because of yer ears?"

"Among other things."

"No one cares about yer big floppy ears, Nutbeam!"

"I'll give ya five dollars to keep quiet."

"No one will laugh at ya, Nutbeam."

"Six dollars!"

"Course, ya never kin tell 'bout some people."

"Seven dollars!"

"Bert Todder's an awful man for laughin'."

"Eight dollars and that's it!"

"It is such a nice place," said Shadrack. "It would be a shame if Graig Allen found out about it being on his property."

"Ten dollars!"

"Well, OK, Nutbeam, but I'll have to tell Dryfly. Bad as I hate him for stealin' me woman, I'll have to tell 'im."

"No! Tell nobody!"

"Him and me will come and see ya once in a while, Nutbeam."

"I don't want you bringin' no one back here!"

"Just Dryfly, Nutbeam."

"What d'ya want to bring 'im back here for?"

Nutbeam knew very well who Dryfly was. He'd heard him play guitar many times.

"For ten dollars, I won't tell a soul yer back here, Nutbeam, 'cept for Dryfly. Him and me will be the only ones to know."

"What's to stop him from tellin' everybody?"

"Oh, ya might have to give him some little thing . . ."

"How do you know he can be trusted?"

"Oh, you can trust Dryfly, Nutbeam. Never did a thing wrong in his life. Leave anything at all layin' around and Dry'd be the last person in the world to ever touch it."

"I don't like it," said Nutbeam. Nutbeam was being black-mailed, and he knew it.

*

When the Atlantic salmon leave the ocean to swim the fresh water rivers to spawn, they stop feeding. They don't feed again until after they've laid their eggs, which sometimes takes three or four months. You can fish over these pregnant fish with all the juicey fat flies, bugs and worms you want, but you might as well try to water a horse that isn't thirsty. They refuse to eat.

Occasionally, these pregnant fish will make a pass at a fly (a roll), and on occasion, they may even go as far as to kill the fly. However, this is really nothing more than recreation. It is these sports-minded salmon (the jocks) that anglers seek. You might say that anglers clean up on the jocks of the school. Palidin Ramsey was sure of only one thing: there had been four jocks in the school that rested in Dr. MacDowell's salmon pool. Palidin Ramsey had four salmon lying dead on the beach.

Palidin was very optimistic. "It could be working," he thought, "but I'm still not sure. There might be some other reason why the fishing's so good today. I'll have to try different flies. Maybe any flyhook, magnetic or not, would take these fish. I need more flies."

Palidin made a little pool out of rocks at the water's edge. He put three of his salmon in it and covered them up with grass and leaves to keep the sun from spoiling them, then headed for the footbridge with the fourth. He carried the salmon directly to Bernie Hanley's store.

"Boy's! What've ya got there!" said Bernie Hanley when he saw the ten-pounder Palidin had with him. "Ain't that a nice one!"

"Just caught it," Palidin proudly announced. "Wanna buy it?"

"Well, by cripes, I could do with a feed o' salmon! How much ya want for it?"

"Want three flyhooks."

"Three flyhooks . . . well, that's a little steep . . . seventy-five cents a piece . . . seventy-five . . . a dollar fifty . . . two-twenty-five . . . well . . . I'll give ya two dollars."

"No, sorry, I'll just take it home."

"OK. Three flyhooks."

Bernie Hanley paid twenty-five cents per flyhook to Bert Todder for tying them. Bernie Hanley was actually getting the salmon for seventy-five cents . . . a dollar, if you included the fly-hook George had stolen from him earlier.

"I want a butterfly, a black bear hair with a green butt, and a cosseboom." Three different patterns along with the "blue charm" George had stolen for him earlier, would greatly enhance the experiment.

Palidin headed back to Dr. MacDowell's pool.

When he got back in the river, he tied on the butterfly and fished for what he figured to be about fifteen minutes. Nothing happened.

He then took out his lodestone and magnetized the hook of the butterfly. He made a cast — Bang! Splash! A salmon grabbed the butterfly.

He landed the salmon and tried the same experiment with the cosseboom. Fifteen minutes with the regular hook produced nothing. He magnetized the hook and was into a salmon (a grilse) after just a few minutes.

It was a very exciting experience for Palidin. He found himself wanting to run home to tell everyone he met, to share his wealth, so to speak. He fought the urge and tied on the black bear hair with the green butt. He performed the same experiment. He achieved the same results.

He now had four salmon and two grilse. More than he could carry. He would have to make two trips. "I'll give Shad one," he thought, "and take the rest home. If this keeps up, I'll start sellin'. I'll buy me a rod of my own, sell some more and buy a car. I'll fish for a living."

*

Dryfly ate Helen MacDonald's corned beef stew with gusto. He was very hungry. He hadn't eaten all day and it was getting late. "Americans eat awful late," he thought. Helen MacDonald had been very careful not to get Dryfly's bowl of chocolate pudding mixed up with the bowls she had prepared for Bill and Lillian Wallace. Dryfly Ramsey's chocolate pudding was laced with Exlax.

"Not too much," Helen had thought. "But enough to teach him a lesson. Enough to keep him running for a while."

During dinner, everyone was in a good mood. Bill Wallace was happy and so was Lillian. Dryfly, although a little uptight about his own table manners, was also happy. The stew was good and the pudding perfect. Helen MacDonald was a good cook.

The topic of conversation (the common denominator) was the river and the salmon. Bill Wallace asked questions and Dryfly answered the best he could. Dryfly didn't know much about salmon, so most of his answers were inspired by the many stories he'd heard during long winter evenings standing around listening to the men talk in Bernie Hanley's store.

"There use to be a lot o' salmon," said Dryfly. "One time Bert Todder was wading the river with a horse and wagon. The salmon were so thick that they were getting caught on the spokes of the wagon. As the wheels turned, the salmon kept flipping up into the box. Bert Todder got enough salmon for the winter, just wading the river."

Bill Wallace laughed loud and long. Both he and Lillian thought it a great story.

Dryfly, liking the laughter, said: "You use to have to get behind a tree to tie yer hook on."

More laughter.

Dryfly blushed, but he was hot . . . . "That was a dry summer," he said, "The salmon use to have to come ashore for a drink."

More laughter.

"What's the biggest salmon you've ever seen?" asked Lillian.

"Well, I don't know how much it weighed, but it was as long as this table," said Dryfly. "It was stuck to an eagle."

"It was stuck to an eagle?"

"Yeah, the eagle had locked his claws in the salmon's back and wouldn' let go. The salmon dived deep and drowned the eagle. The salmon must've been too heavy for the eagle to lift. We found the both of them washed up on the shore down by Tuney's Brook."

"Is that a true story?" asked Bill.

"True as I'm settin' here," said Dryfly, and, indeed, the story was true.

"You know, I haven't caught a salmon all week. I can't imagine what I'm doing wrong," said Bill.

"You'll git one," said Dryfly. "Salmon are funny fish. Once John Kaston fished all week with a sport and didn't ketch a thing. Then, one day they was settin' in the canoe and a salmon jumped right in along side the sport. John killed the salmon and it turned out to be the only one the sport took back with him. That was the only fish they caught all week." That, too, was a true story.

When dinner was over, the three retired to the veranda. Bill gave Dryfly a pack of Lucky Strikes. Bill and Dryfly smoked and talked, Lillian smiled and laughed and looked very pretty. Both Bill and Dryfly loved Lillian Wallace very much.

Ten o'clock rolled around and Bill hinted it was time for Dryfly to go home. Ten o'clock was not late for Lillian, but Bill wanted to discuss a few things with her in private.

"Well, I guess I'd better be goin'," said Dryfly.

"I'll walk a little way with you," said Lillian.

"Good night," said Bill.

"Good night, Bill," said Dryfly.

When they were sure the night was hiding them from Bill's

vision, Dryfly and Lillian held hands. They walked to the edge
of the Cabbage Island Salmon Club property and sat at the base
of a pine tree.

"I had a wonderful day," said Lillian.

"Me too," said Dryfly.

"I like you very much," said Lillian.

"I like you too," said Dryfly.

"I think my father likes you, too."

"Ya think?"

Lillian leaned and kissed Dryfly one cool little peck on the
cheek. It was the first time anyone other than his mother had
ever reached out to kiss him. Dryfly was amazed at how good it
made him feel. It gave him butterflies and made him feel all
warm inside.

"I . . . I . . . "

"Yes?"

"I . . . I . . . " Dryfly wanted to say the magic words (I love
you) but he couldn't seem to come out with them.

"I'd better be goin'," he said.

"There's no great hurry. Dad won't mind as long as I don't
stay too long."

"I know, but it's gettin' late and I . . . "

"I'm really glad you could come to dinner tonight, Dryfly."

"It was good food. I really think I should be goin' now."

"Relax, Dryfly, it's only early."

Dryfly didn't want to go. He would've sat beneath that pine
tree with Lillian all night, but he was getting terrible cramps in
his abdomen. The Helen MacDonald dosage of cabbage and
Exlax was working hand in hand and Dryfly wasn't sure whether
he need let off gas, or indulge in a full scale bout. Either way, he
didn't want to do it in the presence of Lillian Wallace.

"I really gotta be goin'," he said.

"What for?"

Dryfly was too backward and shy to tell her the truth.

"Mom wants me home early tonight," he lied.

"Oh, well, OK. Will I see you tomorrow?"

"Sure."

"Will you walk me back to the camp?"

"Sure."

They stood and started back to the camp.

"Want to go on a picnic tomorrow?" Lillian asked.

"Sure. If you want."

Dryfly was beginning to really suffer and Lillian seemed to walk so very slow.

"It's such a beautiful night," said Lillian. "Look, there's a new moon."

"Yep."

"I love moonlit nights." Lillian squeezed his hand and turned to face him. "I'll be leaving Sunday morning, Dryfly. I'm going to miss you."

"I'll miss you too."

It was clear to Dryfly that Lillian wanted to kiss again, but he was not sure he could hold on much longer. A particularly vicious spasm coursed through his bowels forcing him to cross his legs and bend over. He still would not admit to his agony, however.

"What's wrong?" asked Lillian.

" . . . nothin' . . . thought I saw somethin' on the ground."

"What? I don't see anything."

"Nothin'."

"Are you all right, Dryfly?"

"Yep." Dryfly straightened. "I'm alright."

They moved a few more paces toward the camps. Lillian stopped again. "You know," she said, "it's so quiet here, you can almost hear the silence."

"Yeah, but the flies are eatin' me alive," said Dryfly. "I gotta get out o' here!"

"That's funny, they're not bothering me at all."

"Well, they're botherin' me! I'll see ya later!"

"Kiss me good night?"

Dryfly kissed her quickly. He knew the countdown had started.

"I'll see ya tomorrow," he said, already moving away.

"Good night."

"See ya tomorrow!"

Dryfly walked twenty paces, then ran with desperation into the woods.

*

Shadrack sat on the Tuney Brook bridge until it was too dark for him to see the little trout swimming in the water beneath. Although he was somewhat excited about the events of the day, he kept very still. He did not wave or slap at the mosquitoes and most of them never found him.

"Dryfly stole me woman," thought Shadrack. "Me own fault, though. Should've kissed her when I had the chance. She'd still be with me, if I had've kissed her. Now I got a broken heart and I'm . . . I'm . . . blue, yeah, I'm blue. What's a blue lad feel like, I wonder? What's a man do when he's got a broken heart and blue?"

Shadrack knew what he had told Dryfly. Shadrack knew that he had told Dryfly he and Lillian were lovers; that he and Lillian had even discussed marriage.

"Course, I was lyin'," thought Shad, "but that don't matter, I'll have to show signs of a broken heart, even if I don't care any-more. I could tell 'im I left her for another woman . . . or I left her because I didn't like her cookin'. I'll tell 'im . . . somethin' . . . . What's keepin' 'im so long?"

Another hour passed before Shadrack heard Dryfly coming down the path.

> Beautiful, beautiful brown eyes,
> Beautiful, beautiful brown eyes,
> Beautiful, beautiful brown eyes,
> I'll never love blue eyes agin, sang Dryfly.

"That you, Dryfly?"

Dryfly came to an immediate halt.

"Shad?"

"Yeah. Here on the bridge."

"What're ya doin' here?"

"Waitin' for you!"

Dryfly carefully approached the little bridge. Dryfly was somewhat worried that Shad might be angry. He wasn't afraid.

He felt he'd done nothing wrong, but he wasn't up for a confrontation. He still felt somewhat ill, and his spirits were too good to ruin them with an argument, or whatever Shadrack might have in mind.

"Where ya been all night?" asked Shad.

"I . . . I've been with . . . Bill Wallace."

"How's you and Lillian makin' out? You in love with her, Dry?"

"Naw, jist settin' up there talkin', that's all."

"An awful lot o' talkin', Dry! You been up there all day!"

"Jist talkin', that's all we were doin'."

"I saw you and Lillian walkin' down the front holdin' hands!"

"So?"

"So, where were ya goin'?"

"Lindon Tucker's."

"Walkin' down the front, holdin' hands in broad daylight! Good thing I left her when I did!"

"You left her?"

"Didn' she tell ya?"

"No."

"Course, I left her! Good thing too, by the looks of it, or you'd be holdin' hands with another man's woman! You think about that, Dry?"

"No."

"No! Course ya didn'! You don't think o' nothin', do ya! You never stopped to think o' me and how I might've got hurt. Course, I didn' get hurt, cause I left the jesiless tramp, but it's a good thing for you that I did!"

"Lillian ain't a tramp, Shad."

"Course she's a tramp! Last night me, tonight you, God knows who tomorrow night! That tramp don't care about us lads, Dry! She's prob'ly up there in the camp right now laughin' her head off at ya. Wouldn' surprise me at all!"

"I don't think so, Shad."

"I saw through her, so I did! No woman's gonna make a fool out o' Shadrack Nash!"

Dryfly didn't like what he was hearing. To Dryfly, Lillian

Wallace was not a tramp. To Dryfly, Lillian Wallace was the most refined, wonderful, kind, sweet girl in the world.

"I don't care if she laughs at me," said Dryfly.

Dryfly's love for Lillian Wallace was the first real possession he'd ever had. He knew it might not be a possession that would hang around for very long, but he was going to enjoy it and make the most of it while it lasted. He did not want to fight with Shad, though. He would let Shadrack and anybody else say whatever they wanted. He would not give up the precious moments he was spending with Lillian.

"She kin laugh, and you kin say what you want, I don't care!" said Dryfly.

"And you shouldn' care! She'll be gone in a few days and she'll laugh and make fun o' you, all the way home!"

Dryfly endeavored to change the subject. "What've you been doin' all day, Shad?" he asked.

"I've been . . . I've been . . . You'd never guess who I met up with today, Dry."

ten

Saturday night at dusk, Bill Wallace and Lindon Tucker stood outside the Cabbage Island Salmon Club camps. They were saying good-bye. They would not see each other again for a year. Bill paid Lindon for guiding him and tipped him twenty dollars. Twenty dollars was the biggest tip Lindon Tucker had ever received for guiding. Bill Wallace had had a few drinks and was feeling generous. He could afford to be generous. Bill Wallace was a millionaire who had just purchased a fifty thousand dollar salmon pool for a thousand dollars. Lindon Tucker had been drinking too, and was feeling quite good.

"I didn't catch any salmon this year," said Bill, "but I'll be back next year. I want to put up a cottage next year, Lindon, and by God, I want you to be one of the carpenters."

"Yeah, sure, yeah, sure, sure, sure! Done a bit o' carpenter work. Wouldn' mind workin' on it. Yeah, sure, sure! I'll work on it."

"Well, Lindon, I think I'll get my gear together and go to bed. I've got a long drive tomorrow, and Lillian and I will be rising early.

"It's been good doin' bus'ness, yeah. See ya next year. We'll git lots o' fish next year."

"If we could figure out what that young Palidin Ramsey is doing, we'll catch them alright, Lindon. How many do you think he's caught in the last few days?"

"Well, he got six one day, he told me, so he did. Six, yeah. Six one day and four the next. Yeah, yeah, yeah, six one day and four the next and seven today. That makes . . . six and four and seven . . . how many?"

"Seventeen, I believe, Lindon."

"Seventeen, yeah, yeah, seventeen. Did ya buy a few from him to take back with ya?"

"I sure did, Lindon. I bought eight from him. I'll tell the boys back home that I caught them myself."

"Yes sir, yes sir, yes sir. Tell them ya caught them yerself, yeah, yeah yeah. Yeah. Ha, ha."

"Well, good-night, Lindon."

"Yes sir, yes sir. Good-night."

"We'll see you next year."

"Next year, yeah. Yeah, yeah, next year, yeah. Yep. Take 'er easy."

Bill Wallace escaped into the camp.

Lindon Tucker was in a mood for celebrating and headed for Bernie Hanley's store.

Dan Brennen, Bob Nash, John Kaston, Bert Todder and Stan Tuney were all standing around Bernie Hanley's store gossiping, eating oranges and drinking Sussex ginger ale. When Lindon Tucker arrived, he pulled a pint (already half empty) from his belt, ordered a bottle of ginger ale and treated the boys.

"Yes sir. Yes sir, yes sir, the best sport I ever guided. Tipped me twenty dollars, so he did. Twenty dollars! And, and, and gimme a fishin' rod. Brand new rod! Give it to me, he did. Twenty dollars and a fishin' rod, jist like that! He said, he said, he said, he said, he said, he said, what he said was I want you to have it, he said. Gimme a rod, jist like that, yeah."

"That old lad I was guidin', didn' ketch a fish all week and didn' tip me a cent!" said Stan Tuney.

"My sport fished from daylight to dark, caught four salmon and a grilse and only tipped me two dollars. I reached right in me pocket and give 'im five. Told 'im he might need it to get home on," said Dan Brennen.

"Remember that old lad I was guidin' in April? The old lad that wouldn' piss in the river?" said Bert Todder.

"Yeah, I remember him. Same lad you were guidin' all week, weren't it?" asked Stan.

"Yeah, that's the same old jeser!"

"I never heard that story," said Dan Brennen. "What happened?"

"Well, I was guidin' him in April and he wouldn' piss in the river. I was goin' up the river with that 'Ten Johnson' outboard motor and he was in the front. When he needed a piss, he pulled out this pickle bottle and started to piss in it. The wind was blowin' real hard and the piss kept blowin' back all over me . . . jist kind of a fine spray, if ya know what I mean. I snubbed 'er up some quick, I tell ya! I ain't drinkin' yer piss all the way to Gordon, I told 'im!"

All the men laughed.

"Oh yeah, yeah, yeah," commenced Lindon. "Sold that old shore o' mine. Sold it, yeah. No good, that old shore. Got rid o' it, so I did. Got rid o' it. Might sell the whole place, yet. Move to Fredericton, I think. Move to Fredericton and take 'er easy."

There were no secrets in Brennen Siding. All the men knew that Lindon had sold his property. Somehow, Bert Todder had found out.

"You'll get a job lookin' after that lad's camp when he gets it built, won't ya, Lindon?"

"He didn' say for sure. I might, I might, ya never know, I might! I think I'll sell the whole place and move to Fredericton. Lay right back in Fredericton."

"I'd sell that old place o' mine some quick," said Bert Todder. "That old shore, anyway. Them old shores ain't no good to a man."

"Should be able to sell that old shore o' yours, no trouble, Bert. The mouth o' Todder Brook is right there. There's always salmon at the mouth o' the brook. Why don't ya sell it and get a big chunk o' money for it?" said John Kaston. "Them old shores ain't worth nothin'."

"Ain't worth nothin', no," said Lindon Tucker. "Sold mine, so I did. Yep. Think I'll move to Fredericton. Lay right back, take 'er easy, yeah."

*

Lillian Wallace was not laughing. Fifteen-year-old Lillian Wallace had a tear in her eye. Lillian Wallace said: "I'm going to miss you, Dryfly," and meant it.

"Gonna miss you too," said Dryfly.

"I'll come back next year, Dry. We'll get together again next year."

"A year's a long time," said Dryfly.

"You could come down and stay with us, play at the Red Lion."

"Yeah, maybe."

"Will you write to me?"

"If you write to me."

Over the past few days, Dryfly had spent every possible minute with Lillian Wallace. They walked and talked, sat around on the veranda drinking lemonade and "soda"; they swam and went on picnics and kissed and hugged forty-two thousand and one times.

They were very much in love, but the word "love" was never spoken. Dryfly wanted to say it now. Dryfly didn't want Lillian to walk out of his life without her knowing how he felt, and he wanted to know how she felt about him. He wanted to say, "I love you," and he wanted to hear her say, "I love you, too."

He held her close, smelling the fly repellent on her neck, feeling her warm young body against his own. He kissed the tears from her cheek. "This is it," he thought. "This is the last time I'll hold her. I might never see her again." Dryfly wanted to cry too.

Dryfly would never forget her. He would never forget the few short days and nights they'd had together. He was totally in love — in love with Lillian; in love with the stars and the moon; in love with the river and the warm July night.

Dryfly had wanted to say "I love you" so many times during the past few days, but for some reason, couldn't twist his tongue around the three little words. Now, with tears welling from his eyes, while kissing her tears from her face, while looking into the big, tear-filled blue eyes he adored while feeling her warmth with the reality that he might never see her again, he thought he could say it.

"Lillian," he whispered, "Lillian . . . "

"Yes, Dryfly?"

"Lillian . . . I love you!"

There was a silence, during which Dryfly could only hear their heartbeat and their breathing. Then, Lillian pulled away from him. She looked at his tattered sneakers and ragged jeans, the same shirt she had washed for him three days ago, his hair parted in the middle, his long nose and his eyes. He had tears in his eyes.

Crying with all the spirit of a child, she ran into the camp.

*

Dryfly swung and started walking. He didn't know where he was going and he didn't care. All he knew was that he needed to walk. "I'm in love," he thought. "I'm in love with Lillian Wallace and she's gone. I'm alone. I can cry now." He unleashed a flood of tears.

When he got to the Tuney brook bridge, he found Shad waiting for him. He didn't want Shad to see the tears, but there was no stopping them. He approached Shad and stood before him, weeping like a hurt child.

When Shadrack saw that Dryfly was crying, he did not speak. Neither did Dryfly. They stood eyeing each other, Dryfly crying and Shadrack not knowing what to say. Shadrack knew one thing though: he was sorry for the things he'd said about Lillian Wallace.

"You alright?" said Shadrack, when he finally found words.

"I don't know . . . I guess."

"I'm gonna miss her too," said Shad.

"I love her, Shad!"

"She'll come back, Dryfly. Don't cry. She'll come back."

"Maybe . . . maybe."

"Let me pole you up to Gordon," said Shad. "We'll git some wine at the bootlegger's. We'll have a drink o' wine and talk."

"Wine? I ain't got no money for wine."

"I got that ten dollars Nutbeam gave me. We'll git some wine and have a talk."

"OK. Might as well."

Shadrack and Dryfly went to the Cabbage Island Salmon Club and slid off, quietly so that no one would hear them, in one of the Club's canoes.

Dryfly found some consolation from being on the river and cheered up a bit. The river reflected the blue of the sky, the stars, the moon and the forested hills. Except for the "swish-plunk, swish-plunk" of the pole, and the rippling sound of the canoe cutting the water, all was quiet.

"She didn't say it," thought Dryfly. "She didn't say 'I love you.'"

"You know what, Shad?" said Dryfly a little later. "She's the only woman I ever loved."

"Me too," said Shad.

The boys had one more bond between them.

*

Knock, knock.

"Who's there?"

"Shadrack and Dryfly."

"Ah, Hell!"

Nutbeam arose from his cot, went to the door and opened it. "What d'ya want?"

"We got some wine, Nutbeam," said Shadrack. "Thought maybe you'd like a drink."

Nutbeam had just gotten home from his radio listening trip. He had listened to the "Saturday Night Jamboree" outside of Shirley Ramsey's house. Again he had crept closer to the house so he could peek through the window at Shirley. Shirley was sewing a shirt for Palidin and looked very beautiful to Nutbeam. Nutbeam wanted very much to meet Shirley Ramsey.

Later, lying on his cot, he had given his predicament thought. "She's a good woman. A man should have a woman. Shirley Ramsey needs a man. I could keep her, look after her . . . but what's the use? She'd never look sideways at a lad like me."

"I'm gonna have to do somethin'," Nutbeam said aloud to the

camp. "I'm not gettin' any younger. Let me see . . . I'm forty-six years old. Forty-six and never had a woman. Sweet forty-six and never been kissed."

Nutbeam had spent many hours during the last year, thinking about his lonely situation and had concluded that the loneliness was getting to be too much. He was beginning to talk to himself. "I'm goin' crazy," he said. "Talkin' to yerself is one of the first signs of goin' crazy."

When Shadrack showed up to unlock his little secret, Nutbeam had been very upset, nervous, yes, and even a little afraid. But now, there in the dark, on his cot, Nutbeam felt that maybe Shadrack's appearance had been a blessing in disguise. Maybe the Good Lord was looking after him and had sent Shadrack to find him, to flush him out, to reveal him to the world that he would either have to face, or go insane. Setting all other predicaments aside, Nutbeam, there in the dark, on his cot, was a very troubled and bewildered man. And then:

Knock, knock.

"If I don't face this young fella and play some sort o' game, the young brat will blackmail me. I shouldn' have offered him any money in the first place. And now, he's brought that young Dryfly Ramsey back here in the middle of the night, lookin' to blackmail me. I'll have to face them. I'll have to play some sort o' game."

"Mind if we come in?" said Shadrack

"It's awful late," said Nutbeam.

"Ain't late. Ain't even twelve o'clock."

"What d'ya want?"

"Don't want nothin'. Jist came to visit ya. Was tellin' Dryfly here about ya. He wanted to meet ya."

Nutbeam sighed. "Come in," he said. "But just for a minute!"

"Awful dark in here. Ain't ya got a lamp?"

"Yes, I have a lamp."

"Nutbeam struck a match and lit the lamp.

"Nice place ya got here, Nutbeam," said Dryfly.

"Just an old camp."

"I like it."

147

"Would ya like a drink o' wine?" asked Shad, pulling a bottle of sherry out from under his jacket.

"I haven't had a drink in ten years," said Nutbeam.

"Go ahead, have a drink. It's good stuff. Golden Nut."

"No. I think not."

"Aw, c'mon! Won't hurt ya. Have a drink o' wine. Good for ya. Keeps that lad from starin' at ya." Shad had adopted "Keeps that lad from starin' at ya" from Bert Todder.

Nutbeam stared at the bottle. "Would be nice to have a drink with someone," he thought. He sat by the table and took a small sip of the sweet wine. He thought it was, indeed, quite good.

Shadrack and Dryfly smiled at each other and sat on the cot.

"Bought that with the ten dollars you give me, Nutbeam. Wanted to show ya that I didn't waste the money. Have another drink . . . take a big one, that's no good! Take 'er down! Help yerself!"

Nutbeam took a bigger drink.

"Good stuff," said Nutbeam. "Where'd ya get it?"

"Gordon. From the bootlegger in Gordon. We left another bottle outside, so don't worry about runnin' shy of 'er."

The three sipped from the wine and it wasn't long before they commenced to feel its effects. The conversation flowed a bit easier, and although Nutbeam hadn't really talked any amount in years, he found that the words were coming surprisingly easy. He thought he might even be enjoying himself. The boys weren't making fun of him either, or they didn't seem to be. They actually seemed to like him.

"You play guitar," Nutbeam said to Dryfly.

"How'd ya know that?"

"I know a lot o' things."

"Yeah, I play, but not very good."

"You play good." Nutbeam took another drink.

"You sure have some nice rifles," said Shad.

"You like me rifles?"

"Sure do. What's that one?"

Shad pointed at the rifle he fancied most.

"That's a 30-30. Good gun, that."

"You must get a lot o' deer and moose and stuff," said Shad-rack, still admiring the rifles.

"I get what I need."

"Hey! What's that thing?" asked Dryfly.

"Trumpet."

"Really? What's it for?"

"It's a musical instrument."

"Kin ya play it?"

"Ain't played it much lately."

"Would ya play it fer us Nutbeam?"

"No. Makes too much noise. Can't play it anyway."

"What do we care if it makes noise? There's only the three of us."

"Not tonight."

"Ya know what we should do some night? We should bring the banjo and guiddar back and play some music."

"Ya could sure let loose back here," agreed Dryfly. "No one would ever hear ya back here."

"I can't play very good," said Nutbeam.

"Sure ya kin," said Shadrack. "All ya have to do is practise."

"They'd hear me all over the country."

"Naw! Never in a million years," said Dryfly. "Never hear ya way back here."

"Play it Nutbeam," urged Shad.

"Maybe later."

When the three finished the first bottle of wine, Shad went and retrieved the second bottle. With the ten dollars, he had purchased four bottles. He and Dryfly had consumed one on their way from Gordon. If they finished this one, they still had one left. Shadrack was in a party mood.

Soon Shadrack started to sing. He wasn't much for carrying a melody, but he loved to sing, so he bellowed one dirty song out after another. Between songs, the boys told dirty jokes. Nutbeam was forgetting himself. Nutbeam actually laughed at the dirty songs and jokes. This was the best time that Nutbeam had ever had.

Shad got up and danced around the camp. "Yeah-whoo!" he

whooped. "Yeah-whoo and her name was Maud!" He grabbed
the trumpet and tried to blow into it. Nothing happened.

"Here, Nutbeam old dog, give 'er Hell!"

Nutbeam was getting drunk and caught up in the excitement.
He took a bigger than average drink of the wine, grabbed the
trumpet from Shadrack, stood and commenced to blow.

"BARMP-BARMP-BEEP-BARMP-BARMP!"

Shadrack and Dryfly couldn't believe their ears. At first they
just stared at each other. Then, they smiled at each other. The
smile turned into a chuckle. The chuckle turned into hilarious
laughter. They laughed at Nutbeam's big lips trying to manufac-
ture sounds on the trumpet. They laughed at Nutbeam's big ears
and lanky body. They laughed at the awful noise Nutbeam was
making. But, most of all, they laughed at the reality that there
before them, was none other than the Todder Brook Whooper.

Shadrack was already starting to get ideas.

Staggering homeward in the middle of the night, Shadrack
said to Dryfly: "What d'ya s'pose a nice lad like that would live
his life in the woods for?"

"He's got big floppy ears," said Dryfly.

"Yeah, but there's got to be somethin' else."

"Inferiority comprex," said Dry.

*

At the crack of dawn, Lillian Wallace stirred, rose and got
dressed. She put on her blue shorts, pink blouse and sandals.
Then, she went to the dresser and peered into the mirror. She
combed her hair and looked into her tired, sky-blue eyes. If she
had smiled, her full, young lips would have revealed clean, well-
kept teeth, but Lillian Wallace did not feel like smiling.

When she was satisfied with her appearance, she picked up a
pen from the dresser and jotted down three words on a piece of
paper. She put the note in an envelope, wrote "Dryfly" on it,
started to lick and seal it, but decided against it. Then she, with
envelope in hand, left the room. Three seconds later, she stepped
into the grey, pine-scented Dungarvon morning. Every bird that
could sing was singing.

Lillian needed to think. To think, she needed to walk. She

went down the path, over the hill and across the little bridge Stan Tuney had built over his brook. A fingerling trout swam beneath the bridge, but Lillian Wallace, there in the cool dewy morning, did not take the time to watch it. She would be leaving the Dungarvon in little more than an hour for Stockbridge, Massachusetts and needed to see Dryfly Ramsey one more time . . . or at least be close to him.

She followed the brook until she came to Stan Tuney's field. Crossing the field, she stopped to pick a daisy. She put the daisy in the envelope with the three word note and sealed it.

By the time she got to the railroad, her feet were soaked with dew. She didn't care. She was almost there. In a minute she stopped in front of Shirley Ramsey's house and peered at the window she thought might be Dryfly's.

In the grey dawn, she eyed the drab, paintless structure before her. She eyed the sandy lawn and the car tires. They were cut diametrically in two and placed at the ends of the culvert. A sandy path led to the front door. In another car tire beside the path, Shirley had planted a geranium.

Lillian went to the door and stood for a moment. She wanted to knock, to awaken Dryfly, to hold him, to feel the warmth of his body, to kiss and hug and love him like he'd never been loved before. Lillian Wallace, young and beautiful, alone in a strange land, standing at Shirley Ramsey's door at dawn, whispered: "Sleep tight, Dryfly, my prince of Dungarvon. I love you."

Quietly, so as not to disturb anyone, she slid the envelope beneath the door. Without looking back, she returned to the Cabbage Island Salmon Club.

Back in her room, Lillian sat on her bed to wait for her father to awaken. She knew she would not have to wait long. Bill Wallace wanted to get an early start.

eleven

When Dryfly found the note from Lillian Wallace, he kissed the daisy. As the daisy touched his lips, a teardrop that had been coursing its way down his cheek, dropped to land on the "loves me" petal. The old "She loves me — she loves me not" game would not be necessary.

Dryfly Ramsey was a dreamer.

Dryfly Ramsey had always been a dreamer. When he was a child, he dreamed of cowboys on dynamic white stallions, cacti and coyote calls (there were no coyotes in New Brunswick back then); he dreamed of exotic places like Newcastle and Chatham, Saint John and Fredericton. As he passed through the awkwardness of puberty, his dreams reluctantly changed.

Dryfly didn't have it in mind to give up childhood, but it happened, as it happens to everyone. His dreams had changed from range cowboys to radio cowboys, the guitar being a key implement in the process. He wanted to be like Lee Moore, or Doc Williams. He wanted to live in exotic places like Wheeling, West Virginia or Nashville, Tennessee.

Now, Lillian Wallace had changed things again. The need for the love of a woman stormed in and Dryfly started to experience the cold, ruthless loneliness of adolescence.

Dryfly started taking long walks alone, dreaming of Lillian Wallace. He was seen less often, and whenever he did show up at Bernie Hanley's store to associate with the boys, he was quiet and downcast, always too aware of himself. Shirley Ramsey saw the change in him. She also noticed that Dryfly was paying frequent visits to the piece of mirror that hung above the water buckets. He'd look into the mirror, sigh, comb his hair, look it over and shake his head. When the greased-back hair went "flip-flop," he'd sigh again and sometimes left the house for a lonely walk. Dryfly's introverted state passed quickly, but not without leaving a scar — a change had occurred. Dryfly felt he needed a woman.

"It seems to me, to get the women, ya gotta be in with the in crowd," said Shadrack one evening.

The two teenagers were sitting on the center abutment of the footbridge. They were facing downstream, watching an American fishing the Dr. Martin pool. The American was old and bent and maneuvered his way through the pool with the assistance of a cane.

"The in crowd?" asked Dryfly.

"Yeah. That's the new sayin' around places like Blackville these days."

"What's the difference in the in crowd and the out crowd?"

"Well, the way I see it, the in crowd are lads that got a trucker's wallet with a chain that holds it to yer belt, and jet boots."

"And the out crowd?"

"Lads like us."

"There ain't no girls around here, anyway."

"There are in Blackville. Everybody goes to Blackville these days."

"Maybe that's what we should be doin'.""

"No use. Ain't got a trucker's wallet and jet boots."

*

When Max and John Kaston pulled up in front of Brigham's store in Blackville, the first thing that caught their eyes was a fellow named Lyman MacFee. Lyman MacFee played electric guitar with a country-rock group called "Lyman MacFee and the Cornpoppers." Lyman MacFee did much more than play for weekend dances for five dollars a dance. He was also the president of the Blackville recreation council, a right-wing forward for the Blackville hockey team (The Blackville Aces), and the manager of Brigham's Store Blackville Limited. When Max and John Kaston pulled up in front of Brigham's, they saw Lyman

MacFee diddling "Mutty Musk" and step-dancing on the step that ran across the front of the store.

Max and John Kaston got out of the truck and approached the diddling, dancing Lyman MacFee. When they reached the step, Lyman quit diddling and dancing, swung and said: " 'Mutty Musk!' The best damn tune ever played! Old Ned MacLaggen always said, ya kin tell a good harmonica player when he plays ya 'Mutty Musk' in variations! What kin I do for ya today, boys?"

"I don't know for sure, Lyman, but I was thinkin' I'd like to take a look at yer chainsaws."

"A chainsaw! Now, there's the rig! Come inside! I know just what yer lookin' for! Dee-da-diddle-daddle-diddle-daddle-diddle-daddle-dum . . . "

John and Max followed the diddling Lyman MacFee into what Max thought was probably one of the biggest stores in the world. "It's two stories and must be a hundred feet long," thought Max. "And just look at all this stuff!"

Brigham's Store had everything in it from beds to rifles, shovels to chesterfields, bicycle pumps to phonographs to clothing. Max noticed that they even had a couple of television sets. Max would have loved to have a television, but he knew it would never happen as long as he lived with his father. John Kaston believed that television was the creation of Satan.

Lyman MacFee led them to the corner he had recently cleared to accommodate his newest sales item, the yellow Pioneer chainsaws, the pioneer of the machine that would change Brennen Siding, the Miramichi area, even all of New Brunswick, forever.

"There's what yer lookin' for, right there," said Lyman. "The best outfit to ever hit the woods!"

"Howmuchyouwantfor it?" asked Max, so fast that Lyman wasn't sure if the words were English or not.

Max was a little bit afraid of Lyman; thought he might be lying to them, overpricing the saws, ripping them off. He was also afraid of the saw — it was ugly and heavy. Max had lost twenty pounds working with a bucksaw, but he had gotten used to it. Now this chainsaw would demand even more from him;

he'd lose more weight; he'd have more lumber to contend with; he'd be working longer days. He didn't want to get used to it.

"All three of them are the same price, $249.95 — but they're worth every cent. You kin saw more lumber in a day with them things than ya kin saw with a bucksaw in a week! Randy Carter's young lad's cutting four cord a day with one like this and is home for supper at four o'clock."

"It's a lot o' money, though, ain't it?" said John Kaston to Max, the son who was too contrary to go back to school and become a preacher; Max, the son who even refused to read the Bible or lead in prayers.

"Yep," said Max.

"No money at all," cut in Lyman. "No money when ya think of the wood yer cuttin'! That's not one word a lie, John, four cord a day by himself! Let's take 'er out back and I'll show you how it works."

Out back, Lyman MacFee hauled the pullcord of the chainsaw and a sonorous buzzing noise settled over half the village. The other half of the village could also hear the buzzing, but it was somewhat bearable if one was far enough away.

Lyman MacFee cut into a log he had placed out back for the purpose of demonstrating. The sharp new teeth of the chain cut with great rapidity through the bark, knots and wood of the unfortunate log.

The flying sawdust and the buzzing like so many giant insects frightened and depressed Max Kaston to no end.

Again and again Lyman sawed through the log, then handed the saw to John, who gave it a try. When John had zipped off a couple of blocks, he handed the saw to Max.

John Kaston thought that the chainsaw was, indeed, the best outfit for sawing lumber he'd ever seen. Max, on the other hand, was on the verge of tears. He sawed a couple of blocks, but lost heart quickly and handed the saw back to Lyman MacFee.

"What d'ya think, men? Ya ever see anything like it?"

"She's quite the outfit, alright? What do ya think, Max? Ya think you'd like to work in the woods with that outfit from daylight to dark?"

Max, detecting the sarcasm in John's voice, said: "A lot o' money."

"A man could pay fer it with four or five cord a day."

"She's an awful heavy outfit," said Max.

"Sure it's heavy," put in Lyman, "but ya'll git used to it. Three or four days o' sawin' and ya won't notice the weight at all. And even if it is a little heavy, it's still a lot easier than pushing a bucksaw all day for half the money. Four cord a day . . . that's forty, forty-five dollars every day you work. I tell ya, John, this outfit's gonna change the whole face of lumberin'! I'll put it on yer bill, you take it home and try it fer a few days, and if ya don't like it, bring it back. I guarantee you won't be sorry."

John Kaston took the chainsaw.

*

To a salmon angler, one salmon a day is considered good fishing. To most anglers, one salmon a week is acceptable. It is not unusual for an angler to fish for a week and catch nothing at all.

But, to drive all the way from New York or Boston to Brennen Siding to fish and return with nothing to show for it was looked upon with a certain amount of suspicion by left-behind wives.

"You went all the way to Canada to fish?"

"Yes, my pet."

"So, where's your fish?"

"I didn't catch any, pet."

"Sure!"

While the angler might still be having visions of the Dungarvon River in his memory, the wife was visualizing bars and whorehouses in Montreal, or Quebec. An unsuccessful angler, if he was smart, would buy a salmon to take home with him, make up a tale about the struggles he'd had and keep peace in the family.

Palidin, with his magnetized hook, was catching anywhere from two to eight salmon a day. He did not have a freezer. A dead salmon would not last long outside a freezer on an August day. Palidin had to sell his salmon, or else give them away. He wanted a car. He did not want to give his salmon away. Palidin Ramsey was in business.

Palidin and George Hanley strolled down the Gordon Road discussing the business.

"I'm ketchin' more than I can sell," said Palidin. "There's just not enough sports around here. I need to be sellin' in Blackville, Upper Blackville, Renous, all over the place."

"Sellin' salmon's against the law. Aren't you scared of gettin' caught?"

"I'll be careful. What I need is a car."

"How much money ya got now?"

"Seventy-eight dollars. I'd have a hundred, if I hadn't bought that rod and reel. If I had a couple of hundred, I could buy an old car good enough to get me to Blackville now and again to sell. But, I don't have enough money, that's the problem."

"Maybe you could borrow a car."

"Nobody'd ever lend me a car!"

"I kin get one. I kin git dad's."

"Ya think?"

"Prob'ly. But I'd have to have a cut in the money. You buy me a rod out of the seventy-five dollars and I'll help ya with the fishin', too. We kin be partners."

"I'll think about it," said Palidin, but Palidin was already liking the idea. "I don't have much choice," he thought. "If he can get a car, I'll make him a partner."

David Kaston (Max's older brother) and a girl he was dating from Gordon passed Palidin and George on the road. When they had passed by several yards, Palidin and George turned to watch after them.

"Nice bum," said George.

"She's not bad either," agreed Palidin.

*

Nutbeam was changing, too.

With encouragement from Shadrack and Dryfly, Nutbeam started practicing his trumpet playing again.

"Who cares if they hear me," he said to himself. "I'm not

breaking any laws. If they find me out and Graig Allen runs me off his land, I'll move somewhere else. I'd like to have a bigger camp, anyway."

Nutbeam put the trumpet to his lips and unleashed a blast that put the fear of the devil in the hearts of everyone in Brennen Siding . . . except for Shadrack and Dryfly, that is.

Shadrack and Dryfly thought it was the funniest thing they ever heard. They found themselves going to Bernie Hanley's store every night for no other reason than to hear the stories and surmisals.

"I knew that thing was gonna show up again," said Stan Tuney. "I knowd as soon as I saw them tracks in the woods. Hoof tracks, they were!"

"I think meself, now, as the feller says, meself now, I think it's a jesiless fox," said Lindon Tucker.

"Some fox!" said Shadrack. "Weren't no fox we saw in that woods four year ago!"

"Well, just for certain, what did you boys see back in that woods?" asked Bernie Hanley from behind the counter.

"Was awful dark," said Shadrack, "but I do remember seeing a set o' horns like a cow's."

"And it was as big as a moose, but shaped more like a cat," said Dryfly. "What's a panther look like, anyway?"

"They're a big cat," said Bert Todder, "but I never heard tell o' one with horns — you, Bernie?"

"Ain't never been a cat with horns," said Bernie Hanley.

"It's a wonder you boys weren't tore to pieces," said John Kaston.

"I had the rifle, and was about thirty feet away from 'im. Pulled the old gun up and let him have it from thirty feet away. Aimed right for its forward shoulders and let 'er drift. The thing just swung and looked at me as if I was stupid, turned and struck 'er down through the woods," said Shadrack.

"Just seemed to be floatin'," said Dryfly. "Never made a sound."

"Father Murdock blessed the whooper's grave and it was

never heard after. Maybe if I went back in the woods and prayed, the thing would take off out of here," said John Kaston.

"You ain't a priest," said Bernie Hanley.

"No, you're right! I ain't a priest, I'm a good Christian Baptist and that's a lot better than any priest!"

"Prayin' would work just great," said Bert Todder, "but you're forgettin' one thing. We ain't got a grave, or none that we know of, anyway."

"I was out listenin' to it last night," said Bernie Hanley. "Almost sounded like the thing was tryin' to sing, or somethin'."

"Jist sort o' sings, so it does," said Lindon Tucker. "Heard it meself, yeah. Jist sort o' sings like."

"Ya know what a crowd o' lads should do? We should load our rifles and go back there and hunt the devil down," said Dan Brennen. "Fill 'im full o' lead."

"That's what a lad should do, Dan old boy. Fill 'im full o' lead, that's what I say. Gun the bugger down, yeah."

"You're movin' to Fredericton pretty soon, ain't ya Lindon?" asked Stan Tuney.

"Oh yeah, yeah, yeah! Movin' in the fall, I think, yeah. Takin' off in the fall, takin' off in the fall."

"Ya can't shoot the devil," said John Kaston. "The good Lord is the only medicine for the devil."

"Young Shadrack scared 'im off with one shot," said Bernie Hanley. "Never came back for four years."

"I wouldn't do that," said Dryfly, recognizing the potential problem for Nutbeam. "I wouldn't go back in that woods again! That bullet didn't hurt 'im one bit."

"But it scared him off," put in Bert Todder.

"And you lads were just a couple o' young lads," added Stan Tuney.

Shad also saw that things might be getting out of hand. "That's the thing," said Shadrack. "We was jist kids back then and didn' know no better. We were lucky, that's all! Knowin' what I know now, I wouldn' take a million dollars for goin' into that woods!"

"Well, I say, somethin's gotta be done!" said John Kaston, "and ya don't need a grave to pray! The power o' the Lord is infinite! I'll go back there with the Lord by my side, and smite that demon. You lads ever think o' prayin'?" It was a rare occasion when John Kaston wouldn't take the opportunity to preach. "Just trust in the Lord and it won't matter if it is the devil back there! Yea, though we walk through the valley o' death, we fear no evil, the Bible says!"

"I'll go back, but I ain't takin' no Bible," said Bert Todder. "I'm takin' the 38-55."

"I'll go too, but I'll have to close the store early," said Bernie Hanley.

"I'll take the Bible. That's the only weapon I need," said John Kaston.

"I'll take me shotgun," said Stan Tuney. Stan Tuney didn't think his shotgun would stand up against the devil, but he had no intention of missing out on anything like this. This would be an adventure to lie about for the rest of his life.

"You lads wouldn't go back there tonight, would ya?" asked Dryfly.

"Too late now. We'll go tomorrow night," said Bernie. "We'll meet here at . . . let's say, nine o'clock." Bernie Hanley very much wanted everybody to meet at his store. The gathering would mean a fairly substantial sale of oranges and ginger ale.

Shadrack and Dryfly knew that these men were cunning hunters and trappers — that they had, in a manner of speaking, been living in the woods all their lives and knew it like the backs of their hands. There was a very good possibility that if these men went back Todder Brook, they would find Nutbeam. Nutbeam was squatting on Graig Allen's property, and although he was somewhat more outgoing than he used to be, he still wanted his location kept secret.

Shadrack and Dryfly slipped away from the crowd and headed for the river.

"What are we gonna do?" asked Dryfly.

"I dunno. Tell Nutbeam to quit playin' for awhile, I guess," said Shadrack.

"Listen . . . I can hear him now."

"BLAT, BLAT, BLAT, BARMP-BARMP!" Nutbeam was practicing "The Blue Canadian Rockies," but one would have to stretch the imagination considerably to recognize it.

Although the sound of the trumpet may have been injecting fear and bewilderment into the hearts of everyone else in Brennen Siding, to Shadrack and Dryfly it was what the ear-torturing grunts of an accordian might be to an Italian, or what the monotonously unbearable drone of the bagpipes might be to a Scotsman. It inspired in them a certain nostalgia — the music that brought back the memory of their greatest childhood adventure. It was spooky and mysterious, the substance of childhood curiosity.

"I don't want to see him quit playin'," said Shadrack. "It gives him something to do."

"Me either. I kind of like 'im. These lads around here would never let it rest."

"They ain't got much to think about, that's for sure."

"It's kind o' our fault," said Dryfly. "We're gonna have to do somethin'."

"Let me think for a minute," said Shad. "We're gonna have to do something, you're right there."

*

That night the frost paid Brennen Siding a visit and crystallized a million dewdrops. The dewdrops had been eyeing the northern lights when the frost struck and many of them were holding a flash within. Like tiny prisms, they shone from blades of grass and cucumber leaves, on Shirley Ramsey's geranium and Dan Brennen's tomato plants, on Helen MacDonald's dahlias and Judge Martin's weathervane, on spider webs and all the tombstones (except for one) behind the little Baptist church. On the tombstone that did not sparkle (Clara Tucker's) sat Palidin Ramsey. Clara Tucker had died of gangrene. The gangrene had started in her toe.

The northern lights soughed like the wind and merged to the zenith as if drawn by celestial magnets.

Palidin could vaguely remember Bill Tuney. Bill Tuney

HERB CURTIS

smoked a pipe all his adult life and his lower lip had weakened from the stress, and hung loosely from stained teeth. He had been a lumberman and a guide; he had loved and been loved; had built a home and raised a family. Bill Tuney had liked molasses in his tea.

"Bill Tuney liked molasses in his tea," thought Palidin. "Right now, people still remember Bill Tuney, but in twenty years, they'll only remember that he liked molasses in his tea. In fifty years, this tombstone will be all that is left. Bill Tuney will have left, memory and all."

The house that Bill Tuney built would never become a museum. The barn was falling down already. His son would never become famous or do anything to be remembered for. Stan Tuney did not even like molasses in his tea.

Palidin Ramsey wondered if he, himself, would pass in the same way, unremembered like Bill Tuney and everybody else in the graveyard . . . his brother Bonzie.

"Bonzie was a great little lad," thought Palidin. "Bonzie might have become somebody, had he lived."

Palidin could hear the murmur of the northern lights. He tilted his head back a bit to listen better.

"The cycle," he thought, "like rain, like water, like magnets, like northern lights, like echoes . . . bouncing back and forth through time and space. Sometimes you hear it only once; sometimes the echo returns half a dozen times before it escapes into space . . . but they come back . . . they always come back. From which star do I hear the hoof fall? . . . rain falls on earth to rise again . . . it falls on me to rise again to fall on God . . . rain, magnets, northern lights, hooves . . . sandals . . . "

Palidin decided that he would like to watch the Dungarvon River for a while. He slid from the tombstone and headed for the footbridge. He walked to the center abutment and eyed the dark forest, the sparkling fields, the azure above and the reflections below. The foam-speckled water slid smoothly under the bridge.

"Fish farts," he thought. "Bert Todder will be remembered for naming them fish farts."

Palidin was startled by the appearance of two fishery wardens in a canoe. He saw the wardens, but the wardens did not see him, and without a word or gesture of greeting, they slid quietly past in the way of the river.

"It's poachin' season. Hope nobody's out nettin'," thought Palidin.

When he felt the wardens were far enough down stream so that he himself would be safe from being caught as an accessory, he whooped long and loud. The whoop echoed past the wardens like the proverbial bat out of hell, warning poachers for a mile or more that the enemy approached. "If someone hears the whoop, he'll whoop, too," he thought. "The signal could travel all the way to Renous. The wardens will've wasted their run."

In a moment, Palidin heard footsteps falling on the far end of the bridge.

"Could it be the wardens coming back to get me?" he asked himself. "Could they have seen me after all? No. They're talkin' like two fools. It's Shadrack and Dryfly."

Palidin waited.

"We'll have to hide it somewhere 'till tomorrow night," Dryfly was saying to Shadrack. "Somewhere indoors in case it rains."

"It ain't gonna rain," said Shadrack. "It's gonna be windy and cool tomorrow."

"How ya know that for sure?"

"The northern lights. It's always windy and cool after the northern lights."

"Yeah, I guess you're right. We'll just stash it under a tree somewhere."

"G'day lads," said Palidin.

"Palidin!"

"What you lads up to?"

"Ah . . . ah, jist walkin' around. What're you doin'?"

"Just standin' here."

"Was that you whooped?"

"Yeah. Saw the wardens."

"Runnin' the river?"

"Yeah, two of them."

"Bastards!"

"What've ya got there?"

"Oh . . . this . . . a trumpet."

*

As Shadrack and Dryfly gave Palidin a five-minute spiel (all lies) on where they got the trumpet and what they intended to do with it, Lindon Tucker left his kitchen to "see a man about a horse."

As he made his way to the barn (the chosen building for tonight's annointing), he eyed the northern lights.

"Storm on the ocean," he thought.

Lindon Tucker believed that the northern lights were caused by the sun's reflection off a troubled sea.

"Oh, yeah, yeah, yeah. Be frost tonight and windy tomorrow, yeah."

Lindon stepped into the deep shadows of the barn, sighed contentedly and relieved himself. He sniffed the air — "Yep, gonna be a storm, yeah. I kin smell that pulp mill in Newcastle. Yep. Oh yeah, yep. Pulp mill, yep. Kin always smell that pulp mill before a storm. Yep. Oh yeah, yeah, yeah. Smells like shit, yep."

"Clump." Something moved in the field beyond the barn.

"Clump . . . clump . . . clump."

Lindon eyed the field. The frost, the stars and the northern lights made it just possible for him to see across the dim field to the edge of the forest. He could see nothing unusual in the glittering expanse.

"Clump . . . clump . . . clump." The clumping sound came from the field once again, nearer this time.

"Sounds like a horse walking," thought Lindon, "or a moose."

Then Lindon saw the dark figure standing still about thirty yards away. He thought it might be a cow, or a moose; he wasn't sure. It was hard to see in the dimness of the night. Lindon wasn't even sure that it might not be a tree, although he couldn't recall a tree being in that particular place.

"Yep. Oh yeah, yep. Prob'ly a moose, yeah. Yep. Oh yeah,

yeah, moose, yeah. Moose kin be dangerous this time o' year, yep. Dangerous, yeah. Better git in the house, yeah."

*

The next night, every man in Brennen Siding met at Bernie Hanley's store. While they drank Sussex Ginger Ale and dis-cussed the plan: three dogs, eight rifles and four shotguns waited outside in the cool evening. A Gideon Bible got to go inside with John Kaston. The rifles and shotguns were unaccustomed to hunting this time of year, and had never been fired at a devil. The dogs were not trained hunting dogs, but Bert Todder's dog Skip had a fair reputation for chasing cats. The owners of the dogs had brought them along more to sacrifice than to track. "If the rifle don't down the devil, throw the old dog at 'im and run for dear life!"

"We'll all stick together," said Bernie Hanley, "at least until we know what we're dealin' with back there." They were all standing around in Bernie Hanley's store. In Bernie Hanley's store, Bernie Hanley was in charge.

"OK," said Bert Todder, "Let's go."

"No hurry," said Bernie, thinking that to stall was good for two or three purchases of ginger ale. "The thing never starts yel-pin' till near dark."

"Yeah, but we should be over there when it does," said Bert Todder.

"Oh, yeah, yeah, yep. Never shows up 'till pretty near dark, no. No. No he don't, no."

"If we're gonna wait fer it to start howlin', we should be out-side listenin' fer it, I say," said Dan Brennen.

"Oh, yeah, yeah, yeah. Should be outside, we should. Should be outside so we kin hear it," agreed Lindon Tucker.

John Kaston stood fingering his Bible, looking very thought-ful, like a preacher about ready to take the pulpit. Tonight would be a test of faith for him. If he was successful in his exorcism, he would be the talk of the area. He might even get to preach in the church occasionally. "Dear loving heavenly Father . . . " John Kaston was praying for his dream to come true.

"Anyone want anything before I lock up?" asked Bernie.

Several of the men bought ginger ale, then they all went outside to wait and listen. The sun was dropping behind the horizon, splashing the north-west with shades of red.

"That's a cool breeze," said Bob Nash. "Startin' to feel like fall."

"Gonna head to Fredericton in the fall," said Lindon Tucker. "Oh, yeah, yeah, yeah."

Dan Brennen had hidden a quart of navy rum under the rhubarb leaves that grew along the east side of the store. He fetched it and passed it around. "To keep that lad from lookin' at ya," said Dan. John Kaston refused the shot of courage.

They had just tossed the empty rum bottle back into the rhubarb leaves, when the Todder Brook Whooper let off his mournful cry. As they reached for their rifles, every man in the group thought: "I wish we had more rum."

When the men were crossing the footbridge on their way to Todder Brook, the noise from the forest stopped. All the men came to an abrupt halt and stood on the bridge and listened.

"It stopped," said Lindon Tucker.

"It's just takin' a rest," said Bob Nash. "It's still back there, you kin bet on that."

When the men were entering the forest on the path that led to Nutbeam's camp, the screaming started up again. This time, however, the noise was not coming from the Todder Brook area. It came from what seemed like John Kaston's farm.

"Bless us and save us," whispered John Kaston, squeezing his Bible tightly in his hands, "the devil's on me very own land!"

"What do we do?" asked Bob Nash.

"Only one thing to do," said Bernie Hanley. "He's up at John's."

All the men swung and headed in the direction of John Kaston's. They crossed the Graig Allen field and climbed over the fence into John Kaston's field. The last man, Stan Tuney, had no more than stepped off the cedar rail when the noise stopped. The men all stopped and stood, closer together than usual, and listened once again. They were more than just a little excited. They now felt they were close. Every man stared into the night for a gigantic cat with horns and eyes the size of ash-trays.

"We'll stick together," said Bernie Hanley. "We don't want to shoot each other."

"If the thing's around here," said Dan Brennen, "it's prob'ly hidin' in the shadows of the barn, or one o' the sheds."

The men formed a line and walked, side by side, toward the barn. When they were but thirty feet from it, they stopped and all except John Kaston raised their rifles. Bob Nash flicked on his flashlight. Nothing.

They searched every building on John Kaston's farm, inside and out, but came up with nothing unusual. John and Max Kaston went into the house to check on the Mrs.

"John! John! The thing was right out by the barn!"

"I know, I know! You all right?"

"I'm alright, but the thing's right out there by the barn! What are we gonna do?"

"Don't be scared! Max and me will stay here with ya. Max, go and tell the men that we'll stay here, in case it comes back. Tell them to go on without us!"

Max delivered the message and had no more than re-entered the house when the thing screamed from down on Helen MacDonald's farm. Inside, Max found his father loading the rifle.

"He's down at Helen's place," said Bob Nash.

"Helen'll shit herself," said Stan Tuney.

By the time the men climbed the fence into Helen MacDonald's farm, the noise had stopped once again. When it started screaming again, it was coming from Lindon Tucker's farm. When they arrived at Lindon Tucker's, the thing had stopped again. By the light of Bob Nash's flashlight, they searched all the buildings that belonged to Lindon, but once again came up with nothing. Crossing the field, Bob Nash flicked on the flashlight to check his pocket watch for the time and several of the other men spied the hoofprints of the old bull moose.

"Hoof prints!" said Stan Tunney.

"Right in my field, right in my field, right in my field!" Lindon Tucker was nearly in tears.

Then the noise started up again, up by the footbridge.

That night the Todder Brook Whooper haunted every farm in Brennen Siding.

The next morning, a sleepless Lindon Tucker blew out the kerosene lamp that had been turned as high as it would go without smoking.

"That's it! The time's come! That's it, that's it, I'm gettin' out o' here! Goin' to Fred'icton. Right now . . . soon's I go fishin'. Gotta fish first . . . ."

A week later he would walk to Blackville and catch the SMT bus to Fredericton.

twelve

Palidin Ramsey's business took a complicated twist. On the first day of September, Dr. Macdowell returned to his cottage. He would be there for the whole month of September and half of October. Dr. MacDowell did not want anybody but himself fishing his salmon pool.

Palidin had already been run out of Judge Martin's pools. The judge hadn't minded at first, but then he saw that Palidin was catching too many fish, more than his limit. Palidin had been severely reprimanded and was lucky to get away without being reported to the wardens.

Palidin then tried the Cabbage Island Salmon Club's pool. In September, the Club's business boomed. For the whole month, all five cabins were occupied by American anglers, paying in the vicinity of a hundred dollars a day each for the privilege of staying there and fishing the productive waters. Frank Layton, the club's manager, did not want Palidin to fish in the pool. It was over-crowded already.

Sam Little, from Hartford, Connecticut, ruled his pool as selfishly as everyone else, but he did not own both sides of the river. Across the river from Sam Little's, was the Lindon Tucker pool, which from then on would be called the Bill Wallace Pool.

When Palidin arrived at the Bill Wallace Pool, he found Dan Brennen, Lindon Tucker and Bert Todder, all wading waist-deep, fishing. A little fort of rocks had been constructed at the water's edge, which was occupied by three dead fish — two grilse and a salmon. Palidin sat on a rock to watch and listen. The men were carrying on a leisurely conversation while they fished.

"How big was it?" asked Bert.

"I wouldn' say fer sure, now, but it, now, I wouldn' say fer sure, I wouldn' swear to it, but now it looked to me to be about ten, twelve, fourteen, sixteen pounds. Gottem right behind his pet rock over there. Gets one there everyday, he does, so he does."

"I don't see his car there, now," commented Dan.

"No, no, no. Got his limit. Got his limit twice. Watched him. Got his limit this mornin' and again this afternoon. Got his limit twice and left." It was obvious that Lindon was not happy with the day's activity of Sam Little. Lindon did not like Sam Little one bit. Sam Little fished without a guide ever since he bought the shore from Stan Tuney who lived across the way. Lindon used to guide Sam, but Sam, once he owned river-front property, did not legally need a guide anymore, so Lindon lost out on a month's work every summer.

"Goodday, Ramsey. How's she goin'?" yelled Dan.

"Good," said Palidin. "I see ya got some fish."

These men, like all the men and boys in Brennen Siding, did not like Palidin Ramsey. He was fruity. He read all the time. Dan, particularly, did not like him. With all that knowledge, Palidin might learn and surpass Dan's own limited knowledge. But, on the river, things were different. On the river, although it had never actually been spoken about, it was customary to be courteous, gentlemanly. A rule that all except for the Americans and Monctonians followed. Local anglers, especially, did not like Monctonians.

In Palidin's case, they would tolerate him with a subtle sarcasm.

"Lindon and Bert got them. I ain't seen a thing," said Dan.

"What did you get them on?" asked Palidin.

"Butterfly. Butterfly. Butterfly. Got' im on a butterfly."

"Green butt?"

"Orange. Orange. Orange."

"Got my two on a green butt," said Bert. "The salmon come clean out o' the water for it. Jesus, he hit it hard!" Bert was very pleased with his success and started to sing: "My little blue charm is better than yer yellow cosserboom."

"What're ya workin' at, Palidin?" asked Dan.

Bert Todder laughed: "Ha, ha, ha, tee, hee, sob, sob." The thought that Palidin Ramsey would ever have a job was, indeed, amusing.

"Selling post holes," said Palidin. He did not laugh. He knew the men were making fun of him.

Dan Brennen frowned and spat into the water. He badly wanted to catch a fish — a big one to show the others up. He considered changing flies.

"Only for Lindon and Bert, I might've caught them fish meself," he thought. "Bastards!" Dan didn't like for anyone, other than himself, to catch a fish. He had fished for two hours and was growing impatient with the inactivity. "And now that young arsehole is waitin' to get in!" He made another long, well-executed cast. The fly landed lightly and began its swing on the current. It passed several hotspots, but nothing surfaced or grabbed it.

"The damn nets are ketchin' all the fish," commented Dan.

"'Pon me soul, yeah. Nets are gittin' them, Dan old boy. Nets, yeah. Yeah. Yeah. Couldn' ketch the clap with all them nets in the river, Dan old boy, chummypard."

"Tee, hee, hee. Sob, tee, sob."

"It's not the downriver nets," commented Palidin. "It's the Russians and the Danes fishing off the coast of Greenland."

"It's them damn Frenchmen! Them lads want 'er all!" Dan was disagreeing with Palidin. "Ain't that right, boys?" He was looking for support.

"Frenchmen, yeah, Dan old boy. Frenchmen. Want 'er all, they do," agreed Lindon.

Bert Todder said: "The damn Frenchmen are tryin' to take 'er over!" He was agreeing with Dan, but deep down, he felt Palidin was right . . . but, Dan was older and that was reason enough to agree with him.

Palidin knew their way and shrugged off the conversation.

"I sure put that brat in his place!" thought Dan.

No one spoke for a few minutes. The men fished and scanned

the water's surface with well-trained eyes. A salmon jumped up-stream.

"You're not fishing clean," yelled Palidin.

No one commented.

"Ing," thought Dan. "Fish -ing! Could'n't say fishin', like everyone else!"

Bert Todder was fishing the upper end of the pool. Lindon and Dan were moving too slowly for him. He decided to take a break and waded ashore.

"You go try'er, Palidin. I'm gonna have a smoke."

Palidin stood to let Bert sit down.

"How's George Hanley, these days?" asked Bert.

"I . . . I . . . Good, I think," said Palidin.

Palidin eyed Bert's countenence for a few seconds, trying to see any expression that might betray Bert's motive for asking about George. Bert seemed to know something . . . . "But how?" Palidin asked himself.

"I'll give it a try," said Palidin and walked to the water's edge. He waded waist-deep into the September water, thinking that he should have waders.

Palidin hooked a fish on the first cast. The salmon weighed about ten pounds and used every ounce, the current and every trick it knew, combined it all with strength and fury, to avoid being beached. The hook was embedded deep in its gills, the leader strong, the fisherman skilled. The salmon lost the battle. Palidin killed it and placed it in the pool with Lindon's and Bert's.

Bert Todder and Lindon Tucker seemed genuinely happy with the action, with Palidin's performance. Dan Brennen had left and gone home.

*

On the twentieth of September, the mail came as usual, but this time when Shirley opened the bag, there was a letter in it addressed to her, from Ottawa. It was a notice from the Director of Postal Services, saying that a change in the postal system was occurring. Her address was being changed. RR #5 was replacing Brennen Siding, N.B. The rural post offices were to be replaced by a rural route. On the first of January, Shirley would be out of a job.

Shirley read the letter, put it down, rolled a cigarette, lit up and began to take inventory.

"Jug is married and living in Renous. Oogan is workin' in Newcastle . . . I haven't seen Oogan in six months. Bean is married to Mary Francis Shaw and are havin' their own problems . . . Bean's out o' work and Mary Francis is gonna have their third baby any day. I'll be grandmother agin. Naggy's workin' at Eaton's in Moncton . . . Nagg might be able to help me . . . She's got a good job, don't do nothin' but clerk in that big store. Neenie and Bossy are married and livin' in Gordon. Junior's married to Mary Stuart and still livin' with old Silas. Junior'll get that place when old Silas dies, which shouldn't be too far away . . . I hope. Digger's in Toronto or Leamin'ton or some place. Last time Digger come home, he stayed drunk all the time he was here. Skippy finally married Joe Moon and is livin' in Quarry-ville. They finally got married, thank God . . . done it just after Joe's dog got killed. That just leaves Palidin and Dryfly home with me."

Shirley butted her cigarette and went to the piece of mirror that hung over the water buckets.

"Me hair's startin' to turn grey," she thought. "I ain't but forty-five, I got eight grandchildren and me hair's turnin' grey. Me teeth have just about had the biscuit, too. And I'm gettin' fat . . . I wished I could get rid o' that wart on me cheek."

Shirley sighed. "I won't be gettin' fat this winter when there's nothin' to eat in the house and no money."

Shirley went back to the table and rolled herself another cig-arette.

"Palidin's crazier than the birds," she thought. "Don't know where I went wrong with him. All he does is read and fish. I must've salted twenty salmon. Enough to do the winter . . . but, ya can't live on salty salmon, can ya?

Dryfly's no good either. All he does is play guiddar. Well, I got 'till January. Somethin' might happen before then."

*

By the last week of September, Palidin ran into another com-
plication. He didn't have waders and the water was getting too
cold for comfort.

Palidin had clients all over the Blackville area who wanted
salmon; who paid good money to get them. He could afford to
buy waders, but it was getting late in the season and he felt that
waders at this late date might not be worth the investment. The
salmon would be spawning within a few weeks and people would
quit buying — the waders might not pay for themselves.

George Hanley, Palidin's business partner, was having the
same difficulties; plus, his father was getting suspicious and
didn't want him borrowing the car so often. If one got caught
selling salmon from a car, one not only got fined and jailed;
they'd take the car as well.

Palidin and George sat on two tombstones in the cemetery
behind the Baptist church and discussed the situation.

A giant harvest moon lit up the night. From the forest back
of Todder Brook, came the sound of a trumpet playing "Red
Roses for a Blue Lady.' "

"We got $350.00 between us," said Palidin. "We could buy an
old car for that kind of money."

"Yep. Sure would be nice," said George.

"Mom can't afford to keep me any longer, and I'm no good
for woods work, are you?"

"Never worked in the woods in my life."

"What will we do, George?"

"We could get an old car and head for Fredericton, or someplace. We could get a job in Fredericton. We could hunt up
Graig Allen, tell 'im who we are . . . he might get us a job in no
time."

"I wonder how Lindon Tucker's doing over there?"

"Hard to say. Lindon got a big chunk of money for his shore.
He'll be alright."

"A lot of lads from Blackville are going to Toronto."

"That'd be nice. Livin' in Toronto."

"We should think about it, George."

"Sounds good to me."

*

Dryfly had but one thing on his mind: he was not getting any letters from Lillian. He couldn't write her one, because he had been too dumb to get her address. All he could do was wait.

Shadrack Nash had started to work for his father, cutting logs. Shad did not like working with Bob's new chainsaw any-more than he liked peeling pulp. Dry figured Shad would quit his job in a day or two.

Shad and Dry were spending a great deal of time with Nutbeam. Nutbeam was teaching them how to hunt and trap, and the boys were teaching Nutbeam some new songs to play on the trumpet.

"It just seemed to happen overnight," thought Dryfly. "One day he couldn't play a thing, and the next day he was doin' the very best of a job on 'Red Roses for a Blue Lady.' "

Nutbeam had become a good friend of the boys. His camp was a good place to party and play music. Nutbeam never seemed to care how late they stayed, or how dirty they talked. He'd often cook them up a pan of venison and occasionally sent them to the bootlegger in Gordon for Golden Nut. He never wanted them to share in the cost, but he did ask them to run a few er-rands. Shadrack and Dryfly did much of Nutbeam's shopping at Bernie Hanley's store, thus cutting back on the dreaded trips to Newcastle. They also helped him patch the roof of his camp and gather wood for the winter. The boys did not mind working for Nutbeam. It never seemed like work to them. It was more like play.

Some nights when the boys went to visit Nutbeam, he would not be there and they'd have to wait, sometimes for as much as a couple of hours, for his return. They didn't know where he was going, or for what reason, and he never offered to explain. Nutbeam was spending many evenings listening to Shirley Ramsey's radio.

This turned out to be one of the nights. When Dryfly arrived at Nutbeam's camp, he found it empty. Dryfly sat beside the door to wait.

Dryfly knew that Shadrack might not come tonight, either.

Shadrack was rising at six in the morning these days, and working hard. Shadrack would be too tired to play at nights and would not show up until he finally quit his job. "In about three days," thought Dryfly.

It was very pleasant there by Nutbeam's camp. The evening was warm for September and a big moon rose from the forest to keep him company.

"That moon is shining down on Lillian Wallace the same as it's shinin' down on me," thought Dryfly. "I wish I was with her. I wish she was here."

In his mind's eye, Dryfly visualized Lillian sitting beneath the moon somewhere in the States. He could see her big blue eyes and golden hair, the smile on the lips that had kissed him so gently. "God, let her write to me," he thought.

Dryfly didn't know it, but Lillian Wallace was, indeed, writing to him at that very moment.

"Goodday, Dryfly," said Nutbeam. Dryfly had not heard Nutbeam approaching, and was somewhat startled.

"Godday! How's she goin'?"

"Good."

"Out for a walk?"

"I got a slug o' wine left. Want some?"

"Yeah, maybe."

Nutbeam went into the camp and returned momentarily with a less than half-full bottle of Golden Nut.

Nutbeam was downhearted. He had just returned from watching Shirley Ramsey take a bath. Shirley Ramsey was looking more beautiful to Nutbeam everyday.

Nutbeam sat beside Dryfly, screwed the top off the bottle and they both took a drink. They did not talk for what seemed like a very long time; just eyed the moon and thought of their lovers.

Dryfly was the first one to break the silence. "Ever been in love?" he asked.

Because Nutbeam had been thinking that he was in love with Shirley Ramsey, Dryfly's question surprised him. It seemed as if Dryfly had been reading his thoughts.

THE AMERICANS ARE COMING

"I don't know," said Nutbeam. "It takes two to fall in love. No woman ever looked sideways at me long enough to fall for me."

"Don't you ever get tired of livin' alone?"

"It's better than being feared, or laughed at all the time. I once went to a dance and asked every girl there to dance with me. Not one said yes. Even the homeliest old woman there, laughed and turned me down. People wouldn' even set close to me."

"I don't think yer that homely, Nutbeam."

"You're jist gettin' use to me, that's all."

"It don't matter, anyway," said Dryfly. "Look at me, I'm in love. But it don't matter none. I'll prob'ly never see her agin, anyway. I don't think she loves me as much as I love her."

"Well, you're young and ain't nearly as homely as me. You'll get a woman soon enough."

"Ain't no other woman like this one."

"There ain't no other woman like Shirley Ramsey," thought Nutbeam. "There's lots o' fish in the sea," he said.

Nutbeam wanted to get to know Shirley Ramsey very much, but he didn't know how to set up the opportunity. He had befriended Dryfly, hoping that it might lead somewhere. This was the first private conversation they'd had and Nutbeam sought a way to approach the topic. He drank some more wine, hoping that it would loosen his tongue a little.

"How's yer mother?" asked Nutbeam.

"She's alright."

"Yer father's dead, ain't he?"

"Never saw 'im in me life."

"Yer mother must git awful lonesome with no man around."

"I don't know. Never thought about it."

"She ever look sideways at another man after your father died?"

"I don't know. Not that I know of."

"Yer mother's an awful pretty woman," said Nutbeam.

"She prob'ly was a long time ago."

"Still is."

"I never thought of it before, but Mom never goes anywhere. Stays home all the time. Ain't got a friend."

"Sounds like me."

"She should start goin' to dances or somethin'," said Dryfly. "Maybe she'd meet up with some friends."

"You know what I'd like you to do, Dry?"

"What's that?"

"Ah, ah . . . sing me a song."

Dryfly eyed the moon and thought of Lillian Wallace. He sang: *Roses are bloomin'*
> *Come back to me darlin',*
> *Come back to me darlin'*
> *And never more roam.*

*

"Get up, Shad, it's time to go to work."

"Day four," thought Shadrack. "Another day in the woods and I'll die. I'll die, I'll die, I'll die! I hate it. I'll starve to death before I pick that chainsaw up again!"

"Shad!"

"I'm too sore, Mom! I can't hardly walk!"

"Don't give me that! You get out here and go to the woods right this minute!"

"I tell ya, I'm too sore! I'm pretty near dead! Ya deaf?"

"Sore! Sore! A big boy like you, sore! Your poor old father's been back there for an hour and you layin' in bed sleepin'! Sore, my arse! Now, get out here and eat yer breakfast before I take a stick to ya! Sore! A big man fifteen years old gettin' sore! Hangin' around doin' nothin' like that . . . that . . . that Dryfly Ramsey. No wonder yer lazy, hangin' around with the likes o' that . . . that . . . that tramp! What's ever gonna become o' ya?"

Shad knew there was no stopping his mother. She had the stage, front and center, and would transmit spiel after spiel, condemning every man, woman and child that Shadrack ever as much as said hello to. She would start with Dryfly Ramsey and end with Dryfly Ramsey, but in between she'd find examples of depression and poverty from both ends of the river. She would bring in her own aging, ailing state, Bob's deterioration, the state of Bob's grandfather who had been no more than a no-good tramp. The Bible would come into the picture and how she'd had hopes for Shad to become a minister some day like cousin Ralph. She would yell through the bedroom door for as long as Shad stayed in there.

Shad arose, dressed, toileted and limped into the kitchen. The hard work (running the chainsaw) had stiffened his muscles. He was not lying about being sore. He checked the time, "Nine o'clock," he thought. "Dad will be ugly at me. I was s'pose to be back in the woods at eight. I'm an hour late." He turned on the radio and sat at the table to listen, to wait for his toast and eggs. The radio was turned to CFNB and Jack Fenety said, "Good morning, ladies, and welcome to Facts and Fancy. Today we are coming to you from under overcast skies. Our temperature is expected to remain stable at about 55° and we can expect rain, rain, rain." Jack Fenety went on to read some poetry and a prayer; he sent out birthday greetings to Mrs. Smith who was "a hundred years young today"; he played "The Yellow Rose of Texas" and "Bernadine."

Shad eyed the kitchen window as he ate his eggs and toast. "Please, God, let it rain," he prayed. Shad knew that his father would not work in the rain. Shad knew, by the swiftly moving clouds, that chances were very good he'd get the day off.

At nine-thirty, Jack Fenety played CFNB's rattling, ear-torturing news music and said, "CFNB, where New Brunswick hears the news." Shad didn't care about the news. There was nothing happening outside of Brennen Siding that concerned him. Shad gulped down the last of his tea and headed for the woods.

When Shadrack stepped outside, the September morning greeted him with a light drizzle. "It's gonna rain, it's gonna rain," he sang, "Ya can't work in the rain, Thank God, it's gonna rain." The rain seemed to Shadrack to be a magical rain, for, indeed, the soreness left his limbs with every drop that fell.

On the way back to the worksite, Shadrack met his father coming home.

"Gonna rain," said Bob Nash.

"I figured that," said Shad, "that's why I didn't bother to hurry."

"I covered up the chainsaw and the gas jug," said Bob. Bob Nash didn't want to work that day either. It was mid-September and the salmon (the September run) were here. Bob Nash had it in mind to go fishing.

An hour later, Shadrack announced that he had it in mind to go to Shirley Ramsey's to get the mail. He put on his jacket and headed for the footbridge. The rain was heavier now and slanted in from the southwest. The red checkered Mackinaw did little to keep him dry. Shadrack didn't care if he got wet. "Getting wet is a lot better than working in the woods," he thought.

*

Dryfly awakened to the sounds of Palidin moving about the room, and Shirley talking.

"What are ya gonna be doin' way out there in T'ronta?" Shirley was asking Palidin.

"I don't know," said Palidin. "Get a job . . . work. Ain't nothin' to do around here."

"How ya gonna get there?"

"Train."

"Where ya gittin' the money?"

"I got some money."

"Where'll ya live?"

"I'll get a room."

"Way out there in T'ronta all by yerself! T'ronta's an awful bad place, so it is! No one to cook fer ya, or look after ya . . . it's not like home, ya know, and you'll be all alone!"

"I won't be alone, Momma! George Hanley's goin' too."

Palidin was packing a cardboard box with his belongings. The box was not very big. Palidin only had one extra pair of jeans, a shirt, a pair of shorts and a pair of socks with the heels worn through to put in the box. He found a white T-shirt in the corner — it was dirty, but he threw it in the box anyway.

"How long ya plannin' on stayin'?" asked Shirley.

"I don't know. A month, six months, a year. If I get a job, I'll send ya home some money."

"What if ya don't get a job? What if ya git lonesome?"

"I'll be alright, Mom!"

The tears were threatening to overflow Palidin's eyes. He was getting lonesome already.

Shirley went back into the kitchen to smoke, to cry, to think things over.

"Poor little Paladin," she thought, "only sixteen, way up in T'ronta! I might never see him agin!"

Palidin sat on the bed to talk to Dryfly.

"I'm goin' to Toronto," he said.

"No? Yeah! What for?"

"Gotta get a job. Ain't nothin' to do around here."

"When ya comin' back?"

"I don't know for sure."

"Did I hear ya say George Hanley's goin' too?"

"Yeah. We're catching the train in half an hour. Will you stay home and look after Mom?"

"I don't know. I guess."

"Mom's losing the Post Office. She's gonna need a lot o' help. I'll send ya's some money soon's I get on my feet."

"You won't be scared up there?"

Palidin shrugged.

"Gonna miss ya, Pal."

"You won't miss me. You'll be too busy courtin' all the women."

"Ain't no women around here."

"Dry?"

"Yeah?"

"'Member me catching all them salmon?"

"Yeah."

"Well, there's a trick to it."

"A trick?"

"Yeah, and I'm gonna tell ya the trick, but I don't want you to tell anybody else. It's a good trick and it could make us rich some day. Promise not to tell it?"

"Sure."

Palidin proceeded to tell Dryfly the ins and outs of magnetizing salmon flies. When he was sure that Dryfly understood completely, he gave Dryfly the little lodestone he'd been using.

"Works every time," said Palidin. "Now, I gotta go. The train'll be here any minute."

"Be good, Pal."

"Yeah. You too."

In the kitchen, Palidin stopped to kiss Shirley goodbye.

"I love you, Mom." he said.

"I love you too, Pal. You know you kin always come home, Pal. You know where your home is."

"I know, Mom. I'll send ya money, Mom. Don't you worry."

Palidin forced back the tears as he eyed the ugly, the laughed at, the forsaken woman. "My mother in Helen MacDonald's hand-me-down dress . . . her hair is starting to turn grey . . . the most beautiful mother in the whole world," he thought.

"Don't cry, Mom," said Palidin, and quickly, so as not to change his mind, he picked up the box and left.

On the way to the Brennen Siding sidinghouse, where he would meet the train, Palidin passed Shadrack Nash on the road. Shadrack was limping slightly and looked soaked to the skin.

"See ya Shad," were the only words spoken, and Palidin made no attempt to hide the fact that he was capable of crying.

At Shirley Ramsey's house, Shadrack sensed that something dramatic had just occurred.

"What's wrong with Palidin?" Shadrack asked Dryfly.

"Him and George Hanley eloped," said Dry.

thirteen

On the twenty-ninth of October, Shirley opened the mailbag and found but three letters in it: a bill for John Kaston from Lyman MacFee, a letter from R.M. Crenshaw (Boston, Massachusetts) for Frank Layton, the manager of the Cabbage Island Salmon Club, and a red envelope with Dryfly Ramsey, Brennen Siding, N.B. written neatly on it in blue ink.

Ecstasy is not a strong enough word to describe how Dryfly felt when he saw the envelope. When Shirley passed it to him, he could not contain himself. He jumped for joy. It was one of the happiest moments of his entire life.

His joy was so obviously imprinted upon his countenance that Shirley, too, was stirred by his emotions.

"Thanks, Mom!" Dryfly hurried into his room and shut the door.

As she put the other two letters in their rightful compartments in the Post Office, she wiped a tear from her cheek and whispered: "Poor little darlin'."

Dryfly threw himself on the bed and eyed the envelope.

"Lillian Wallace," he whispered, "I love you, I love you, I love you!"

He sniffed the envelope and thought he could vaguely smell the scent of fly repellent. "Some kind of perfume, anyway," he thought.

He carefully tore the end off the envelope and removed the pink pages. There were four of them, all folded neatly. "What a girl!" he thought. "What a wonderful, wonderful girl!"

He prolonged opening the letter, wanting to savour the feeling, the moment.

"I just want to see one word," he thought. "The one magic word from the most beautiful girl in the world."

Before he began to read, he sniffed the paper once more and kissed it.

> *Dear Dryfly,*
>
> *I'm sorry I took so long to write. I'm the world's greatest procrastinator!*
>
> *How are you and what have you been doing? Did you go to work guiding? How's Shadrack?*

Lillian wrote about going back to school, the turning of the leaves and the harvest moon; she wrote about her plans to return to the Dungarvon River, her father's plans for building a cottage, a recent trip to New York and a new friend (Rick) she'd met in school. She did not write "I love you" in her letter, but at the very end she wrote: "I miss you very much. I'll always be very fond of you. Love, Lillian." It was the "I miss you very much. I'll always be very fond of you. Love, Lillian" that Dryfly read over and over and over.

Dryfly showed the letter to Shadrack. Shadrack was noticeably envious and that made Dryfly happy, for that put him one up on Shadrack in the women department. Shadrack figured that he, too, had dated Lillian and therefore they were even.

Dryfly read his letter to Nutbeam and after the "Love, Lillian" said:

"What do you think o' that, Nutbeam?"

"That's a good letter! A real good letter! I think she likes you a lot, Dryfly. But who's this Rick lad?"

"I don't know. Some lad in school, I s'pose."

Nutbeam sensed that Rick was mentioned for a reason. He didn't want Dryfly to be overly optimistic. "She mentioned him twice. Could be a boyfriend," he said.

"Could be." Dryfly had given the same thought consideration, but he didn't want to think about it.

Nutbeam was more impressed with the letter than Dryfly realized. Nutbeam was not just impressed with what Lillian wrote, but he was fascinated with the whole concept of letter writing. Nutbeam had encountered an additional problem in the Shirley

Ramsey venture — not being able to write. If one can't write, one does not have letters to mail. In Brennen Siding, if one does not have letters to mail, one might never enter the realm of Shirley Ramsey's love nest.

"You gonna answer the letter?" asked Nutbeam.

"Yeah, prob'ly."

"Wished I could write," said Nutbeam.

"Anyone can write. Didn' you ever go to school?"

"I didn't start to school until I was ten years old . . . I think me father and mother was ashamed of me . . . thought I was re-tarded. When I was ten they figured I maybe knew something and sent me off to school where everyone my age had the jump on me by four years. They not only laughed at me being ugly, but they thought I was stupid, too. They use to gang up and play tricks on me . . . and sometimes even beat me up. I raised a fuss and me parents let me stay home."

Nutbeam seemed very sad. "I couldn' go nowhere, Dryfly," he said.

"If you could write, who would you write to, Nutbeam?"

"Aunt Johannah, prob'ly. She's the only one that was nice to me. I'd like to find out who's dead and how they're all doin'."

"Me or Shad could write letters for ya," said Dryfly. "I ain't a real good writer, but I could scratch something out for ya."

"Maybe . . . maybe."

"You got any paper and a pencil?"

"No. Ain't got anything like that."

"There's paper and pencils in Bernie Hanley's store. I could pick some up for ya."

"Maybe . . . maybe."

"You'll need envelopes, too."

"Yeah. Might work. How's your mother doin'?"

"She's alright. Awful lonesome for Palidin, though."

"A woman like that shouldn't be lonesome," thought Nut-beam. "She ever hear from him?" he asked.

"Not yet. I guess she's worried about him. She's worried about the Post Office closin' too."

"When's the Post Office closin'?" asked Nutbeam.

"First o' the year."

"Don't leave much time," thought Nutbeam, "two months and some."

"What's she gonna do for a livin' when the Post Office closes?"

"Dunno. Somethin'll turn up."

"Maybe," said Nutbeam. "Maybe."

*

Lindon Tucker left his room on Pine Street and walked toward the Carleton Street bridge. This was the second time that day that he had walked "over town." The first time "over town," he'd gone to the bank and withdrawn two hundred dollars. This time he walked toward the hotel. Lindon Tucker always walked — he did not like spending seventy-five cents on a taxi. He didn't like spending seven dollars a week for his room with kitchen privileges, either, and he did not like having to buy things like meat and potatoes. In Brennen Siding, he did not have to pay rent. In Brennen Siding, Lindon grew his own potatoes and every fall he would shoot a deer, or a moose, and salt half a barrel of salmon. Lindon Tucker did not like spending money on anything. Lindon Tucker did not like Fredericton very much at all. .

Brennen Siding and the people he knew there was his whole life. He thought of them day and night with an aching heart. He longed to be walking on the footbridge, or through the forest; he missed his Sussex ginger ale with the boys at Bernie Hanley's store and he missed listening to the radio in his own kitchen and going behind a shed to "see a man about a horse." He found the people in Fredericton cold. They rarely spoke to him on the street. On the few times he did manage to strike up a conversation he was as agreeable as he could be — to no avail. They invariably walked away, to leave him once again, alone.

"How kin ya be so alone with so many people around?" he asked himself many, many times. "I'd go home, if I thought that devil would leave me alone, so I would. Oh yeah, yeah, yeah: Home, yeah. Yep."

Another depressing thing in Lindon Tucker's life was his landlord, Arthur McGarrity. To Lindon Tucker, Arthur McGarrity and his wife Monique were something lower than worms. Arthur and Monique McGarrity took great pleasure in beating the living daylights out of their five-year-old son, Bobby. If Bobby whimpered in the night, Arthur or Monique would stomp into his room and "SLAM, BANG, THRASH!" Bobby would be inflicted with a new set of welts and bruises. Lindon did not know what to do about the beatings. He figured it was not his place to interfere with the goings on of someone else's family. Lindon gritted his teeth and remained silent — silent and alone.

This night, Lindon decided that he didn't want to hear the child being beaten anymore. Last night's beating had been more severe than usual. That day, he had gone to the bank and withdrew two hundred dollars with the thought in mind to go on a drunk. He decided that the hotel would be a good place to start. "Maybe at the hotel, someone will talk to me."

When Lindon Tucker entered through the glass doors of the hotel, he was met by a good-looking young gentleman in a red jacket with brass buttons.

"Checking in, sir?" asked the bellman.

"You work here?" asked Lindon.

"Yes, sir," said the bellman and thought, "No, no, I'm dressed in this outfit because I'm a monkey grinder."

"Kin ya git drunk here?" asked Lindon.

"There's a bar right in there, sir."

Lindon headed across the lobby toward the lounge. Inside, he sat at the bar and waited for service. The lounge was nearly full and the bartender was very busy.

"What would you like?" yelled the bartender.

"Gimme a glass o' roy whiskey and a bottle o' Moosehead," yelled Lindon and scanned the other people at the bar to see if his order was making an impression. He smiled and winked at a couple of people, but no one seemed to take notice.

"A single or a double?" asked the bartender.

"Yeah, sure," said Lindon.

The bartender poured Lindon nearly a double. He recognized Lindon as a country hick and would shortpour him all evening long.

Lindon tossed the rye down and chased it with a quaff of ale. "Gimme another roy," he said.

*

Shirley Ramsey took a line-by-line, grey-hair-by-grey-hair inspection of her body. Palidin was gone, and she, for the first time in many years, had the privacy to undress completely without the possibility of being interrupted. Dryfly never came home until at least midnight.

Shirley Ramsey scanned her leg — "varicose veins, but not too bad." She scanned her belly — "bigger than Bert Todder's," she thought.

Bert Todder was a bachelor who did his own cooking. His diet consisted primarily of potatoes. Sometimes he'd cook a piece of salmon or venison to accompany the potatoes, and he ate many, many oranges and drank much ginger ale at Bernie Hanley's store, but primarily, he ate potatoes. For supper, he'd boil as many as ten and would not hesitate to eat the whole lot. If he left any, he'd have them fried for breakfast. He had the biggest belly in Brennen Siding.

When Bert Todder was asked why he let his belly get so big, he replied: "When ya got a good set o' tools, ya should build a shed over them. Tee, hee, ha, ha, sob, sob."

Shirley eyed her breasts. They depressed her. They tapered from chest to nipple like skin hankerchiefs with a marble dropped in each one.

She noticed how brown her skin was. "That's the Indian in me," she said aloud to the kitchen.

Her eyes also indicated Micmac ancestry. Her great-great-grandmother had been a Micmac Indian from the Northwest. Her grandfather had been an immigrant from Ireland. She had the dark eyes, skin, hair, and high cheekbones of the Micmac. Her nose, mouth and chin were Irish. Her great-grandmother had been English; her grandmother Dutch and her mother Scottish. Her children had blue eyes and did not look Indian at all Shirley bathed, donned her best dress (the Helen MacDonald hand-me-down), and went to the table to smoke, think and take inventory.

"There's one thing I kin say," she thought, "I raised a family."

Shirley was the youngest of nine children. Her mother had given birth to her under the very capable hands of a midwife. The midwife had delivered all nine children successfully. It was not the midwife's fault that Shirley's mother had taken one look at the baby (Shirley) — said: "It's a girl," and passed away. It was as though she was giving up her space, air and baby-making ability to Shirley.

Shirley spent the first twelve years of her life developing a body. At twelve she had been quite beautiful, with brown hair, dark eyes and an attractive smile. She had developed a sleek young body that yearned to be fondled, caressed and loved, but it wasn't until she reached the age of fourteen that she was able to put her body to the test. After just one night with Buck Ramsey, she learned that her body was as good for making babies as her mother's.

At the ages of 16 and 14 respectively, Buck and Shirley married. Junior was born three months later. At first, luck seemed to be with them; Buck's father died and left Buck the crumbling old house and gravel pit. They moved in and waited for someone to buy the gravel, but no construction was applied to the road that year. Buck didn't have a job and couldn't get one. He was forced to seek employment in Fredericton, and then in Saint John, where he found part-time labor loading ships. In Saint John, Buck also found a thirty-five year old widow to live with. As the relationship with the widow grew, Buck returned to Brennen Siding less and less.

Buck had never loved Shirley and Shirley had never loved Buck. They got married because they "had to" — Shirley was pregnant. He didn't love the widow either, but life was a hell of a lot easier in Saint John. As Shirley began to deteriorate under the stress and wear of baby-making, poverty and aging, Buck started to find her too unattractive for his tastes, and eventually even found her repulsive — repulsive, that is, until he got drunk. When Buck Ramsey got drunk, he stayed that way for three or four days. On about the third day, he'd start feeling sorry for himself and Shirley, head for Brennen Siding, stay drunk all the time he was there, make a baby and head back to Saint John, hung over and broke.

After making Dryfly, Buck returned to Saint John to find his thirty-five-year-old widow in bed with another man. With no money and no place to live, he took to bumming on the streets. On this meagre income, he did not eat much. His main source of nourishment became wine.

After several months, he moved to Fredericton, and for a matter of a year or so, it seemed he might pull himself together. He got a job as a janitor, bought himself a guitar and a new radio. He moved into a room on Charlotte Street and even managed to save a few hundred dollars. Then, he started drinking again. On the third day of overindulgence, he thought of Shirley. He would have gone to Brennen Siding, but for one thing — even Buck Ramsey didn't have the gall to face Shirley after eleven years of not being around to help her raise the family. He took some of his money and went to Saint John to see his widow instead.

The Saint John widow saw him coming and locked the door. Buck bought more wine and went in search of his cronies down by the wharf.

Most of the degenerates he knew had either died, or moved away in the year he'd been away and he found himself alone, drunk, cold and without shelter in the middle of February. He lay down by a crate, cuddled himself to keep warm, drank some more wine and passed out. In the middle of the night, a foghorn woke him up briefly. He looked about him to see a ship and an unloaded cargo, a few lights and drifting snow.

"Good-day," he said to himself, "I suppose I ain't havin' too hard a time!"

He then went back to sleep, never to awaken.

"At least I raised a family," spoke Shirley once more to the kitchen.

But now, with Palidin in Toronto, or wherever he was, and Dryfly running the roads night and day, Shirley was alone. The loneliness closed in on her like a coffin lid. With her family she had been poor, but never lonely. There had been rough moments when she hadn't known where the next meal was coming from, but there had always been someone to hold onto.

"I'm gettin' old," she thought. "My family's gone and I'm all alone. Nobody loves me, nobody cares . . . Hail Mary, full of grace . . . "

*

Shadrack Nash was very unhappy. His mother and father nagged him constantly.

"Go to work," they'd yell. "If ya don't go to work, go to school! Ya can't lay around the house and play the banjo for the rest of your life!"

Shadrack was getting so annoyed with the constant nagging that he started playing the banjo just to drown out their voices. The banjo playing did not help the situation. The constant plucking of the sonorous strings was eating at the ends of Bob and Elva's nerves. There was never a moment's peace in the house.

Bob Nash had just read the same paragraph of the *Family Herald* three times. Elva had just added three stitches too many to a sock she was knitting. Shadrack had just played "Will the Circle Be Unbroken" for the twentieth time.

"I could throw something at him," thought Bob.

"I could stab him with a knitting needle," thought Elva.

"John Deere, John Deere, John Deere . . . good tractor . . . John Deere . . . . Damn! I'm losing my mind." Bob Nash was reading the John Deere tractor ad on the back cover of the *Family Herald*. He wanted to read the article inside on scabby potatoes, but he couldn't concentrate. The banjo seemed to be getting louder and louder.

Finally, Bob started to roll the *Family Herald* into a tight round tube. His nerves were screaming for help and he was about to come to the rescue. Bob stood. "I'll beat the shit out of him," he thought. "A good thrashin's just what he needs."

Shadrack did not see Bob's approach.

"WHACK!" went the *Family Herald*.

"BOING!" went the banjo.

"What the . . . "

"WHACK! WHACK! WHACK!"

"Stop it!"

"Take that (WHACK!) you little bastard . . . and that (WHACK!)."

Bob Nash hit Shadrack on top of the head with the *Family Herald*. To Bob, it felt very good. To Shadrack, it stung and startled him so that he dropped the banjo. Shad knew from experience, from the look in Bob's eyes, that he was in for a thrashing. Shad was uncertain about what he had done to deserve it, but he knew it was too late to discuss it.

"WHACK! WHACK! WHACK! WHACK!"

Everytime Bob hit Shad, he felt better. The silence of the banjo and the "whack" of the *Family Herald* on Shad's body was like music to his ears, a pacifying symphony that conquered and replaced "Will The Circle Be Unbroken."

"I could do this all night," thought Bob. "WHACK, WHACK, WHACK . . . WHACK . . . a black eye, WHACK, a bloody nose, WHACK, a bruised arm: WHACK on the bum, WHACK on the leg, WHACK on the shoulder . . . . " Bob Nash, for the moment, was gloriously insane. The nagging wife and the lazy, banjo-playing boy had removed a brick from his structure; he had been pushed temporarily over the edge.

"WHACK, WHACK!"

At first, Shad saw it as just another beating, but soon enough he began to realize that things were getting out of control. He realized he was cornered, that there was no escape. He was being attacked by his father and was more than just a little leery about fighting back. He took a couple of more blows. They were getting harder and they weren't slowing down. There was a strange "wild" look in his father's eyes. Shad knew that he had to do something. "But what? I can't hit my father . . . ." "WHACK!"

Shadrack tensed his muscles and gathered his strength. He made a blind dive at Bob. "Thud!" It was like colliding with a load of bricks.

"WHACK! WHACK!"

Elva Nash watched contentedly. The beating was a tension release for her too. "Shad's getting what he deserves," she thought.

Once again Shad cringed and gathered his strength, and once again made a plunge. "Thump!" Bob Nash was still solid.

"Might as well run into a brick wall," thought Shad.

By now, Shad too had lost all reason. He started counting for his next attack. "One, two, three . . . " He could have been counting bricks.

At the count of three, Shad's foot connected with Bob's crotch, a definite weak point in the wall. On the count of four the *Family Herald* loosened and fell from Bob's hand. On the count of five, Shad saw his father fall to this knees in agony — "Thump!" like a load of bricks. On the count of six, Shadrack dashed for the door. Seven, eight . . . . On the count of nine, Shad glanced over his shoulder to see if he was being pursued. He saw Bob Nash kneeling, holding on to himself. Shad gave a frightened glance at his astonished mother.

"Dad's a brick short of a load!" he yelled, and ran from the house.

*

Dryfly returned to Nutbeam's camp with a pencil, paper and envelopes. He sat at the table across from Nutbeam and the two began to contrive a letter. The letter was to Johanna Banks in Mars Hill, Maine.

"What d'ya want to say?" asked Dryfly.

"You ready?"

"Yep. All ready."

"Dear Johannah, how are you, I am fine, hope you are the same. Dryfly is writing this letter for me. What's going on in

Mars Hill? Was it a good year for potatoes? Is Ned dead yet? How's Willy? I am fine and living in Canada. How's Alex and Norah?"

Nutbeam ran out of things to say. "What'll I say now?" He asked.

"Ah . . . how about the weather? Tell'er how the weather is."

"The weather's good. How's the weather in Mars Hill? It was cold here last night. It will soon be winter."

Dryfly wrote down Nutbeam's dictations with many misspellings and little punctuation.

"Ya think that's enough?" asked Nutbeam when Dryfly had scratched out the word "winter."

"I don't know . . . maybe."

"Put, 'Yours, Nutbeam' on it and that'll do."

Dryfly finished off the letter and put it in an envelope. He wrote "Johanna Banks, Mars Hill, Maine" on it and sealed it.

"Ya want me to mail it for ya, Nutbeam?"

"No, no, that's alright. I'll mail it."

"Wouldn't be any trouble."

"No, that's alright, I'll mail it."

Nutbeam held the letter up and looked at it proudly. He then took it to the shelf beside the stove and laid it down carefully, as if it was breakable, beside a pot. He put a block of birch in the stove and went back to the table. He turned the lamp down a bit. The fire in the stove lulled them with snaps and crackles. The camp was cozy and warm.

"Thanks for writing that letter, Dry. You're a good lad."

"No trouble. Any time."

*

A knock sounded at Nutbeam's door.

"That you, Shad?" yelled Nutbeam.

"It's me, Shadrack," came the muffled voice through the door.

Nutbeam unlatched and opened the door and in stepped the battered and bruised Shadrack Nash. He was limping and had a bloody nose and a swollen eye. The eye was already starting to turn black.

"What you run into, a bear?" asked Dryfly.

"Dad's gone crazy! . . . Beat me up!" panted Shad. "Kicked him in the nuts! . . . I'm done for!"

"You kicked Bob in the nuts?" Dryfly was amazed.

"I'm a dead man! He'll kill me! He'll stomp me into the ground! He'll chew me up and spit me out! He'll . . . "

"Holy dyin'!" said Dryfly, "he'll shoot ya sure as hell! What're ya gonna do?!"

"I don't know, I don't know, I don't know," said Shad, like Lindon Tucker. "I'm dead, I'm dead, I'm dead, I'm dead . . . !"

Shadrack paced back and forth in the tiny camp until Dryfly jumped up and told him to sit down. Shad sat in Dryfly's chair, his breath coming in puffs that caused the lamp to flutter. Nutbeam's ears seemed to flap like wings in the dancing light.

"Take it easy," said Nutbeam, "he'll get over it. He jist got ugly for awhile that's all."

"You don't know my father," said Shadrack. "He'll kill me and not think twice!"

"So, what are you gonna do?"

"Can't go home, I know that!"

"You'll have to hide out at my place," suggested Dryfly.

Shadrack was not thinking too clearly, but he knew immediately he did not want to stay at Shirley Ramsey's. Something like staying with Shirley Ramsey would not be at all good for the reputation. "No, that's all right. I'll think o' something," he said.

"You could maybe stay here with Nutbeam!" offered Dryfly. "This is a great hideout!"

"There's no place for ya to stay here," said Nutbeam.

"He could sleep on the floor," said Dryfly.

"Ya couldn' sleep on that old hard floor," said Nutbeam, "and besides, they'll come lookin' for 'im."

"But they'll never find him here!"

"They'll come lookin' and they'll find him!"

"They never found you!"

"That's different. They're not looking for me."

"I can't go home, I know that much."

"You go home and I bet yer father will've forgot all about it. He ain't out to kill ya. You shouldn't have kicked him anyway! You shouldn' kick yer father!"

"I had to, Nutbeam! He would've killed me!"

"I don't believe he would've killed ya."

"Maybe you'd let me stay for just a while," said Shadrack. "Just until I figure out what I should do."

"They'll come lookin' for ya," argued Nutbeam.

"Just for a couple o' days," said Shadrack.

"They'll find ya sure as hell."

"Just for tonight, then. I'll feel things out tomorrow."

"I don't like it."

"C'mon, Nutbeam, just for the night!"

"I don't know."

"Please?"

"Well . . . "

"Ah, thanks, Nutbeam! You're a pal!"

"Just for the night!"

*

When Lindon Tucker starts feeling his liquor, he likes to talk, or at least, likes to repeat the things other people say. Lindon was sitting at the bar. After the second double rye, he swung and eyed the gentleman sitting on the stool beside him. Lindon thought the gentleman was wearing either a black or purple suit; he wasn't sure, the room was dimly lit. He had a black vandyke beard, but otherwise, his head was as bald as an egg. He had one of those timeless faces. Lindon couldn't tell if he was thirty-five or much older. Oddly, for the lighting was very low, the gentleman wore sunglasses, hiding whatever lines of wisdom, happiness and pain (age) the eyes might have revealed.

Lindon scanned the candle-lit room, then came back to eye the stranger whose glasses reflected the light like cat eyes.

"How come yer warin' smoked glasses in here?" asked Lindon.

"Shade. I like the shade." The gentleman's voice was soft and deep.

"Oh, yeah. Shade, yeah. OK. Shade."

The gentleman was eyeing Lindon's mackinaw, which he didn't remove despite the room's exceptional warmth.

"Are you cold?" he asked.

"Oh, yeah. Yeah. Cool enough, yeah."

The gentleman removed his eyes from Lindon and lifted his head as if to eye someone across the room.

"Lookin' for someone? What're ya lookin' at ? Ya could see better without them glasses on."

"A lovely lady across the way."

"Ha, ha, ha, yes, sir. Yes. Oh yeah, yep. Quite the lady, yep. You from around here, are ya?"

"I'm from . . . the south," said the gentleman.

"Hot country? Hot country? Hot country?"

"It can get hot. It can get very hot."

"What do ya do fer a livin'?"

"I'm a musician. I play the violin."

"Yeah? Yeah? Like the fiddle, you mean?"

"Yes. Like the fiddle." The gentleman nodded toward the corner of the room to where a small triangular stage was located. "I'm here tonight," he said.

"Good, good, good. Like the fiddle. Always liked the fiddle. Play somethin' fer us. Give us a tune. You know 'Mutty Musk,' do ya?"

"I'm not familiar with it. Perhaps I could play you something else."

"Sure, sure, sure. Don't matter. Anything at all."

The gentleman checked his watch. "It's about time," he said. Standing up, he nodded farewell to Lindon, nodded to the lady across the room and headed for the stage.

In a minute the gentleman and two other musicians started to play. Lindon was not familiar with the melody and he thought it was unbearably loud. But as if he were in a Miramichi dance-hall, he commenced to stomp his feet and whoop. "Drive 'er!" he yelled. "Walk back on'er! Whoop! Yea-whooooo! Keep 'er close to the floor!"

Then Lindon felt the eyes upon him. There were more people

looking at him than at the men on the stage. He quieted down and ordered another drink.

"Sober crowd," he said. "The music ain't that great, anyway."

The bartender served Lindon another drink, which he tossed back as if it were water. He chased it once again with ale. He was feeling very good and wanted to talk to someone, but he noticed that nobody was sitting near him at the bar. He contemplated moving to another seat and eyed the room for a likely place. He spotted the lady the fiddle player had been eyeing and was surprised that she was eyeing him. He nodded. She nodded back. He winked. She smiled.

"Hm," he thought. "If I had another drink, I'd give that lady a little rub."

He ordered and was served once again. He tossed the rye back, eyeing the woman all the while. He felt he nearly had enough confidence. One more drink and he'd confront her.

But then, to his surprise, the middle-aged woman with the red hair and dark-rimmed glasses, left her table and moved to the stool next to Lindon. She ordered a screwdriver and lit a Rothman's.

Lindon eyed her with blurred vision.

The woman saw Lindon staring, smiled and said: "Hi."

Lindon leaned toward her and shouted above the music. "Havin' a little drink, are ya?"

The woman nodded and smiled. "From around here?" she asked.

"Brennen Siding!" he yelled. "Brennen Siding! Blackville!"

"Oh! You're from God's country."

"The Devil's country, devil's country, devil's country, more like it! Ho! Ha, ha, ha! Boys! Ya havin' a little drink, are ya?"

The screwdriver was served and the woman started digging into her purse for money. She removed her gloves, a make-up kit, a package of Spearmint gum and a handkerchief. She removed a little black book, her eyeglass case and a ring of keys. The bartender waited patiently. From her purse, the woman removed a pen, a cigarette lighter, several kleenex, a nail file and a hair brush. Her wallet was the last thing to be removed.

"How much?" asked the woman.

"Same as before. $1.25."

"Oh, my goodness," said the lady. "I seem to be out of cash. Would you cash a check for me?"

"I'm sorry, Ma'am. It's against the rules."

"Well, what am I to do?"

"I'll have to take your drink back, Ma'am."

"Oh! I'm so embarassed!"

"I'll get that," said Lindon. "I'll get that. Let me buy that . . . hic . . . how much?"

"$1.25."

Lindon paid for the drink and noticed that the woman seemed impressed with the wad of bills. She inched her stool closer to Lindon's.

"Thank-you very much," she said.

"No trouble, no trouble, no trouble. There's lots more where that came from."

"Oh! What do you do for a living?"

"Nothin', nothin', nothin'! Don't have to work. Guide some. Don't have to work!"

Lindon Tucker was wearing heavy woollen (APH) pants and a plaid Mackinaw coat. Lindon Tucker with his pot belly, unshaven face and missing cuspids, did not look like a doctor, or a lawyer.

"Oh," said the woman. "I'd have thought you was a doctor or a lawyer."

"No, no, no; could, could, could, might, might, ya never know, might. Bartender! Get me and this here little lady another drink."

"You shouldn't be spending your money on me," said the woman sweetly, placing her hand on Lindon's thigh.

"Lots more where that come from! Make them big ones, bartender! Never mind them little sips! Make 'em big ones!"

The bartender poured them two doubles and sat them in front of Lindon and the woman. "Nine dollars," he said.

"Nine dollars!" exclaimed Lindon.

"Yeah, they're triples."

"Oh, oh, oh well then." Lindon paid the bartender.

An hour went by and Lindon grew more and more intoxicated. The woman got prettier and prettier, and very, very friendly. It became quite clear to Lindon that she wanted him to get a room in the hotel.

At first he didn't know how to bring the issue up, but a couple of more doubles looked after that little holdup.

"What d'ya say we get a room, little lady?" said Lindon.

"Oh, my goodness, I hardly know you!"

"Get to know me, git to know me! Git to know me in a room!"

"Well, I guess I could party a little bit. Got any booze?"

"Booze?"

"Vodka, rye, rum, something to drink?"

"No, but there's lot's of it here! Could get it here!"

"Would you be so kind as to sell my friend here a bottle of vodka, bartender?" said the woman.

"I'd have to sell it by the ounce," cautioned the bartender.

"Give us some vodker!" yelled Lindon.

The bartender reached under the bar and sat up a forty ounce bottle of vodka. "Fifty dollars." he said.

The music had been wearing on Lindon. He hadn't liked one tune the band played all evening. But, as he left the room with his little lady, he heard them playing the first tune he was familiar with: "The Devil's Dream." Lindon whooped as he was going through the door.

At the front desk, after paying for a room, Lindon noticed that he only had seventy-five dollars left. His only comment was: "Jesus."

He was more than just a little upset, but he decided to worry about the spending later. "Right now, there's something else that needs spending," he thought.

"You know somethin' (hic) darlin'?" said Lindon, as they entered room 405, "I don't even know yer (hic) name."

"Call me Molly, darlin'."

"MOLLY, MY NAME'S LINDON TUCKER! THE BEST MAN

TO EVER SHIT A TURD IN THE DUNGARVON RIVER! HA, HA, HA, WHOOP!"

"You sit on the bed, darlin', and I'll pour us a drink."

Molly found two glasses in the bathroom and poured them each a drink. She poured one ounce in her own drink and topped it off with water. In Lindon's glass, she poured five ounces of straight vodka. She delivered Lindon his drink, they toasted (clink). "Down the hatch," she said and drank her glass empty. Not to be outdone by a little lady, Lindon downed his glass also.

For five minutes, Lindon raved, fondled and boasted; then he went to sleep.

Molly took Lindon's seventy-five dollars. She took his pocket watch and Zippo lighter. She considered taking the rest of the vodka. "Why not?" she said, "I might need it for another sucker at the bar."

As she was leaving the room, she said, "Good-night, Lindon," to the best man to ever shit a turd in the Dungarvon River.

*

Shadrack stayed up as late as he could and talked to Nutbeam. Nutbeam stayed awake much longer than he wanted to, talking to Shadrack. At four o'clock a.m., Shad sat on Nutbeam's cot, yawning. At five o'clock, Shadrack was fast asleep on Nutbeam's cot. Nutbeam only had the one cot and therefore had no place to sleep. He was left sitting alone at the table. The lamp beside him was turned low, so that Nutbeam appeared as a silhouette with an incredibly strange face. His big lips gave him a negroid appearance, although his white skin and blue eyes denied any possibility of black ancestry. His ears in the shadow on the wall behind him made him look like a Labrador Retriever. His nose was so long that two of him back to back would have looked like a pickaxe. Nutbeam was staring at the letter Dryfly had written for him.

Dryfly had tried his best to write well, but the address, crooked and slanted, indicated he needed much practice.

"I wish I could write good like that," thought Nutbeam.

Nutbeam didn't like the fact that Shadrack had stolen his

cot, but he figured it would soon be time to rise anyway. Nut-beam knew that Shadrack couldn't possibly stay with him for very long and that Shadrack surely knew that too. With a fleeting inspection, one could easily see that the camp was not designed to accommodate more than one person. Nutbeam had an idea for Shadrack and planned to tell him as soon as he awakened. For the moment, though, going to the post office had to be planned.

"If she laughs," he thought, "I'll just pretend I don't know what she's laughin' at. I'll buy a stamp and tell her . . . tell her . . . tell her I like her dress or somethin'." Nutbeam knew that conversation with Shirley would not be easy. To Nutbeam, Shirley Ramsey was a beautiful woman and he was an ugly man. "No ugly man ever won the heart of a beautiful woman," he thought.

"If I could get that woman," he thought, "I'd be the happiest man in the world. I'd make her happy, too. I'd fix up the house and build a permanent woodshed. There'd be enough room in the shed to keep enough wood to last a year, plus room to hang a couple of deer and a moose. I'd plant whatever land she has with potatoes and vegetables and build a root cellar in the gravel pit. If I could get that woman, I wouldn't care if people laughed at me. I'd take her to dances in the village and to church on Sundays . . . and I'd get some nice clothes to wear . . . maybe I'd even buy that old farm and this woodlot from Graig Allen, build a barn, a new house, the works. Dryfly could live with us and sing to us at nights. Other nights, while Dry's running the roads, we could sit and talk 'till maybe twelve o'clock and then go to bed."

To go to bed with somebody, to actually feel the warmth of another body next to his, to reach out in the night and find somebody beside him and to make love to somebody had never been anything more than fantasy for Nutbeam.

*

Shadrack awakened to the smell of bacon frying. Nutbeam was cooking them a breakfast of bacon, eggs and biscuits.

"Mornin' Nutbeam. Sorry 'bout takin yer bed. Guess I must've fell asleep."

"Don't matter. Had some figurin' to do, anyway."

The two sat at the table and ate. Conversation was nothing more than an occasional comment. Shadrack had talked himself out during the night and had only slept a couple of hours. He was sore, his clothes were crumpled, he was homeless and broke, there was nothing much to say. Nutbeam had something to say, but the presence of the weary boy sitting across from him, shoulders slumped with the stress of guilt, fear and emptiness, gave the matter a certain delicacy that needed time. Nutbeam would hold off until after breakfast.

Shadrack ate slowly, giving each morsel the consideration of a scrambling mind. Over a bit of bacon, he looked around the tiny camp. "It's mornin' and the sun is high in the sky," he thought, "but it's always night time in here."

When you go to bed at four or five in the morning after a night's rendezvous with the river and sky, you find yourself dreamed out, and so you dream a dreamless sleep. The river creeps into your soul, like a god or a demon, sought on possessing you and holding you in her lush valleys. Shad had been playing on the river a great deal for the past several months and had found great comfort and joy in its grasp, but now the river was starting to reject him. It's just not the same in the autumn. The river tends to give you the cold shoulder after her bout with the frosts and the northeast rains. Shad was losing his friend, the river, and the time spent was being replaced by the restlessness of the idle. He had replaced the river with the banjo and was playing it fanatically. He was plucking fantastic, mind-boggling little melodies from the strings and flew off with them into dreams. Bob Nash found the banjo playing a beautiful thing, an accomplishment for his boy. But in his envy, it was a rasp that constantly filed his nerves, driving him from the house, or more drastically, into the arms of Elva. Bob Nash found that the Elva he once loved was not there anymore. Elva was a bitch, Shad played the banjo and Bob was given to fits of argument and temper — no warmth, no communication, no love — an unfit place to live.

Over a bit of egg, Shad eyed Nutbeam — the mysterious, tall man who looked like an elf, who lived alone in a tiny camp with no windows that smelled of kerosene and woodsmoke — Nutbeam, the Todder Brook Whooper, the man who haunted everyone in Brennen Siding in one way or another. This man was like the river — he summoned dreams from within you. Where John Kaston claimed to know the Lord, Shadrack Nash could claim to know Nutbeam. Nutbeam was something for Shadrack to hold on to.

Shadrack hadn't held or kissed his mother and father since he was five years old. It was the absence of love, warmth and communication that sent him to the river, Nutbeam and Dryfly.

After breakfast, Nutbeam opened the door to let the light of day in. He cleared the breakfast dishes from the table and replaced them with two tin cups. He poured the tea and sat to confront Shadrack.

"Shad," he began, "I've been thinking."

"Yeah?"

"I've been thinking about letters."

"Letters?"

"Yeah. Writin' letters. Kin you write a letter, Shad?"

"I s'pose, I don't know."

"I can't," said Nutbeam.

"I know. So?"

"So, I wish I had gone to school."

"So, why didn' ya?"

"Because I was weak."

"You was weak, Nutbeam?"

"When I tried to go to school, everyone laughed and made fun o' me. The other kids thought I was a freak and threw rocks at me, wouldn' let me into their games, and I . . . I use to think it was them that was weak." Nutbeam grinned thoughtfully and shook his head negatively. "Wasn't them, Shad, it was me that was weak. I was too weak to stand up to them."

"So you didn' go back to school anymore?"

"You know, Shad, I've been thinkin' a lot lately. I've been thinkin' that I got the best ears of any man in this whole world. I've been thinking that I should've held me head right back and stepped into that school like I owned it; walked around not just like I was as good as everybody else, but better. Hey boy, I can hear a robin sing from across the river! I kin hear a deer walkin' from a hundred yards away! I kin hear yer heart beatin'!"

"So, what are ya comin' at, Nutbeam?"

"I think they would've left me alone after a while if I hadn' been so weak. I think I would've had friends and maybe even a woman. But, instead, I crawled back here in this camp, no good to anyone, even meself."

Nutbeam rose from the table and walked to the open door. He stood thoughtfully for a moment, gazing at the generous colors of autumn in the forest around him.

"You like girls, Shad?"

"Pretty likely."

"When I was fifteen I wanted a girl so bad that I use to wish on the evening star and pray to the moon. One night, I was walking and a heart-shaped cloud drifted up so that the moon looked as if it was framed by a heart. I took it as an omen that said, 'Don't worry, Nutbeam old boy, love will come to you.'"

"And did it?"

"A few days later I met this girl I'd never seen before. She was very nice to me; said she was stayin' at a neighbor's house and that she would like for me to come a callin'. She said she'd be waitin' in the kitchen for me at eight o'clock."

"So, did ya go?"

"Yep. I went and knocked on the kitchen door at eight o'clock, feeling on top o' the world. Can you imagine how I felt, knowing that a pretty little lady was waiting for me inside?"

"Yeah, sort of."

"Can you imagine how it felt when I found out that it wasn't a girl at all, but one of a bunch of boys that were playin' a trick on me? The girl opened the door slightly and talked sweet-talk to me for a minute, then threw the door open all the way to reveal six other boys all laughing their heads off."

"So did you hit the bastard?"

"No! I was too weak! I crawled into a deeper hole and cried for two weeks! Are you gonna do that, Shad? Are you gonna crawl into a hole and live in the woods like me?"

"Well . . . I . . . I . . ."

"Shad, what I'm sayin' to ya is, get off your ass!"

"So, what am I to do?"

"I think you should start goin' to school! You're a smart lad, Shad! You could be an engineer some day!"

"You're starting to sound like me mother!" said Shad.

"Then maybe you should be listenin' to yer mother!"

"My mother don't know nothin'! She ain't never been anywhere!"

"Just like you'll be, if ya don't go to school."

Shadrack was beginning to sweat a little. He did not expect this line of talk from Nutbeam and he did not like what he was hearing.

"But why would I wanna go back to school?!"

"Because you don't wanna live like me, a hermit for the rest of your life!"

"Ah, you're crazy!"

"A little bit crazy, maybe, and you'll be a little crazy too, if you live alone long enough! What about the girls, Shad? Do you think that a girl wants a man with no schoolin' and lives in a cave in the woods?"

"No."

"You like workin' in the woods, Shad?"

"No."

"You think you're ever gonna git a job doin' anything else, with schoolin' like you got?"

"No . . . maybe, I don't know!"

"Put it this way, Shad: you'd have it easy! As long as you went to school, you wouldn' be expected to work in the woods. You'd be hangin' around with young girls everyday and everyone would look up to you. You'd have 'er made!"

"I don't want to talk about it, Nutbeam. I thought you and me was friends!"

"We are friends, Shad. You and Dryfly are the only friends I got."

"So, leave me alone!"

"Well, you think about what I've said," said Nutbeam.

Nutbeam saw he had talked enough. Shadrack had a contrary nature; to push him would only make matters worse.

"You think about it, Shad. I'm goin' for a walk."

Nutbeam stepped into the autumn day feeling more confident than he'd ever felt before in his life; his talk to Shad had been good therapy. With the letter addressed to Johannah Banks in his hip pocket, he headed for the Post Office. He walked to the edge of the forest and for the first time in nearly nine years, stepped out without concern for who might see him.

On the footbridge, Nutbeam came face to face with Lindon Tucker.

"Hello, Lindon," he said.

"G'day, G'day, G'day, G'day," said Lindon.

Lindon was in a good mood. He was home again. Any other time, he might have been nervous in the presence of Nutbeam, but today, Nutbeam could have been an old friend.

Lindon's pleasantness, his I'm-happy-just-to-see-you attitude, encouraged Nutbeam. "This is going to be a good day," he thought.

fourteen

The Cabbage Island Salmon Club Camps were vacant and closed for the winter. They would re-open on April 15th, when the club members and guests returned to fish the black salmon.

Shadrack sat on the same veranda where he'd sat with Lillian Wallace. The river was quiet and uneventful — no swimming or canoeing, no fishermen laughing, talking and wading about. The river, too, was closed for the winter.

Shadrack had the worst case of depression he'd ever had. "Dad and Mom don't love me, Dryfly stole the only woman I've ever loved and now Nutbeam's turned agin me! The homely bastard! They all want me to do what they want," he thought.

Shad knew that Nutbeam's suggestion to go back to school was practical enough and would probably solve most of his problems, but Shadrack Nash did not like being manipulated and told what to do. If he went back to school, the decision to do so would have to be his own. "If I go back to school, I'll have to go suckin' up to Mom and Dad," he thought. "What I really should do is leave. Run away and never come back."

"No sense runnin' away," thought Shad. "I got no money and I got no schoolin'! I might as well be dead! I'll jump in the river and drown. I'll drown and wash up on the shore for someone to find all bird-picked and wormy like Bonzie Ramsey was when .they found him. They'll be sorry then, I bet ya!"

Shadrack Nash was very depressed, but he was not suicidal. He was too curious about the future, the cars, the money, the women to seriously consider death.

"Maybe I could get into one of these camps and stay for a while," he thought. "If I stay here and sneak around like Nutbeam, they might all think I'm dead, anyway. They could look for me all they wanted, but they'd never find me. They'll drag the river and everything. Dad and Mom will cry their hearts out thinkin' they beat me the last time they saw me."

Shadrack rose and started checking the windows. He checked all the windows on three cabins before he found one that was slightly ajar. He opened it and climbed over the sill. He was in! He looked about at the paintings of wildlife, the mounted deer-heads and salmon; at the sofas and chairs, at the carpets and fireplace.

"Hello! No house, I suppose! I suppose I ain't got no place to hide out!"

Shadrack inspected the cabin. In the living-room, he found dozens of books, a rack completely stacked with rifles and shotguns. A drawer underneath the rifle rack was filled with boxes of ammunition. He found fishing rods and boxes of fly-hooks and a full case of various kinds of liquor. In a bedroom drawer, he found three dollars and change that someone had obviously forgotten about.

Shad cracked the seal on a bottle of Glen Livet and took a drink. He sat on the sofa, put his feet on the coffee table and sized up the situation.

"No food," he thought. "I'll have to figure out a way of gettin' food. There's everything else here, though."

Shadrack guzzled another drink. The depression drifted off into oblivion.

"I got 'er made," he thought.

*

Nutbeam walked to Shirley Ramsey's with powerful, deliberate strides. He did not once stop. He did not dare to stop. To stop, even for an instant, might give the old inferiority complex a chance to slip into his plans, to undermine his determination. Nutbeam knew himself very well. He knew the limitations of his confidence. He was following providence. He had no specific course of action. His confidence was holding up quite well as of yet (he hadn't shied away from Lindon Tucker), but Lindon Tucker was not his concern. Shirley Ramsey would be the ultimate test.

And then there was the house. And then there was the door. His heart was pounding from a combination of walking fast and the excitement of seeing Shirley Ramsey. He knocked.

"Come in."

The voice was muffled from the depths of the house, but Nutbeam could hear it loud and clear. He heard its softness, its femininity — the Goddess had spoken.

"Come in," came the gentle feminine voice once again. Yes, the voice was gentle and feminine, but to Nutbeam it could have been the thunderous bellow of a goddess who could tear him apart.

Nutbeam turned the knob, then let it go quickly, as though it was red hot and had burned him. He heard Shirley's footsteps approaching from inside. She was only a few steps from the door. He eyed the corner of the house and contemplated hiding.

The door opened and there before him stood the Goddess in her hand-me-down dress. The Goddess was as afraid of Nutbeam as he was of her.

When Shirley opened the door to see Nutbeam standing on her step, she didn't know what to do. Her ability to speak leaped from her mouth and into thin air.

"The mysterious man from the woods! He's come to kill me, sure as hell!" she thought.

Nutbeam couldn't find words either, but he was together enough to know that something had to be done. He handed her the letter.

"I . . . I . . . I . . . " tried Nutbeam.

Shirley looked down at the envelope.

"Five cents," she said.

"Fi . . . five cents?"

"The stamp."

Nutbeam started frantically searching his pockets for a coin. There wasn't any. He came up with a five dollar bill, handed it to her.

"I'll get your change," said Shirley and practically ran into the Post Office. She opened her cash box and fumbled through the few bills and coins. She dropped a quarter, made a dive for it, stumbled and nearly fell. She glanced over her shoulder to make sure that Nutbeam hadn't followed her into the office. She managed to count out $4.95, took a deep breath and went back to the open door.

"Your change," she said, but there was nobody there. Nutbeam had vanished.

*

Dryfly removed Lillian's letter from its hiding place under the mattress, unfolded it and commenced to read. He read from beginning to end, then went to the word "love" and eyed it thoughtfully.

He heard a knock on the door.

"Who could that be?" he asked himself. "Nobody knocks around here."

Dryfly was lying on the bed. He heard Shirley responding to the knock, so did not bother to rise.

Dryfly sniffed the letter. When it first arrived he could detect the slight scent of perfume, or perhaps fly repellent. The letter was now ragged and crumpled and the scent of whatever it was was long gone. Dryfly closed his eyes, visualized Lillian's lips, and kissed the letter.

"If you could only read my thoughts," he thought. "I love you, Lillian. I must write to you. But . . . what will I say?"

Dryfly rose, found a scribbler and pencil, then returned to his bed. Lying down, which did nothing to improve his calligraphy, he began to write:

Dear Lillian,

How are you? I am fine. Hope you are the same.

Dryfly wanted to spill his heart. He wanted to say: I miss you and I love you, but instead he wrote, "It was good to hear from you." He wanted to say: I'm crazy about you and I need you, but instead he wrote "It's been a good fall. The sun is shining here today. How's your father?" Dryfly wanted to spill his heart, but instead he wrote about Shadrack, his mother, Palidin and Nutbeam. He wrote about the river, the hunting season, the autumn colors and the fact that new boards were needed on the footbridge.

He finished the letter off by saying: "Hope to see you next summer. Love, Dryfly."

"It's a good letter," he thought, "I've managed to squeeze in the word 'love.' "

He folded and fit the letter into an envelope, addressed it and went to the kitchen to give it to Shirley to mail. He didn't have a nickel for a stamp, but he knew that Shirley would send it off for him.

"Who was that at the door, Mom?" he asked.

"You'd never believe it!"

"Who?"

"That Nutbeam fella'."

"Nutbeam? Here?"

"Yeah. Wanted to mail a letter. Give me five dollars and left without his change."

"Did he say anything?"

"No. I came in here to get his change and when I went back to the door, he was gone."

"Odd."

"Yeah. It was."

"Would you stamp this letter for me, Mom?"

Shirley took the letter and read the name and address.

"You think about her a lot, don't you, Dry?"

"Some."

"She's a fine lady. Pretty, too," said Shirley, then thought, "She'll never get caught with the likes of one o' us."

Shirley stamped the envelope.

"What do ya make o' Nutbeam?" she asked.

"Don't know. Wanted to mail a letter, I guess."

"The letter was to somebody in Maine. He's got floppy ears, Dry. You'd have laughed to see him."

"Did you laugh?"

"No, I was too scared to laugh."

"That's good."

"Have you ever seen him, Dry?"

"Yeah, I've seen him. He's alright. He won't hurt ya. He's a nice lad, really."

"I wonder why he didn't wait for the change?"

*

The Italians make a cigar that is too strong to inhale. They're about three inches long and tapered. They're hard on the outside. They're good for smoking while you fish. They don't absorb moisture from your hands and when it's raining, they'll stay lit longer. They also smell like the dickens and keep away pesty insects like mosquitoes and blackflies. Parodys, they're called. Shadrack found a box of Parodys on the mantle.

He lit one up and flew into a fit of coughing. "Not bad!" he thought.

Shad puffed on the smelly cigar and nipped straight from the bottle, the Glen Livet. Shad was not a thief at heart. He would never steal anything he thought anyone would care about. He figured the American owners of the Cabbage Island Salmon Club were rich and would never miss the scotch or the cigars and therefore, it was perfectly alright to take it. "They prob'ly don't even know they left it here," he thought.

Shad had sat to think, but something was toying with his concentration. He found himself much too happy to give much thought to being depressed. How could one think seriously about running away or committing suicide, while grinning from ear to ear? Instead of thinking about his problems, he carried his scotch to the big window that faced the river, had another nip and bit on the cigar.

"My name's Shaddy Nashville," he said. "I'm a zecative in the nylon industry. I'm from Bangah Maine."

Shadrack started to sing: "I once had a sweetheart, but now I got none! She's gone and left me for somebody neeeeeeeew! La, la, la, la, la, la, la to the red, white and blue! Whoop!"

"Ladies and gentlemen! Star of stage and screen! The great Shadrack Nash!"

Another little nip.

"Hey, boy! Fetch ma Wada's and auvis! I'm goin' to the riva!" Shad's fabrication of the American accent was better than he knew. Shad didn't care if his accent was correct or not. Shad didn't give a fiddler's wink about anything.

"Are you mine, rich or poor? Tell me darlin' are ya sure? La, la, la, la, la, . . . whoopo! WE HAW AND HER NAME WAS MAUD!"

In his mind, Shad was not standing alone in an empty cottage. In his mind, he was facing an audience of thousands of people. He was a powerful performer, with an audience so captivated he could do whatever he wanted and they'd be pleased.

"Ladies and gen'lmen, I don't give a damn about anything," he shouted. "The whole world can go piss up a stump, for all I care! WHOOP! When I was but a little boy before I went to school, I had a fleet of forty sail, I called the ships o' yule! Ya'll like that, ladies and gen'lemen? Ya'll like me little poem?!! Thank you, thank you, thank you!"

Then something made a noise in the kitchen. It sounded to Shad like something falling from a shelf. It startled Shad into silence. He stopped to listen.

"Hello?" he called.

Suddenly, although he was glowing from the scotch and a little breathless from his performance, the cabin seemed cold and clammy — too quiet. He had the sensation that someone was looking over his shoulder. The cigar was getting to him, so that when he stopped to listen, all he could hear was his own wheezing lungs.

"Is there someone in the kitchen?" he yelled. "Cause if there is, ya'd better show yerself, 'cause Shadrack Nash ain't scared o' nothin'."

Still holding the Glen Livet, Shad made his way down the hall. The kitchen was across the hall from the bathroom. The bathroom door was shut. Shad debated whether the door had been open or shut when he'd passed it during his earlier exploration of the cabin.

"Had to be closed," he thought. "Nobody here but me."

He stepped into the kitchen.

Nothing unusual. He couldn't see anything out of place. Nothing visible had fallen.

"Must've been a rat," he thought. "A mouse, or a rat in the cupboard."

"Here's to ya, rat!" He toasted and drank from the bottle. The scotch gave him courage. He stepped back into the hall. He opened the bathroom door.

Empty.

He flicked the Parody butt into the toilet. There was no water in the toilet, but he missed anyway and the Parody stood on its end, straight up, on the edge of the porceline rim.

"Ha! I'd never do that again in a million years," he thought. "Ha! That's even more than you could lie about!"

Shad shrugged, snapped his fingers rhythmically and danced his way back to the livingroom, singing: "Oh, doe, doe, doe, dee, dee; dee yodle dodle day hee hoo; comoss evaw, my name is yod-lein' Euclid, dee yodle dodle day hee hoo!" This time he sang louder, with more gusto, as if he were playing to a noisy, difficult audience. He especially chose the song "Yodeling Euclid" as an attention getter.

And when he stepped back into the livingroom, there, star-ing at him, sad, and undignified, was his audience — the salmon, the moosehead, the deerhead.

Where at first they had looked majestic and beautiful, they now looked grotesque and . . . undignified. They stared at him with unblinking eyes, watching his every move, hating him for what he was; hating him for being human. On the deerhead, you could actually see the seam where the throat had been cut.

"Dryfly," whispered Shad. "I wish Dryfly was here." He might as well have said: "No man is an island."

He was being scrutinized by the mounted animals; he was alone; the cabin was cold and damp; he heard another noise in the kitchen! This time it sounded like something scratching, like a puppy at the door.

Shad knew there were no puppies in Brennen Siding.

He contemplated investigating, decided against it. "I just checked it," he thought.

Shad hurriedly filled his pockets with Parodys, the mounted animals watching him all the while . . . and perhaps other eyes as well, he wasn't sure. He just had the feeling that he might get caught. He felt he had to work quickly.

He took some Parodys, the money and last, but not least, a bottle of Canadian Club whiskey.

He headed for Shirley Ramsey's.

*

Nutbeam entered his camp and shut the door. Lately, he had been lighting the lamp more often, but today he did not. The darkness and gloom of the camp fit his mood. He lay down on the cot.

"I made a fool of myself," he thought. "She must be laughing her head off."

He closed his eyes and envisioned Shirley standing in the doorway . . . small, somewhat afraid.

"I've ruined it all," he thought. " I should've known that nothin' good would ever happen to me!"

The cot was comfortable and Nutbeam was feeling very tired.

"Why did I run?" he asked himself. "Why was I so afraid of her? Did she see how scared I was? Did I really make a fool of myself? But . . . she didn't laugh . . . she didn't laugh."

"I'm alone," he whispered to the camp. "I'm all alone."

Nutbeam slept and dreamed of running on a footbridge that ran into infinity. He ran and ran and ran.

Knock, knock, knock.

"Huh?"

"Nutbeam, old boy!"

"Huh?"

"Hey, Nutbeam, chummy pard!"

Still half asleep, Nutbeam unlatched the door and let Shadrack and Dryfly in.

Shadrack was carrying a bottle of whiskey, the contents of which had been half consumed. Both Shadrack and Dryfly reeked of the rye. Dryfly was carrying his guitar.

"What're ya doin' in the dark, Nutbeam?"

"I was sleepin'," said Nutbeam, yawning so that his big, wide-open mouth was like a black hole amid the gloom.

Nutbeam lit the lamp.

"Have a drink, Nutbeam, old dog! Clean 'er up! There's lot's more where that come from!"

"Where'd ya git it?" asked Nutbeam. Nutbeam knew by the size of the bottle and the quality of the rye that they hadn't bought it at the bootlegger's.

"Don't you worry 'bout where we got it, old pal! Here, chummy pard, have a cigar!"

Nutbeam had only slept for two hours and hadn't eaten since morning. The rye shot through his system so that he could feel the effects of the first small drink. It was good. He took another drink, and then a bigger one, and one more. The party began.

When the rye was empty, Shad reached outside the door and pulled in a second bottle, broke the seal and passed it around.

The three were sitting at the table, and as all drunken conversations do, this one too got dangerously personal.

"Ya know, Nutbeam, you're the best lad in the world!" said Shad. "Nobody ever used me any better than you!"

"It's good havin' you boys around," said Nutbeam. "I've been alone for too long."

"You know (hic) what I did today, boys? . . . I wrote to Lillian Wallace! (hic) I love 'er (hic), you know that?!"

"I've been thinkin' over what you've been sayin', Nutbeam," said Shad, "and you're right! I should go back to school! I'm no jeesily good in the woods!"

At this point of the party, all three were more or less talking at the same time.

"Do you know what it's like being locked up in a place like this?!" said Nutbeam. "What'll happen when a man gets old?! No family! No woman! Alone!"

"I'm the lonesomest man in the world!" said Dryfly as if stating something so profound that he had to yell it out. "Do you have any (hic), do you have any idea what it's like to not be able to see or touch the woman you love?!"

"I know what it's like!" said Nutbeam. "You're damned right I know what it's like!"

"I'm gonna go back to school and rub all them women in Blackville, become rich and famous and own the Cabbage Island Salmon Club. Lay right back and drink and smoke cigars, do a little fishin'."

"I'm in love with her, I tell ya!"

"I'm in love with the most beautiful woman in the whole world!" shouted Nutbeam, as if he were arguing a point.

"If she's nearby, you gotter made," said Dryfly.

"She's near alright!"

"Mine's way the hell down in the States!"

"Then go to her, for Jesus sake!"

"Can't!"

"Go! Go! Tell 'er you love 'er! I would!" said Nutbeam.

"I'd have to go to Blackville school," said Shad. "Kin you just see me in that big school?!"

"Does she know you're in love (hic), in love with her?" asked Dry.

"No! No! No, she don't know!"

"You know what's wrong with you, Nutbeam? (hic) You gotta feriority comprex!"

"I'm goin' home and tellin' Mom I'm goin' back to school!" said Shad. "I'm tellin' her right now!"

"No! Wait! You can't go now! You're drunk, ya jeezer!"

"I went to see her, Dry. Went to see her and failed!" said Nutbeam, practically in tears.

"I heard Joe Louis on the radio, Nut. He said the first rule in boxin' is to never give up. You're just down, Nutbeam. Don't let Mom bother ya. You ain't beaten yet!"

"How'd you know I was talkin' 'bout yer mother?"

"I know a lot o' things, " said Dryfly.

*

Elva and Bob Nash sat in the parlour. Elva was knitting Shadrack a pair of mitts. Bob was rocking, thumping his heel on the floor each time the chair rocked forward.

They heard the kitchen door open, Shadrack's uneven footsteps. In a moment, Shad appeared in the parlour door. He was pale, his hair was messed up, he needed a bath and was obviously drunk.

"Mom? Dad? I'm . . . pretty drunk!" said Shadrack.

Neither Elva or Bob commented.

"I know you'll wanna . . . wanna beat me up, but . . . but, before ya do, I got somethin' to say."

"I don't want no sass from the likes of you!" said Bob.

"I n'ain't . . . ain't gonna ssshass ya. First thing Monday mornin', I'm goin' to ssschool!"

"Who in the hell you think you are, comin' in this house smellin' like dirty old liquor?!" snapped Elva.

"God damned tramp!" said Bob.

"Monday mornin', goin' to school to make somethin' o' meself."

"A little boy like you drinkin' that dirty old liquor! What's the world comin' to ?!"

"A big boy like you goin' back to school in . . . in grade seven! The other lads will be only half yer size!"

"I don't care," said Shad.

"You don't care! Boys! You don't care!" said Bob, then yelled: "It's about time you started to care!"

"You make me sick!" yelled Elva.

"Get into that bathroom and clean yerself up!" yelled Bob.

"School alright! You'll go to school or I'll skin you alive!" said Elva.

"And you won't be stayin' home and playin' hooky either!" said Bob.

"RIGHT NOW, I SAY!"

"DO AS YER TOLD!"

"NOW!"

Shad staggered to the bathroom, making no effort to hide his tears.

"All he needed was a good beatin'," said Bob.

fifteen

Nutbeam looked down at the fresh deer tracks at his feet. This was the fourth set of prints he'd seen in the last few hundred feet. "Four deer," he thought, "all heading toward the brook. These tracks should all lead to a trail sooner or later . . . a trail that they all follow."

Nutbeam followed the tracks for a hundred yards or so, and did, indeed, come to a path frequently travelled by deer. A lesser hunter would have followed the deer trail, but Nutbeam knew better. He sat to wait . . . Nutbeam knew you don't follow a deer — "Sit and wait and they come to you. Might take an hour, might take as long as two days, but they'll come," thought Nutbeam. Nutbeam sat with his back against a tree. He stood the cocked rifle beside him.

While waiting for the deer to show up, Nutbeam's mind was elsewhere. "The hunt's as good as over," he thought. "Deer are stupid." Shirley Ramsey, on the other hand, was a more perplexing matter. "This whole thing might work. If it doesn't, there's no harm done, anyway. All it'll do is make life a little easier."

There were no leaves left on the trees, so that Nutbeam had a clear view of the trail. The November wind prophesied winter. "It'll soon snow," thought Nutbeam. "Meat'll keep good from now on."

Nutbeam sat there for four hours and the sun was nesting well down in the northwest before he heard it.

"Snort" went the deer.

In one swift movement, Nutbeam grabbed his rifle and positioned himself.

"Calm down," he thought. "There's nothin' to be excited about."

He still couldn't see the deer, but he could hear it snort, and he could hear its hooves falling and crunching the dried leaves on the frozen ground. He waited.

"Crunch . . . crunch . . . crunch . . . snort . . . crunch."

The deer approached slowly, cautiously, sensing danger, smelling Nutbeam.

"It could be a human," said the deer, "but I'm not quite sure."

"Crunch . . . crunch . . . crunch . . . "

The deer poked its head from behind a fir tree.

"Sniff-sniff. I probably should flash my tail. There's definitely something at the foot of that tree up there. I'll circle around and see if I can get a better look at it."

The deer crunched its way to an easterly point where it could better see Nutbeam. "It's a human, alright," said the deer. "I guess I'd better flash and dash."

When the deer leaped, Nutbeam swiftly shouldered his rifle and pulled the trigger.

A gigantic bell went "BOING" in the deer's head; the legs buckled, the deer collapsed.

*

"Where ya goin'? asked Elva Nash.

"To Bernie Hanley's store."

"Got some money?"

"Dad gave me five dollars."

"Don't spend it all foolish."

"See ya later, Mom," said Shad, and stepped into the cool November evening. He was feeling good and stepping high; he had a sense of direction; it was Saturday night and he was bound for Blackville.

"I'm in with the in crowd! I go where the in crowd goes. I'm in with the in crowd, And I know what the in crowd knows!" sang Shad, loud, arrogantly.

Shad was not doing great in school; he had a lot of catching up to do. His higher-than-average intelligence and mild interest was helping him along, however, and things were improving. He would not pass at Christmas, but would probably grade in the spring.

His relationship with Bob and Elva was improving, too. It had required a simple solution; stay out of their presence as often as possible . . . .

As he was crossing the river on the footbridge, he noticed that the river was frozen almost completely in. There was but one hole in the ice, about twenty feet long and ten feet wide. It was six o'clock and nearly dark, and the hole appeared black, cold and forbidding in the blue-grey light.

"An air hole," thought Shad. "Could stay there all winter. Dangerous thing, an air hole." Shad was remembering a story about somebody who had walked into an air hole while crossing on the ice on a dark night. There was another story, too, about a child who had skated into one.

Shad made a mental note that the air hole was located just above Dr. MacDowell's cabin, in front of John Kaston's place. "I might be skating there later on in the winter," he thought.

Shad stopped on the center abutment for a minute to take in the twilit scenery. The river frozen had a new beauty to it — a ribbon of ice dividing farms and forests.

"I'd like to build a cabin on the river down in front of home sometime," he thought. "Of course, Dad'll probably sell the shore to a rich American. He could do with a thousand or two."

"See ya next spring, old river," he said. "See ya when you're thawed out agin."

*

Eleven men and boys stood around Bernie Hanley's store, eating chocolate bars and drinking Orange Crush.

"Soon be gettin' snow," said Dan Brennen.

"Oh yeah, yeah, yeah. Gonna snow for sure, Dan, yeah. Looks like snow tonight, I noticed, yeah, Dan old boy," said Lindon Tucker.

"Kind o' warm, though," said Bernie Hanley. "Might come in rain."

"Rain, yeah. That's true, yeah. Might come in rain, I was thinkin' too. That's right, yeah, Bernie, could come in rain."

"How was Fredericton, Lindon?" asked Bert Todder.

"Quite a place, quite a place. Lots o' women, lots o' women.

Lived right there on Pine Street, yeah. Went to the hotel one night, yeah, so I did, one night, yeah. Oh yeah, yeah, yeah. Hotel, yeah. Quite a place!"

"Women ain't much good, if ya can't get yer hands on them," chuckled Dan Brennen. "Did ya get your hands on them, Lindon?"

"Got me hands on them all right! No trouble there! Ha, ha, ha, ha! Got me hands on them alright, Dan old boy. There's, there's, there's, there's no trouble passin' the hand on them ladies!"

All the men laughed. For the moment, Lindon was the center of attention. Everyone knew how Lindon would act when confronted with a female, and didn't believe a word he was saying. Lindon was always good for a laugh.

"Everyone should be livin' in Fred'icton," said Lindon. "Lots o' women, lots o' women. I, I, I, I, I met up with some kind o' fancy woman, I, I, I, so I did. Earrings on, smokin' a big long tailor-made cigarette. Fancy lady, she was. Met 'er at the hotel, I did, yeah, so I did. Got a room. Got a room right there in the hotel, so we did."

"Did ya put the lad to 'er?" asked Stan Tuney.

"Put the lad to'er, alright! Ho! No I didn'! No! No! No, I suppose I didn't put it to 'er none! Ha, ha! Oh, yeah, yeah, yeah. Put it to 'er, I did! Right there in the hotel room. Drunk a whole bottle o' this stuff she called vodker. There wasn't a drop left in the mornin'! Woke up and I was all alone, yep. Jist as well, though. Jist as well."

"Was she good?"

"Ha, Ha, Ha! Good! I guess she was good! Ho! No she wasn't! Ho! The very best, so she was!"

"Did ya see Graig Allen while you was over there?" asked John Kaston, who was getting somewhat annoyed with all the dirty talk.

"Never saw Graig, no. No, I never saw Graig. Right there, too, but I never saw him. Been over there for years, Graig has. Workin' at the cotton mill, I think. Someone said Graig was at the cotton mill."

"Never comes back, does he?" said Bob Nash. "Sold his land to Dr. MacDowell and never cried crack 'till he hit Fredericton. Never came back."

"A man should go and see him, you know," said Dan Brennen.

"Ya'll never guess who I saw on the bridge the other mornin'," said Lindon Tucker.

"Graig?"

"No, no, no, no, not Graig, no. Walkin' cross the bridge I was. Saw that Nutbeam fella. Nutbeam. Nutbeam, know who I mean? Nutbeam. Met him on the bridge."

"What'd he say? What'd he say?"

"Just said g'day. G'day, he said. Just said g'day."

"What'd you say?"

"I said, I said, I said, I said, I said G'day, Nutbeam, old Nutbeam, old boy, I said . . . . He never said nothin', jist kept walkin'. He's got the biggest ears, look o' here, I ever saw in my life! Ya never saw the like o' them! Big as that pound cake there! Homeliest man ya ever want to meet!"

"I heard now," lied Stan Tuney, "that he don't cook one thing he eats! Use to being up north someplace. They don't cook their meat in the Yukon, you know."

"How do ya know he don't cook his food?" asked Shadrack.

"Well, if he don't cook his meat he might be from the Yukon, who knows?"

"I heard everything that sticks out on 'im is a foot long," said Bert Todder, "his ears, nose, everything."

"His tool would just look like a young pig with no ears," put in Dan Brennen.

"That's what that Albert Johnson was suppose to look like," said Stan Tuney. "Albert Johnson was from up north, ya know. Shot all them Mounties! I wouldn' be surprised if that's who he is!"

"They captured Albert Johnson, didn' they?" asked Bert Todder.

"They never knew for sure," said Stan Tuney. "They thought they got'im, but they never knew for sure."

"Homeliest man I ever saw," said Lindon Tucker. "Just said g'day, was all he said."

"You ever hear from yer boy, George, Bernie?" asked Bert Todder.

"Got a letter from 'im yesterday," said Bernie Hanley.

"News from Paladin," thought Dryfly, perking up to listen.

"Said he was workin' in a bakery. Place called Richmond Hill."

"Thought he went to Toronto," said Bert.

"No, no, Richmond Hill. Young Palidin, now, is workin' in Toronto, though. Got 'imself a job workin' with a newspaper, deliverin' papers or somethin'."

"And George is workin' in a bakery! Boys! Sounds like a pretty good job to me! I bet ya he's makin' good money, too!" said Bert.

"They'll be back," said Bernie. "Ya couldn' keep that young Palidin away from the river! Best fisherman I ever saw, Palidin was."

"He could ketch 'em when nobody else could," said Bob Nash. "He use to borry that old rod o' Shad's and bring us up a salmon every other day."

"I bought about ten from him," said Bernie.

"How ya s'pose he did it?" asked Dan Brennen. "I fished all one day and never saw a thing. Young Palidin came over the hill, made two casts and 'bang,' gotta ten pounder."

"He seemed to just know how to do it," said Bert Todder.

"He'll be back," said Bernie Hanley. "You'd never get them young lads to stay away from the river for any length o' time."

*

Shadrack and Dryfly left the store and stepped into the dark, windy November evening. It was Saturday night and Shadrack was getting restless . . . .

"There's nothin' to do around here," said Shad. "I'm bored."

"We could take a walk to Gordon," suggested Dryfly. "Might be some girls around."

"No girls in Gordon. Blackville's the place to go. There's about three hundred girls in Blackville school and they all hang around the canteen on Saturday nights. Why don't we see if we can hitch a ride to Blackville, Dry?"

"No, I don't think so. I don't know anyone in Blackville, Shad."

"I do, Dry. I know lots o' lads."

"I don't think so, Shad. We'd never get a ride, anyway."

Since Shadrack started to school in Blackville, Dryfly was seeing a great change in him. Shadrack was beginning to speak differently, to use words like algebra, math, classroom, corridor, cafeteria, and other words that Dryfly had no comprehension of. Shadrack was making new friends at school, too, and often spoke of Gary Perkins, Polly Saunders and David Carlyle. "That Mary Wilson's a cool chick," or "That Don Monroe's a cool cat," Shad would say, and Dryfly would be left feeling totally alienated.

Shadrack stayed over a couple of nights with a new friend called Peter Bower. Peter Bower's parents possessed a television that Shad and Peter watched as much and as often as they could. This new apparatus was inspiring Shadrack to use terms and words like "River Boat, Darin McGavin, Rin-tin-tin, Time for Juniors, Jim Bowie and The Last of the Mohegans."

With school, homework and visits to Peter Bower's house to watch television occupying much of Shadrack's time, Dryfly was finding himself alone more and more. It seemed that the duo were drifting apart.

"We could go to the canteen and get a wiener and chip," said Shad.

"A what?"

"Wieners and french fries."

"Cost a lot o' money, wouldn' it?"

"I got a few bucks. C'mon Dry, let's go."

"An awful long ways; what if we got way down there and can't find a way home?"

"We'll walk. Dad said he use to walk it all the time. It's only ten or twelve miles."

"Well, alright," said Dryfly. "I'll go, if we can catch a ride."

Dryfly had conceded for adventure's sake, but he was hoping there'd be no Blackville-bound traffic on the Gordon road.

They had waited on the road in front of Bernie Hanley's store for an hour when Ally Dunphy showed up. Ally Dunphy had hunted the deep forests of Dungarvon until it was too dark to see. On his way home to Blackville, in his 1958 Ford, Ally stopped at Bernie Hanley's store for a snack. When he was getting back into his car, a red-haired lad approached him.

"You goin' to Blackville?" asked the lad.

"Sure am."

"Kin me and Dryfly get a ride with you?"

"Sure can."

In thirty minutes, Shadrack and Dryfly found themselves standing in front of LeBlanc's Canteen in Blackville.

*

With the coming of the chainsaw, more money and cars, came the necessity to improve the byroads. Shirley Ramsey sold $160.00 worth of gravel during the summer of 1962. Cars and gravelled roads made Blackville a center of commerce and entertainment for all the surrounding settlements. Blackville, being more accessible, became a meeting place. Every weekend, young people would crowd on the backs of pickup trucks, or in old cars and head for Blackville. Sometimes there'd be a movie to go to, sometimes a dance, but mostly the teenagers would just walk up and down the street from one take-out restaurant (canteen) to another. There were three canteens in Blackville. No more than 500 yards separated one from the others.

"What do we do now?" asked Dryfly.

"Let's walk down to the other canteen," said Shad.

When they arrived at the second canteen, Shad suggested that they check out the third. From the third, they walked back to the second, stood around for a few minutes, then walked back to LeBlanc's. They had done everything there was to do in Blackville, except eat. Shadrack and Dryfly completed the social itinerary for Friday night in Blackville by ordering a paper dish full of french fries and three wieners each.

They were just finishing their snack when Peter Bower showed up with Jim MacNeil, Gary Perkins and David Carlyle.

"G'day, Shadrack. How's she goin'?"

"The very best, Peter."

"Who are you?" asked Peter.

"Dryfly Ramsey," answered Dryfly.

"Dryfly Ramsey! Any relation to Shirley Ramsey?" asked Peter. One of the other boys chuckled.

"Me mother," said Dryfly.

The boys all glanced at each other and grinned.

"What brings you guys out of the woods?" asked David Carlyle.

"Come to chase the chicks," said Shadrack.

"What happened to your hair, Dryfly?" asked Jim MacNeil.

Dryfly scanned the four Blackville boys in their clean black pants, the expensive jackets with the collars turned up, the black jet boots, the trucker's wallets chained to their belts, jutting from their hip pockets, the rings, wrist-watches and the well-groomed Elvis Presley haircuts.

Until now, Dryfly had forgotten that he wasn't very well dressed and that his hair was parted in the middle.

Shadrack scanned Dryfly and saw, maybe for the first time, what the other boys were seeing — the straight brown hair parted in the middle, the ragged jeans that Shad himself had given to him, the mackinaw coat, the black rubber boots with the red soles, the long nose. Shadrack was even more conscious of Dryfly's appearance than was Dryfly, and wished he hadn't brought him along. He had wanted Dryfly for company, in case he had to walk the twelve miles home, alone. He hadn't anticipated that Dryfly might jeopardize whatever chance he might have of being in with the in crowd.

"Where ya get the boots, Dryfly?" asked Gary Perkins, making no attempt whatsoever to hide the mockery in his voice.

Shadrack eyed the grinning Blackville boys and knew he would have to make a decision — go with the in crowd, or be out with Dryfly Ramsey. He decided to try and play it down the middle. He grinned, but not for mockery's sake. He grinned to try and keep it light.

Shy and very uncomfortable, Dryfly blushed and looked down at himself. The discomfort grew as he compared his own clothes to the others. He said nothing. He wanted to go home to Brennen Siding.

"How's your mother?" asked Peter Bower, nudging David Carlyle and winking at Gary Perkins. Peter Bower, for the moment, was the leader of the pack.

Dryfly wondered how the Blackville boys knew his mother. He didn't know that the byword "Shirley Ramsey" had leaked into Blackville.

People in Blackville took their children on Sunday drives past Shirley's, pointed and said: "Look, kids! There's Shirley Ramsey's house." The kids would all look at the epitome of local poverty: the sagging, paintless house, the dirt lawn, the car tires on each side of the driveway culvert. Ogling arrows of curiosity, they might think: "Shirley Ramsey . . . the woman who invented the culvert ends."

"Shirley Ramsey's boy, boys!" laughed Jim MacNeil. "Great boots, Dryfly!"

Shad made a stab at changing the subject. "What's goin' on, boys?" he asked.

"There's a dance at the public hall," said Peter Bower. "Goin'?"

"I don't know, might."

"Ya might as well. That's where the chicks are."

"I dunno," said Shad, shrugging, eyeing Dryfly.

"C'mon, Shad! Get with it!" said David Carlyle.

"Polly was askin' about ya, Shad."

"Was she?!"

"She'll be at the dance, Shad."

"S'pose!?"

"Saw her down the road."

"C'mon, Shad!"

Shad continued to eye Dryfly. "Dryfly is gonna have to learn to handle it," he thought.

"Great! Let's go," said Shad.

Dryfly wasn't invited, but he had nothing else to do, so he followed the others. He walked behind, ashamed of his clothing and his hair, still wishing he was home. Dryfly did not like

Blackville and he did not like the boys in the in crowd. "At least by walking behind, they don't make fun of me," he thought.

When they got to the public hall, they lined up at the ticket booth and, one by one, paid to enter. From the stage within came the harmony of Lyman MacFee and the Cornpoppers, singing, "Wake Up Little Susie." When it was Shad's turn to pay, he turned to Dryfly, said, "I ain't got enough money for both of us, Dryfly. Why don't you try to sneak in?"

"I'll get caught," said Dryfly.

"No you won't. Just wait 'till nobody's watchin'. You can do it!"

A lump had suddenly developed in the back of Dryfly's throat. He was being abandoned. He swallowed the lump.

"I'll wait out here," he said.

Shad shrugged and followed the Blackville boys into the hall, leaving Dryfly alone on the steps.

Dryfly waited on the steps of the public hall for what seemed like a very long time. Men and women came and went, but few paid much notice to Dryfly, and Dryfly hoped it would remain that way. As a matter of fact, Dryfly wanted to hide. "How could Shad do this to me! Some friend!"

By the time an hour had passed, Dryfly was feeling very cold in the damp night air. He was also bored and a little bit afraid. Some men had gathered around on the steps to drink some wine and Dryfly sensed that trouble was brewing.

Some fellow by the name of Kelly was displeased for some reason or other with a fellow named Benny Crawford.

"You're nothin' but a rotten bastard!" said Kelly.

"I ain't scared o' no Kelly that ever walked!" said Benny.

"By Jesus, I came here to dance, not fight, but I'll beat the shit out o' the likes o' you!" said Kelly.

"C'mon and fight then! I'd just love wipin' the street up with you! C'mon! C'MON AND FIGHT!"

Kelly and Benny threw off their coats and squared off in the street in front of the hall. Someone ran into the hall and yelled, "Fight!" The hall emptied — the fight needed an audience.

Until the crowd gathered, Kelly and Benny were having a verbal fight with the intention that whoever had the biggest vocabulary of swear words would win. Sticks and stones were discussed, but as long as they were only being discussed, nobody would get hurt. But now, they had an audience and the pressure was on.

"Hit him Kelly! Hit the bastard!" somebody yelled.

"Don't take that off 'im, Benny! Plant the rotten jeser!"

Kelly made a swing for Benny and missed. Benny made a kick for Kelly and also missed. They stood then, eyeing each other, breathing heavily, obviously very nervous about the showdown, wishing it was over.

Kelly thought that a bluff might discourage his foe, and flew into a spiel of swear words and threats that would make a dead priest turn over in his grave. He touched on the apes and how they were related to the whole of the Crawford family; he spoke of the peculiar smell the Crawfords had picked up doing the only thing that Crawfords were good for — shovelling shit; he recalled that there was never an exceptional mind in the entire history of the Crawford family; he left nothing out that he considered worth a swear word or ten or twelve. At a climactic point of his spiel, for effect, he hit Benny on the shoulder and whooped, saying: "Take that, ya sonuvawhore! Ya think I'm scared o' you?"

Benny Crawford hit back, catching Kelly on the arm.

The two backed off again and yelled a few more obscenities. Kelly made a kick at Benny. Benny took a swing at Kelly. They still remained unscarred.

The crowd were choosing sides a bit, and Dryfly sensed a potential brawl. He didn't like what he was seeing and hearing, and he didn't want to get involved. He looked around for Shad. The crowd was completely encircling the reluctant fighters and Dry saw that Shad was on the other side of the circle, standing, acting cool, with his friends and some fat girl.

"There never was a Kelly any good!" yelled Benny Crawford.

"Look who's talkin', ya yellow bastard!" yelled Kelly.

"Hit 'im Kelly!" yelled somebody from the crowd.

"You stay out of this!" yelled someone else.

The audience was growing. People were coming from their houses to watch the fun, and the canteens emptied. The circle in front of the hall expanded and the whole street was blocked off to traffic. There was a lineup of thirty cars waiting to get through.

Benny Crawford's two sisters showed up and were crying loudly and calling: "Benny, don't fight! C'mon home, Benny!"

"Here," said a man who was standing beside Dryfly, "Hold this! Look after this for me."

The man passed Dryfly a bottle of sherry and stepped into the circle. "You lads want to fight?" he asked. "You lads wanna take on a good man?!"

Everyone in the crowd hushed. The fighters shifted their eyes nervously, unable to hold the steady gaze of this new man on the scene.

"We don't want no trouble with you," said Kelly.

"Well, if you're gonna ruin this dance fightin', you're gonna have to do it over me!"

"We got nothin' against you," said Benny Crawford.

"I don't wanna fight with you," said Kelly. "Me and you was always good friends."

"We don't want no trouble with you, Herman," said Benny.

Herman Burns had now taken over the show. Herman Burns was six-foot-four and muscular. He weighed nearly twice as much as either Kelly or Benny Crawford. He towered over them and everyone else. He was like a snake eyeing two unfortunate mice while a horde of other mice watched on. Everyone knew that Herman Burns was a dangerous man.

"We don't want to fight no more," said Kelly.

"But I thought you wanted to fight," urged Herman. "Looked to me that you fellers were lookin' for a fight! Well, if ya want to fight, C'MON!"

Herman Burns kicked Benny Crawford as hard as he could, breaking a rib and leaving him bent and moaning on the ground.

Kelly started crying and begging Herman not to do likewise

to him. Herman hit Kelly on the brow, knocking him out cold. The fight was over. Everyone was admiring Herman for his great victory. Herman walked around like a rooster sucking up the sweetness of popularity.

"No, s'pose he can't fight none!" someone behind Dryfly said.

"He beat the both of them, just like that!" said someone else.

With arms and shoulders back and chest thrust out, Herman Burns walked up to Dryfly. Dryfly handed Herman his wine.

"Thanks, lad," said Herman.

Herman unscrewed the cap and took a drink. He then handed the bottle to Dryfly. "Have a drink," he said.

Dry drank from the bottle of sweet sherry.

"What's your name?" asked Herman.

"Dryfly Ramsey."

Other boys were gathering around Herman and Dryfly. Herman looked Dryfly up and down, saw the poverty and the fear.

"You're a friend," said Herman, and offering his hand for Dryfly to shake, said: "Put 'er there."

Dryfly shook the huge calloused hand. It looked to the other boys that Dryfly and Herman were the best of friends.

"Better not tangle with Dryfly Ramsey," thought Peter Bower.

"Goin' inside?" asked Herman.

"No, I don't think so."

"C'mon, Dryfly. There's a bunch o' young women in there, and they're lookin' for you."

When Dryfly walked past the ticket booth with Herman Burns, no one asked him for a ticket. When he stepped into the hall with Herman's arm resting on his shoulder, the in crowd did not laugh at him.

*

Shirley Ramsey made a fire and put the kettle on. An inch of snow had fallen in the night and half-melted in the morning sun; it dappled the drab November landscape. Dryfly had walked all the way from Blackville during the night and was still sleeping.

Shirley made a pot of tea, poured some into a mug and a little onto a plate. Into the tea on her plate, she sprinkled some brown sugar, dipped her bread into it and ate. Shirley Ramsey either had bread dipped into pork fat and molasses, or bread dipped into tea and brown sugar, every morning for breakfast. While she ate, she listened to Jack Fenety on the radio. "CFNB — where New Brunswick hears the news," said Jack, then went on to talk about the political dreams and schemes of Hugh John Flemming and John Diefenbaker. After the news, Jack played, "Up On The Housetop," a Christmas song by Gene Autry.

"Christmas," thought Shirley. "T'would be nice to have some money for Christmas. I wonder if Palidin will come home. I hope the poor little lad is doing well."

After smoking a couple of cigarettes, Shirley put on her coat and boots, tied a red scarf over her hair and went for a walk around the gravel pit.

The gravel pit was getting a little bigger each year. Shirley's land was nearly all dug up. What land was left around the pit's periphery was covered with hawthorn and blueberry bushes, and the occasional fir tree. The Ramsey boys had harvested the land completely and the fir trees had sprouted and grown within the last ten years.

"They're jist right fer Christmas trees," thought Shirley. "Dry could cut them and sell them to Rudy Baxter."

Rudy Baxter, from Blackville, owned a truck. Every November, Rudy Baxter bought a thousand Christmas trees from the locals and trucked them to Boston.

"We'd have a little money for Christmas," thought Shirley. "Not much, but a little. Dry could snare a few rabbits, too, and sell them to the Frenchmen down river."

With the Post Office closing at the end of December, and with the selling of Christmas trees and rabbits, Shirley saw the ends meeting until the end of January, no further. After that, times would be tough.

Shirley thought of the tough times in the past. She was thinking of the past a lot lately. She recalled that her father, Bub, had raised his family almost entirely on moose, salmon and potatoes. With no wife and nine children ranging from ages one to twelve, Bub had no time for a regular job, so there was no money for clothes. The children were brought up on hand-me-downs. Shirley had never worn a new dress in her life.

Shirley remembered how Bub would play both mother and father, cook and work the potato field by day, and poach salmon, moose and deer at night.

"There was always something to eat," she thought. "We weren't poor then like I am now, or at least, not as poor as I will be by the time February rolls around."

The bleak gravel pit sprawled before her, a cavity forever threatening her land.

"Another year and that'll be gone, too," she thought. "Never thought ya could run out of gravel."

Shirley heard the distant whistle of the mail train and went to the house for the mailbag. Then, she walked to the siding house for the exchange. When she returned home, Dryfly was awake and sitting at the kitchen table.

"I walked all the way home from Blackville last night," announced Dryfly. "I'm pretty near dead!"

"What took ya to Blackville?"

"Ended up at the dance. Saw a fight, too!"

"Who?"

"Some Kelly fella and another lad. Herman Burns broke it up."

"Herman Burns? He's related to Lester Burns. Use to hang around Brennen Siding a lot when he was a young lad. Nice boy, too. Him and Junior was good friends. Herman could've been a boxer, if he had've got the right trainin'."

"He's some kind o' big and rugged."

"He got that from the Pringles. His mother was a Pringle. All the Pringles were big."

"I wouldn' want to cross 'im!"

"There's some Christmas trees around the pit, Dry."

"Yeah?"

"Big enough to cut. You could earn us some money for Christmas."

"Is there lots o' them?"

"Couple o' hundred, maybe."

"That's a good idea, I'll go at it first thing Monday."

"I'll get ya some rabbit wire, too. Soon's the snow gets on to stay, you could snare some rabbits."

"Sure. I might even do some trappin' this year."

"No luck in trappin'."

"What's the difference between snarin' and trappin'?"

"I don't know, but everyone always said that trappers never had any luck. I guess God don't mind if ya snare rabbits, there's so many of them."

"Know what ya kin git me fer Christmas, Mom?"

"What?"

"A new set o' guitar strings. Them ones on the guitar are hardly fit to play on. They're startin' to unravel."

"Maybe. The fire's gettin' low, Dry. Would you get me some wood?"

Dryfly groaned as he stood. Both his feet and legs were sore from the long walk from Blackville the previous night. It had snowed a little bit while they walked, which did nothing to make the trek any easier. Dryfly recalled thinking that he wasn't going to make it; that he would never do it again, supposing he did hear the best music he had ever heard. At the dance, Dryfly had enjoyed Lyman MacFee and the Cornpoppers very much. Dryfly put on his coat and limped his way to the woodshed.

"MOM!" he yelled from the shed. "MOM! COME 'ERE QUICK!"

Shirley heard the excitement in Dry's voice and ran to see what was the matter.

When she got to the shed, she found Dryfly standing looking up at the hanging carcass of a deer — gutted, skinned and cleaned.

"Where'd ya git the deer, Dry?" she asked, eyeing the most meat she'd seen in years.

"I didn' get it! It was just here! Don't know where it came from!"

"He was poachin' last night," thought Shirley.

"Nutbeam did it," thought Dryfly.

sixteen

Shadrack and Dryfly were making frequent visits to one of the cabins owned by the members of the Cabbage Island Salmon Club. A dozen forty-ounce bottles of liquor had been left in the cabin in September, and by Christmas, due to Shadrack and Dryfly's little parties, only three were left. The hearth of the stone fireplace was piled up with Parody and cigarette butts and ashes; the sofa cushions were strewn about; the hardwood floors were tracked up with sand and leaves and pine-tree needles, courtesy of rubber boots and gumshoes.

"They got lots o' money," said Shadrack, "they'll never miss the stuff."

"Maybe we should move to the other camp," said Dryfly. "God knows what's in the other ones!"

"I checked them all out," said Shad. "All locked."

"Shit's gonna hit the fan when them lads come back and find all their liquor and cigars gone."

"They won't even remember how much they left."

"I hope you're right."

It was the 24th of December and Shad and Dry were having a few drinks to help them get into the spirit of Christmas. Outside the frosty windows that looked down over the frozen Dungarvon river, the temperature was about five below zero; inside, it could have been colder, they weren't sure. They didn't plan to stay long, anyway. "Jist enough to get feelin' good," was their plan.

"I hope I get them jet boots for Christmas," said Shadrack. "I'd like to have a trucker's wallet, too."

"Did you pass in school?"

"Jist failed French and not by much."

237

"You'll get the boots."

"Maybe."

"Ya like goin' to school, Shad?"

"Not too bad, once ya get used to it. Lots o' girls."

"Yeah. No good for me though. I don't feel like running 'round on Lillian."

"You're crazy, Dry. I bet she hardly remembers who you are. You'll be lucky to ever see her agin."

Dryfly shrugged at the possibility. "Those Blackville women wouldn' go out with me anyway," he thought. He didn't realize it, but he was beginning to sound like Nutbeam.

"You ever think about going back to school, Dry?"

"I'm gettin' too old. I'm pretty near sixteen."

"So?"

"So, I'd be in the same grade with all them little kids. I wouldn' look none too stupid, would I! Me, a big lad o' sixteen, settin' in school with a bunch o' little kids!"

"Maybe you could learn at home and ketch up."

"How would I do that?"

"I don't know. Find out."

"Ya think Nutbeam's home yet?"

"He might be. The train should've come by now."

"Let's go back and check him out."

*

Nutbeam sold six hundred dollars worth of fox, bobcat, mink, weasel and beaver pelts to his Jewish buyer in Newcastle and went shopping. He bought himself a complete set of clothing which included Stanfield's underwear, pants, shirt, woollen socks, another parka and two pairs of boots. He also bought a trucker's wallet, a pipe and tobacco, a half gallon of Lamb's rum, a turkey and six yards of linen, black with red roses on it. Needless to say, when he left the train to make his way to Todder Brook, he was more than just a little burdened. The foot of snow on the ground didn't make the walking any easier, and although it was zero degrees out, Nutbeam was sweating and panting by the time he reached his camp.

He placed everything on the table and proceeded to build a fire in the stove. He made a pot of tea, poured himself a mug full, spiked it with an ounce or so of rum, then sat to contemplate his situation.

"If the boys show up soon, the better the plan will work," he thought. "If they don't show up, I'll have to play Santa Claus."

From his pocket, Nutbeam removed the $350.00 left over from his shopping spree. He went to his cot, reached underneath and removed a shoe box. He removed the top and added the $350.00, adding considerably to the bills already in the box.

"One day I'll get Dryfly to count it for me," he thought. "Another day, me and Dry will go to Fredericton and visit that Graig Allen fella; see how much he's askin' for the old farm. Old Doctor MacDowell only bought the shore . . . there must be a couple o' hundred acres of woodland and pasture left, maybe more. I'll build a house on the old foundation and live normal . . . no more hiding like a . . . a bear."

He put the shoe box back in its hiding place, added a bit more courage (rum) to his tea and sat once again.

"Let me see . . . " he thought, " . . . deer, a bunch of partridge, a can o' tobacco . . . and this." He slapped the turkey.

He rubbed his fingers across the linen with the roses on it.

"Ho, ho, ho! Merry Christmas, little lady!" he said. Then, he heard the crunching of approaching footsteps in the snow outside.

Knock-knock-knock.

Nutbeam went to the door, unlatched it and welcomed the boys.

"Come in! Come in!" he said.

"G'day Nutbeam."

"G'day, G'day."

"How's she goin', boys?"

"We were here earlier," said Shad. "You weren't home."

"Went to Newcastle. Sold me furs."

"Get a good price?"

"Real good."

"See ya got a turkey," said Dry.

"You boys want a drink?" asked Nutbeam.

"Sure."

"Might have a small one."

Nutbeam poured each of the boys a drink and touched up his own. It was evident by the grin on his face that he was in a jolly mood.

"That turkey ain't all I bought today," said Nutbeam, raising his tin mug as if to toast the turkey.

The boys waited.

"Wanna know what else I bought, boys?"

"Yeah."

"Sure."

"Well . . . I got meself two pairs o' boots."

"Yeah?"

"Two pair?"

"Two pairs o' boots. Want to see 'em?"

"Sure."

Nutbeam took the boxes from the table and opened one.

"I bought meself these here jet boots."

Nutbeam took a boot from the box and passed it to Shad.

"Boys! Nice boot!" said Shad, admiring the soft, shiny black leather. "Try it on, Nutbeam."

Nutbeam took the boot from Shad, removed his gumshoe and slid his foot into it. It slipped on easily, a good fit for his over-sized foot.

"Nice!" said Dry. "You'll get the women with them on!"

"Boys!" said Shad.

Nutbeam grinned.

"Let's see the other pair," said Dry.

Nutbeam removed the cover of the second box and exposed the second pair of shiny black jet boots.

"They're just the same!" exclaimed Shadrack. "Why two pair the same?"

"Didn' know which ones would fit," said Nutbeam. "Let me try these ones on."

Nutbeam kicked off the first boot and tried on one from the

second pair. He barely got the end of his foot into the boot before it tightened. "This pair's too small," he said. "Here, you try it on, Shad."

Shad removed his gumshoe, put his foot in the jet boot and flopped it around. "Way too big for me," he said. "They must be a ten, I take a seven. You try it on, Dry."

Dryfly slid off his red and black rubbers and tried on the expensive leather boot.

"Perfect," he said. "Boys, they're nice!"

"Sure are," said Shad.

"Too bad I didn' have the money to buy them from ya," said Dry. "Too bad ya have to take them back."

"I ain't takin' them back," said Nutbeam. "I got them for you."

Dryfly's mouth fell open.

"They're yours," said Nutbeam.

"Mine?"

"All yours."

"You mean it?"

"They're yours."

Dryfly wanted to whoop a whoop that would echo across the Dungarvon woods. Dryfly wanted to dance and laugh and sing. Instead, a lump lodged in the back of his throat and for a moment it seemed he would cry.

"They're the nicest boots I ever saw in my whole life," said Dryfly. He threw his arms around Nutbeam and squeezed, hiding his tears the best he could behind Nutbeam's big floppy ears. At that moment Dryfly loved the trumpet-playing, Dungarvon-whooping, mysterious hermit as much as he loved . . . Lillian Wallace? . . . Shirley Ramsey?

"Thanks, Nutbeam," he whispered.

"Sit down," said Nutbeam, somewhat embarrassed by the unaccustomed affection. "They're only an old pair o' boots."

Shad was smiling with envy. He tossed back his rum, said: "Merry Christmas, boys!"

"And for you," said Nutbeam, "this here."

Nutbeam handed Shad a small brown paper bag. Shad

reached in the bag and pulled out the trucker's wallet — the wallet with the golden chain and belt attachment — the wallet Shadrack wanted.

"Hello! No wallet!" said Shad. "S'pose I ain't gonna look none too cool or nothin', am I?! Good day! S'pose the women ain't gonna like that none! No! No! No they ain't! No!"

"You're a saint, Nutbeam," said Dryfly.

"A real saint! A creamatarter!" agreed Shadrack.

"I got a good price for me fur, " said Nutbeam. "Decided to share the wealth."

"Thanks, Nutbeam."

"Yeah, thanks a whole lot. You're a saint and a half."

"Now, for your mother, Dryfly, I got this can of tobacco, that turkey and this pretty cloth."

"For Mom?"

"For Shirley?"

"Yes sir! She's entitled to a good Christmas, too. Merry Christmas, boys! Have another drink!"

The boys and Nutbeam drank the rum straight from the bottle. They were all in very high spirits.

Two hours later, after much talking and laughing, Shad and Dry departed Nutbeam's camp. They followed the moonlit path homeward through the forest and fields. High on rum, the winter wind did not nip at their heels as it would have otherwise.

Leisurely they walked, carried their goods, talked and laughed until, as usual, they separated at the footbridge.

Crossing the bridge, heavily laden with the turkey, tobacco, linen and boots, Dryfly stopped to rest and take in the scenery. The moon was full and bright. The river, except for the airhole in front of John Kaston's, was frozen and silent, sleeping beneath the ice and trillions of snowflakes: its blanket.

As Dryfly focused in on the airhole, he thought he could see somebody standing beside it. He was not sure if it was a person; it could have been an animal, perhaps a deer drinking from the open water. It wasn't moving, so Dryfly couldn't really tell if, or if not, the thing was a thing, or just an extended arm of the airhole itself, or perhaps a stake, put there to warn skaters of the thin periphery of ice.

He shrugged off his curiosity, turned and gazed downstream for a while. There, he could see Lindon Tucker's house, its windows reflecting the moon, but no detectable light coming from within. He could also see the sheds and barn, their symmetrical lines jutting from the snow-clad field. "Like something from a Christmas card," he thought.

He could not see the swing, but he pictured it in his mind — the swing, Lillian Wallace, the butterfly, the summer's day.

"All I really wanted for Christmas was Lillian Wallace," he said to the night, turned and walked toward the warmth of home.

*

Max Kaston eyed himself in the mirror. He had a scratch on his thin and sunken right cheek. A wood chip had hurled from his axe and hit him there the previous day while limbing a hemlock. His right eye was puffy from the slap he received from John for the incidental oath he had sworn.

It was Christmas Eve and Max was very lonesome and depressed. Earlier in the evening, he and John had quarrelled again when John wanted him to go to church with him. Max had been tired, felt ugly and unpopular, had said: "No! I'm not going."

When John slapped him, Max conjured up every ounce of control he could find to keep from slapping him back.

Max had seen Palidin Ramsey fight at school many years ago. The confrontation had been between Palidin and Joey Layton. Palidin had been so calm and cool and Joey had been so out of control. Joey called Palidin a coward and a fruit and Palidin hadn't batted an eye. He just stared into Joey's eyes, intensely enough to cause Joey to shiver with uncertainty. Joey was backing down when Palidin made his mistake. He dropped his eyes and when he did, Joey slapped him.

It would have been a victory for Joey in the eyes of all the boys watching, but Palidin did something scary, almost eerie. He

243

immediately regained his equipoise and turned the other cheek. It so befuddled Joey that he stepped back as if shocked and ran into the school, shamed and crying like the child he was.

Instead of slapping his father back, Max tried the Palidin Ramsey trick. It infuriated John.

"Blasphemy!" yelled John, slapped Max once again and stormed off to church.

The second slap had been harder and stung, but it hadn't neared his other eye. However, its injury to Max had been far greater than any infliction he had ever before been subjected to. It was that one last slap from his father that accomplished all that John ever set out to do — it broke Max's spirit.

Greatly despondent in the wake of that slap that still seemed to echo throughout the room, Max eyed himself. His eyes filled and tears like rivulets coursed their way down his cheeks. His body convulsed as he released sob after sob.

"I can't!" he sobbed. "I can't become a preacher! Why doesn't Dad understand?!"

One by one, the people of Brennen Siding flashed through his tormented mind. Lindon Tucker: a bachelor, uneducated, going nowhere, half out of his mind. Stan Tuney: alone, a bachelor with no ambition, nothing left to sell, nothing left to live for but lies. Dan Brennen: losing his battle to be better than everyone else, primarily because he was growing old and wisdom was telling him that he would never succeed. Bob Nash: forever in a state of unrest, contrary, never smiling. Bert Todder: who laughed at everything and everyone, perhaps the wisest of all the men in his simplicity . . . but, going nowhere as well. Shadrack Nash and Dryfly Ramsey: following along to the same tune, toward the same destiny, as if it were an inalterable direction, a tradition.

"My father," thought Max, " . . . and me. I'm just like my father. I could've been a preacher if I had've gone to school. But, I don't want to become a preacher! I couldn't preach to save my soul!"

Suddenly, Max threw his shoulders back as if some unknown power had taken control of him. The fatigue left him; he felt strong and capable. In the mirror, his reflection stared back at him with cold hard eyes — expressionless, the jaw set in determination. A warmth coursed through his body, the hair stood up on his neck; he thought he might even be getting an erection.

The reaction came from the ultimate of negative thoughts — suicide. But the ensuing effects were nothing he'd ever before anticipated. As if in a trance, he walked to the coat-rack, donned his jacket and headed for the river. He was still in the same state when he found himself staring at the airhole. The water rushed, black and cold from beneath the ice on which he stood.

He did not know why he stopped when he did. His full intention had been to walk into it. It was as if he had to size up the eerie, hooded figure of death — and the choice was still his: jump, or remain and fight.

The moon danced on the troubled surface of the water; the wind, stronger here on the river, slapped at his clothing. The cold, exhilarating Dungarvon air and water were having their effects on him, too. If something irrational and demonic had touched him back in the house, the great outdoors was trying to reverse the trance. There were the moon and the stars; the river and the forest, seen through the crystal-clear moonlit air. There were the farms with their lights glowing warmly within (he could see Lindon Tucker's from the river in front of John Kaston's), and the bridge . . . there was somebody walking on the bridge.

Max suddenly realized that he was outside, at night, alone. There he was, by himself, on the river at night and not afraid. He looked around as if he'd never seen the night before. It was not all that dark. He always thought the night was black and formidable, that it was occupied with wraiths and evil spirits that blended with the darkness.

But he was standing in a quite different world — one of beauty and serenity — where the stars and moon enchanted the land and all that lived there.

The figure on the bridge walked leisurely along, stopped for a moment, then continued on at a slightly faster pace.

Max shifted his attention to a red, glowing planet, northeast of the moon, its light distorted and exaggerated as it shone through his cloud-like breath.

"Jump, or remain and fight," he whispered.

And then, echoing across the forest from the direction of Todder Brook came the sound of a lone trumpet being played, so far off, so clear in the still night.

Nutbeam, basking in the glow of his rum and generosity, was celebrating still. He was playing "Silent Night" for all of Brennen Siding to hear.

"Stand and fight," said Max, turned and walked slowly home, enjoying his newly-found world.

*

On Christmas morning, Dryfly awakened to the smell of onions frying. Shirley had already risen and was frying some strips of venison, onions and eggs. Dryfly rose, dressed and went to the kitchen.

"Mornin'," said Shirley, "Merry Christmas."

"Merry Christmas," said Dryfly.

"Cold mornin', must be thirty below. Fire feels good," said Shirley.

Dryfly went to the stove and stood soaking up the heat. "Sure does," he said.

"I'm cookin' us up a great big feed, Dry."

"I see that. Sure smells great. Would ya like your present?"

"You got me a present, Dry?"

"T'weren't much. Didn' have much money."

"You didn' have to buy me nothin', Dry."

Dryfly went to his bedroom and returned with a gift, crudely wrapped in brown paper.

Shirley unwrapped the rectangular mirror with the white plastic frame.

"It's beautiful, Dry! It's the prettiest mirror I ever saw! It must've cost a lot o' money, Dry."

"Wasn't much."

"It's the best Christmas present I ever got, Dry! Thanks! Thanks a whole lot."

"Ya like it?"

"I love it! I'll throw that old thing away and hang this new one up so's you and me kin see how good-looking we are, Dry," said Shirley with a toothless grin.

Dryfly was happy and smiled, too.

"I have a gift for you, too, Dry."

"Yeah?"

"It ain't much," said Shirley, passing Dryfly a small package wrapped in brown paper.

Dryfly ripped the paper off a pair of grey woollen mitts.

"Nice mitts, Mom! Thanks a lot! They fit, too."

"Good. I thought you might need them this winter doin' your snarin', or trappin', or whatever."

Dryfly had a slight twinge of disappointment. He did not get the guitar strings. He knew, however, that the mitts were more important.

"You're right, Mom, ya can't do nothin' without good mitts," he said.

"Glad they fit," said Shirley.

"I got something else for ya, Mom."

"More?"

"Not from me. From Nutbeam."

"From Nutbeam?"

"Yeah. He got ya somethin' for Christmas."

"But, why?"

"Don't know. Nice lad. Got me and Shad stuff, too."

Dryfly had hidden the can of tobacco, the turkey and the cloth in the livingroom where he hoped Shirley wouldn't find it. He went and got them and gave them to her.

"It's beautiful," she said, fingering the black cloth with the red roses on it, " . . . and the turkey . . . and . . . and tobacco . . . why, Dry?"

"Don't know. Nice lad. Give me a pair of boots."

Dryfly had left his boots in the bedroom. He retrieved them for Shirley to see.

Shirley eyed the boots that Dryfly set before her.

"They must have cost a fortune!" she said.

"I know. Nice lad."

"Is that where you go all the time, Dry?"

"Yeah. Me and Nutbeam and Shad is good friends. Nice lad to do that, eh?"

"I just can't figure out why, Dry! Did he leave the deer and them partridge, too?"

"I think so. He never said."

"Strange, eh?"

"Nice lad."

"If we keep all these presents, we'll have to give him something, won't we?"

"Didn' know he'd got them till yesterday. We ain't got no money to get him presents anyway."

"Do you think we should keep them, then?"

"Don't know. Nice boots."

"He lives all alone, don't he?"

"Yeah. Has a little camp."

"Maybe we could invite him over for supper or somethin'."

"Ya think?"

"He's not crazy, or somethin', is he?"

"Kind o' homely to look at. Doubt if he'd come."

"Why? Is he shy?"

"Don't like people much. People laugh at 'im."

Shirley sighed. "Know how he feels," she said.

"He's a real nice lad, though, Mom."

"After breakfast, you go talk to him, Dry. Supper's the least we kin give 'im."

Shirley Ramsey was uncertain of what the outcome might be in having this mysterious, but obviously kind, generous and sensitive man in for supper, but she was willing to take the chance. Shirley Ramsey had the Christmas spirit. She wanted to give and share. Shirley saw a can of tobacco here, boots there, venison in the frying pan, the cloth and the turkey on the table.

*

Dryfly Ramsey, as much as he wanted to, did not wear his new boots to Nutbeam's camp. "Walkin' in the snow would ruin them," he decided.

After the brisk walk through the bright, frosty afternoon, he knocked on Nutbeam's door.

"Come in," he heard Nutbeam say, "the door's unlatched."

Dryfly opened the door and stepped into the camp, kicking the snow from his feet as he crossed the threshold.

"No more latching the door," greeted Nutbeam. "Only ones that comes is you and Shad, anyway. I've always kept that door latched, but no more, Dryfly. You kin step right in here any time you like!"

"Cold day." said Dryfly. "Been out?"

"Was out and fed some moose birds earlier. They're around every day lately."

"Yeah, I saw one back the trail."

"What brings you back here on Christmas day?"

"Mom says thanks for the cloth. She wants you to come and have supper with us," said Dryfly.

To Nutbeam, Dryfly could have just announced him a lottery winner. His heart quickened, butterflies took to flight in his stomach; he felt scared. Never in his wildest fantasies had he thought this dream would come true. Never in his wildest dreams had he thought that this fantasy would become a reality.

"She wants me to come for supper?" asked Nutbeam, afraid he had misunderstood.

"Got that great big turkey. Someone has to eat it," said Dryfly.

Nutbeam stood and ran his fingers through his hair. Decisions had to be made. "Should I, or shouldn't I go? What would I say? How would I act?"

"Dryfly . . . I don't know . . . I don't know if I can."

"Why? You ain't scared o' Mom, are ya?"

"Well . . . I don't know . . . I don't . . . I never talked to a woman before!"

"Mom's not a woman . . . I mean, Mom's just Mom."

Scrambled remnants of forty-two-thousand-and-one dreams unfolded before Nutbeam. He saw himself walking through the forest on moonlit nights, dreaming of having Shirley Ramsey by his side. He saw himself standing at the edge of darkness watching Shirley Ramsey listening to Kid Baker sing. He saw himself shooting a deer, thinking that with each bit of venison consumed, Shirley Ramsey would be, indeed, consuming a portion of his good will for her. He saw dreams of holding her, whispering "Rest, Shirley, take it easy" into her ear.

"What did she say?" asked Nutbeam.

"She just said go get Nutbeam for supper." Nutbeam was beginning to pace and Dryfly could see that he was beside himself. "I think she likes you, Nutbeam. Mentions you every once in a while. She's been wanting to meet ya, I think."

"Then she wants me for sure?"

"Pretty likely! She was just sayin' the other day that she thought it funny that you never drop in."

"That's for the boots," thought Dryfly.

"I don't know, Dry, I . . . "

"She's got that big turkey in the oven already, Nutbeam. Gonna put extra potatoes and stuff on, too."

"I don't know . . . I'm . . . I'm so strange. People act funny when they see me."

"That's because you are strange, ya old jeser! Get yer coat and c'mon! It must be four o'clock already and supper's at five!"

Nutbeam put on his coat.

"The big test," he thought. "Am I a man or a mouse?"

*

When Nutbeam and Dryfly entered Shirley Ramsey's house, Nutbeam shut the door behind him, stood and waited. He was wearing his parka and the hood was hiding his face. He was reluctant to lift the hood and expose his ears. Shirley Ramsey stood before him. The house smelled of roasting turkey.

" 'Day." grunted Nutbeam. Although somewhat slumped, he still towered over her, so that she eyed him as one might eye a giant, with the evidence of wonder in her eyes.

"Take yer coat off," said Shirley. "Supper's almost ready."

Nutbeam removed his parka in one swift movement, watching the delicate little woman to see if she would laugh or scream.

Shirley did neither.

"C'mon. Sit down by the table, Nutbeam," said Dryfly.

Dryfly and Nutbeam sat by the table. Shirley started puttering around the stove.

"You from around here?" asked Shirley.

"No. From Maine."

"You American?"

"I guess so."

"We're all Canadians around here."

"Yeah?"

"Yeah. 'Cept for the sports on the river. You a sport?"

"Just a man," said Nutbeam.

Dryfly sat eyeing his boots. The boots were sitting beside the bedroom door and he was preoccupied with their presence.

Shirley checked the carrots and the potatoes to see if they were cooked. Then she removed the golden brown turkey from the oven.

"Smells good," said Nutbeam.

"It was awful good o' you," said Shirley.

"Good to be here," said Nutbeam.

"Set the table, Dryfly," said Shirley.

Dryfly snapped out of his boot-induced trance and went to the cupboard for plates, knives and forks.

Nutbeam was beginning to relax a little. Shirley, who had been as nervous as Nutbeam, was also beginning to relax.

"He's more funny than scarey, once ya git use to him," she thought.

"Ain't so bad," thought Nutbeam. "She ain't laughin'. I'm doin' OK."

"Kin I help do somethin'?" asked Nutbeam.

"Got everything just about ready," said Shirley. "Bring them plates over here, Dry."

When she was satisfied with the quality of the gravy, Shirley began loading the plates. She sat across from Nutbeam and the three commenced to eat.

"Don't eat with yer fingers, Dryfly, use yer fork."

"Ain't got a fork. Only had two."

"Then get a spoon."

Dryfly went to the cupboard, got a spoon, returned to his seat by the table and dug in.

The three were hungry. Busy eating, the conversation all but died.

"Good stuff," said Dryfly.

"Best meal I had in ages," said Nutbeam.

"There's plenty more on the stove. Have some salt," said Shirley.

When they could eat no more, Shirley made tea and served it in mugs, two of which had broken handles. She gave the good one to Nutbeam.

Dryfly drank his tea quickly. Dryfly was not interested in tea. He was getting restless and wanted to see if Shadrack had gotten jet boots for Christmas. Dryfly was in a dilemma. He felt he shouldn't leave his mother and Nutbeam alone — Nutbeam was shy; his mother nervous around strangers. Dryfly considered leaving and taking Nutbeam with him, but he knew Nutbeam would not want to go to Bob Nash's.

"Have you travelled a lot?" asked Shirley.

"No. Left Maine and come here. That's all the travellin' I ever did."

"I was to Rogersville once," said Shirley. "All French in Rogersville. Burn down the woods so's they kin git a job fightin' fire."

"Sons o' whores!" said Dry.

"Frenchmen," said Nutbeam.

"They paint their houses funny colors," said Shirley.

"Shit brindle," said Dry.

"Frenchmen," said Nutbeam.

Nutbeam eyed the crucifix and rosary beads on Shirley's wall. "You a Cath'lic?" he asked.

"Yeah. Only Cath'lic around here," said Shirley.

"I'm a Cath'lic," said Nutbeam. "Ain't been to church in years, though."

"Me nuther," said Shirley.

"Gotta go all the way to Blackville or Renous to church," said Dryfly.

"John Diefenbaker's a Baptist, ain't he?" asked Shirley.

"Prob'ly," said Nutbeam.

"Baptists don't play cards," said Shirley.

"Some do," said Dryfly, "Shad does."

"Shadrack Nash ain't nothin'," said Shirley. "Devil's gonna get him."

"Devil's already got 'im," said Nutbeam smiling.

Nutbeam had big lips that fringed a big mouth. When Nutbeam smiled, it was like opening up a piano's keyboard. It seemed he had forty-two-thousand-and-one teeth. Nutbeam's mouth was so big that one would not have difficulty envisioning his face disappearing when he yawned. Nutbeam, when he smiled, looked like the sun with floppy ears. When Nutbeam smiled, Shirley Ramsey thought he looked incredibly funny and smiled also. When Shirley Ramsey smiled, which was rare, there wasn't a tooth to be seen. Nutbeam found Shirley's toothless smile amusing and his smile grew even broader. When Nutbeam's smile broadened, so did Shirley's. When Shirley's smile broadened, Nutbeam chuckled. When Nutbeam chuckled, Shirley chuckled also. When Shirley chuckled, Nutbeam chuckled a chuckle that turned to laughter. When Nutbeam laughed, Shirley laughed. The harder Shirley laughed, the harder Nutbeam laughed. Nutbeam was the funniest looking man Shirley had ever seen and seeing him giggle and laugh (the distorted huge mouth, the big nose, the squinted eyes, the big ears flopping as his head bobbed) was, indeed, an hilarious thing to see. Shirley laughed hysterically, as if she hadn't laughed for forty-two-thousand-and-one years. The more laughter that sprung from Shirley's toothless mouth, the harder Nutbeam laughed. Things were getting out of hand. Dryfly, accustomed as he was to both Nutbeam's and Shirley's features, saw nothing unusual at all and couldn't quite understand all the laughter. Surely Nutbeam's comment about the devil already having Shad was not that funny. Yet, Dryfly had never seen his mother or Nutbeam so out of control ever before. It was good to hear, like music to his ears. Dryfly laughed too. "Ha, ha, ha, ha, ha, ha," repeated itself forty-two-thousand-and-one times, stopped for a brief breather, then continued for forty-two-thousand-and-one more times. The laughter shattered all the fear, crushed the shyness, unlocked forty-two-thousand-and-two inhibitions and broke the ice. The laughter engulfed Nutbeam with a sense of warmth and love and well-being. He had never been happier. He loved Shirley with all his heart. Shirley Ramsey thought that Nutbeam was the funniest, handsomest, most wonderful man she'd seen in her entire life.

seventeen

Bob Nash, Dan Brennen, Bert Todder, John Kaston, Stan Tuney and Lindon Tucker all stood around in Bernie Hanley's store, talking to Bernie, eating oranges and drinking Sussex Ginger Ale.

It was April and all the men except for John and Bernie were discussing their current jobs, guiding American sportsmen.

Most of them had spent a great deal of the winter looking forward to the day they could go guiding; to the day when the ice had finally cleared from the river; to the day when they could put their canoes in the river and attach their outboard motors; to the day when they could watch and listen to the first spring birds nesting and frolicking about; but now that the day had come, they felt they should complain.

"Boys, it was some cold out there on the river today!" said Dan. "The eyes frosted right up on me fishin' rod."

"Them old sports don't seem to mind it, though, do they?" put in Bob Nash.

"Me? I'd hardly be bothered carrying one o' them old black salmon from the river," lied Stan Tuney.

"Them lads like them though," said Dan. "Pay good money to fish them! Set out there on the river in the wind and rain and like 'er great. I wouldn' eat a black salmon if I was starvin' to death!"

No one in Brennen Siding would admit to eating the spring, sea-bound, spawned-out salmon, except for Shirley Ramsey. Black salmon, as they were called, was poor people's food.

"Them Amuricans like 'em, though, yeah. Yeah. Like 'er great, they do, so they do, yeah. Eat anything at all, them lads," agreed Lindon Tucker.

"'Pon me soul, yeah, that's true. They'll eat anything ya set in front o' them. I saw a lad eatin' a steak the other day that couldn' been cooked anymore than five or ten minutes. The blood was runnin' right out of it!" said Bert Todder.

"Make ya sick!" said Stan Tuney, who, like everybody else in Brennen Siding, did not like rare meat.

"Yeah, that's right, yeah. Eat anything at all, so they will, yeah," said Lindon.

"That old lad I'm guidin' didn' wanna quit tonight 'till pretty near dark," said Bert.

"And they'll work ya's on Sundays, too!" said John Kaston. "Sinners. Sinners. That's all they are."

John Kaston was not paying much attention to what was being said. He was preoccupied with his new religion. He had applied and gotten accepted to a sub-denominational school in Fredericton and was due to begin a six-week course that would make him a preacher. All he had to do was leave the Baptist church, accept Jesus as his own personal savior and prove that he could read and speak clearly enough to be understood. He had already purchased a new suit, tie and shoes and had presented his twelve-hundred-dollar check (the initiation fee) to the master of the school.

It was a drastic step for him. He would've settled for Max becoming a preacher, but when Max sold a freight car of pulp and headed for St. Catharines, Ontario, in March, John was left with no alternative. The worst thing that could happen was to fail the course and he was told that nobody with twelve hundred dollars in his pocket and the Holy Ghost by his side had ever failed.

"I caught about a ten-pounder this mornin'," said Bert Todder, "so thin and weak, hardly kicked at all when I pulled him into the boat. Give it to Shirley Ramsey, I did. Dropped it off on me way here tonight."

"That Nutbeam lad there, was he?" asked Bernie Hanley.

"That's what I was goin' to tell ya," said Bert. "He was settin' right back, him and Shirley, jist the two o' them. He's there half the time. Great lookin' couple, they are. You ain't careful, Lindon, you're gonna lose yer woman."

"Ain't my woman, so she ain't! No, no, don't need that fer a woman!"

"Tee, hee, hee, sob, snort, sniff!"

"I heard, now, I ain't sayin' who told me, but I heard that Shirley and that lad was thinkin' 'bout gittin' married," put in Stan Tuney. Stan hadn't actually heard it, but he had thought it so much, and had seen Nutbeam crossing the field so often that he actually believed he had heard it.

"Boys! A man would have to be awful hard up for a woman, wouldn' he?!" said Dan Brennen.

"Oh, I don't know . . . she might be pretty nice in the morning," said Bert Todder. "If I was you, Lindon, I wouldn' let her slip away so easy. She'd be a good woman for you, Lindon. Tee, hee, hee, sob, snort, sniff!"

"You could take her fer walks every night in the gravel pit, Lindon," said Dan Brennen.

"Don't need no Shirley Ramsey, I don't! I kin tell ya that right now, don't need no Shirley Ramsey. Got meself a little lady in Fredericton, so I have. Me little vodker drinker."

"Oh, but that Shirley'd be pretty nice, Lindon. All dressed right up, goin' fer walks in the pit, cookin' ya up a nice black salmon every night fer supper. Tee, hee, hee, sob, snort, sniff!"

"She's still young enough to have two or three young lads for ya, Lindon," laughed Stan Tuney.

"I think Lindon might've had a crack at 'er already. That Dryfly kind o' looks like Lindon, don't ya think boys?"

"He ain't mine," said Lindon, his face beginning to colour a bit. "He, he, he, he, ain't mine. Might be yours, might be yours, Bert. Ain't my young lad!"

The men could hear the temper rising in Lindon's voice and knew they had carried the joke far enough. Lindon was simple-minded and no one wanted to find out what he'd do if pushed too far. The topic changed.

They talked about cars, gold in the Yukon, the price of pulp . . . periodically, Bert Todder allowed that it was time he went home, but as usual, he was the last to leave.

*

When Dryfly Ramsey and Lillian Wallace met in late June, they did not run toward each other in slow motion across a field of daisies and clover, with open arms.

Dryfly figured that Lillian would be starting her summer holidays any time after the middle of June, and he was checking the Cabbage Island Salmon Club twice a day in anticipation of her return. He missed her arrival. She came late at night. They met on the Tuney Brook bridge the next afternoon.

Her presence startled him. Ten feet apart, they stood motionless, staring as if afraid, their hearts pounding.

"Hello, Dryfly," said Lillian.

"Hi. How are you?" Dryfly's voice seemed timid and weak.

"I'm back . . . ." Lillian smiled.

"I'm . . . I'm glad to see ya."

"How have you been?"

"Good. You?"

"Fine."

Dryfly had dreamed of this moment countless times, had always thought he'd embrace her, kiss her, tell her how he'd spent a year dreaming of how beautiful she looked, smelled, was, and how much he loved her. But now, although he wanted to, he couldn't. He thought she might think him forward, presumptuous. After all, she was a rich American and not some backwoods hussy like the kind Shad Nash courted. This was Lillian Wallace. This was the most wonderful girl in the whole world. He was not sure what to do. He felt shy.

Lillian, too, felt confused. She had often thought of Dryfly, but she'd had a busy year; had gone to school, travelled on holidays, dated other boys — Rick. But here stood Dryfly Ramsey . . . and there was something about him . . . not his looks . . . he was thin, had a long nose, hair parted in the middle . . . not his expensive boots . . . and yet (perhaps she saw the adoration in his eyes) there was something attractive about him.

Dryfly was trembling with excitment. He moved closer, looked into the brook for trout, saw one, looked at Lillian, said: "Yer father here?"

"Yes. He's gone fishing."

Lillian moved closer. They could now reach out and touch each other, but instead, they looked into the water.

"And how's Shadrack doing?"

"Good. Don't see him much. Goes to Blackville a lot."

Dryfly moved closer again. They were now standing shoulder to shoulder, gazing into the water. He could feel her warmth and smell that wonderful insect repellent she wore. He was fighting a losing battle trying to contain himself. Another minute and he would embrace her . . . and then, to his surprise and great delight, she touched his arm. It was a touch light as a feather, but it zapped him with energy, unleashing adrenalin from a supply he had never realized was there. Without further premeditation, he swung to her and took her in his arms, holding her close. They hugged for a long blissful moment until, breathless, they parted to gaze into each other's eyes.

"I missed you an awful lot," said Dryfly.

"I missed you, too," said Lillian. "Why do I feel this way?" she asked herself. "What is it about him?"

And then they kissed. It was that gentle kiss they both remembered and they made sure they kept it that way — fragile, the caress of a butterfly, the Dryfly-Lillian kiss.

They embraced again.

Dryfly sniffed the shampoo-scented, silky blond hair. "I love the smell of your hair," he said.

"Do you?" Lillian's voice was like that of a little girl.

Dryfly withdrew far enough so that he could kiss her brow.

"I love your forehead."

He kissed her eyes.

"I love your eyes."

He kissed her cheeks.

"I love your cheeks."

Lillian smiled.

He kissed her nose.

"I love your nose."

He stopped kissing, hugged her instead.

"What about my mouth?" she asked.

"That speaks for itself," said Dryfly.

*

On the tenth of July, Shirley Ramsey and Nutbeam met Palidin at the train. The first thing Palidin noticed was Shirley's new dress, black with red roses on it. The second thing he noticed was her cleanliness, the permed hair and the new dentures when she smiled. He noticed Nutbeam, pleasant-looking enough, but with the biggest ears he'd ever seen. He saw Nutbeam touch Shirley with familiarity and her girlish response, her stimulated spirit, the poise within her he'd never seen before.

Shirley saw a change in Palidin, too. She saw the hair, cut by a real barber; the clothes, snug and clean and new; she saw a far-off look in his eyes and a little grin when he eyed the little red siding house. When he left he had a cardboard box, now he carried real leather luggage: two pieces, a big bag and a small one.

"It's good to have you home, Pal."

"I wouldn't miss your wedding for the world," said Palidin and turned to Nutbeam, held out his hand for shaking and said: "Palidin."

Nutbeam shook the hand and smiled, seemed to lose a great portion of his face behind it, and said: "Nutbeam. Welcome home."

"Are you doin' OK?" asked Shirley.

"I'm doing the very best," said Palidin and gave Shirley a hug.

"Do you mind?" she asked.

"I think it's the best decision you ever made."

"Thanks, Pal."

They started walking, Nutbeam holding her left hand and Palidin her right.

Palidin scanned the fields with their houses and barns. "Everything's so small," he thought. "They used to seem big, but now they're tiny." When Palidin left Brennen Siding, Stan Tuney's barn had been the biggest building he'd ever seen. Now, it looked tiny and shabby, needing paint. The fields that once seemed so large, now all together seemed small in comparison with some of the farms he'd seen east and west of Aurora and Newmarket. He also eyed the narrow dirt road and realized he hadn't seen one since he left home.

As if reading his thoughts, Nutbeam asked: "Big place, Toronto?"

"You wouldn't believe it."

"You must be glad to be back. Are you stayin'?" asked Shirley.

"Only for the wedding. I have a job. I have to go back."

"What're ya workin' at?"

"I work for a newspaper . . . learning to write."

"Sounds like a good job," said Nutbeam.

"Not much money in it . . . in Canada."

"Dryfly got a job."

"Oh yeah? What doing?"

"He's workin' on puttin' up Bill Wallace's camp. Bill Wallace is the father of that girl he's chasin'."

"Ha! Can't he catch her?"

"Oh, I think he can ketch her alright," said Nutbeam, "he's at the club, or out walkin' with her every spare minute he can find."

"Good. He must be happy."

"It'll never come to no good," said Shirley. "She's too far away. He should be chasin' someone handy."

"Ya never know," said Nutbeam.

As they approached Shirley's house, one word echoed through Palidin's mind: Poverty.

And as if Nutbeam had read his thoughts once again, he said: "I bought the old Graig Allen property. Dry and me are buildin' a house on it, soon's he's done workin' on the Wallace camp."

"Great! Good news!" said Palidin.

"You could write about it in the T'ronta newspaper," said Shirley, smiling.

Nutbeam and Palidin both chuckled.

"I just might," said Palidin. "I just might. Don't tear this old house down, Nutbeam. I'll need a picture."

*

After unpacking for his three-day visit, Palidin pulled himself away from the many questions Nutbeam and Shirley were asking and went for a walk. He walked through the forest all the way to the big hollow. At the edge of the barren, he removed his clothes, hung them on a spruce tree for a beacon, then ran freely to the boulder that jutted from the barren's center. He stopped in front of the boulder to read his inscription.

Probe the atom,
Ponder the echoes of the wise.
There lie the secrets to the universe.

"There's something wrong with it," he thought. "I don't know what it is, but there's something wrong. I was so much younger when I wrote that; a boy . . . and it looks just as it did when I wrote it. The only thing I'll ever write that will last . . . and there's something wrong with it.

But why did I write it? . . . oh yes, echoes . . . the cycle. The echoes and the cycle, the answer to all my fears and superstitions. I guess they had more substance than just accepting everything as being the work of the devil, or ghosts. You can explain everything with echoes and circles, in the same way you can say that God did it, or the devil did it, or ghosts, or fairies . . . put them all inside a man and call it fear. We haunt each other."

Palidin sat on the boulder, letting the sun tan his body. It felt good to be back. "My heart's here," he thought. "One day I'll come back to Brennen Siding and retire. I'll sell my idea for magnetizing hooks and retire."

A breeze suddenly came up and swept across his naked body, cool and titillating. He leaned back and lay on the boulder, staring straight up. Looking up, he could not see the grassy barren or the trees on the horizon; he saw only the sky, the sun and a black bird circling far above, far enough away that he could not identify for certain what kind of bird it was, far enough away that he could barely hear its mournful call. It circled higher and higher and got smaller and smaller until it finally disappeared into the azure.

"Circling me like it must have circled Bonzie," thought Palidin. "The cycle. Everything works in cycles — the salmon, the bees, the birds, the earth, the universe . . . magnets and echoes."

Palidin thought he could hear someone walking "splash,

splush, splush" on the barren. He listened to see if he could iden-tify it as being a man, or an animal. It would be very embarrassing for him to be caught naked by someone like Dan Brennen or Bert Todder . . . or anyone.

And then a child's voice called out, "Whoop! Over here!" He sat up and searched the barren for a long breathless moment. He heard the call of the bird once again.

There was nobody there.